FORREST WOLLINSKY VAMPIRE HUNTER

PREDESTINED CROSSROADS

LEONARD D. HILLEY II

Illustrated by
DANIELA OWERGOOR

For Christal, as always.

FOREWORD

"For almost every decision we make, there's always an unforeseen consequence not discovered until after it's too late."—Forrest Wollinsky

CHAPTER 1

 inter 1889

THE JOURNEY TO DELIVER VARAK, the half-blood vampire, to the Archdiocese in Freiburg, Germany was one of the harshest routes I had ever traveled, not to mention, one of the most depressing.

When I had promised Albert the Were-rat that my father and I would escort the child across several countries to the proposed destination, my ambition had not taken into account the approaching fierce winter. Due to the rugged terrain, the frigid winds, and snow mixed with ice, traveling was painstakingly slow. Several times we had encountered mountain passes that were too treacherous to cross, forcing us to find an inn, seek an alternate route, or set up a campsite in the shelter of a crag until the road was cleared.

In many ways the obstacles seemed to dictate that delivering this child to the archbishop was being frowned upon by Fate and by the higher powers that had chosen me as a Vampire Hunter. These hindrances were warnings we were meant to heed, but acting upon my promise to Albert and due to my undying stubbornness, we continued onward.

This half-blood child was diabolical and should not be allowed to live. As an infant he appeared harmless, and indeed that was true, at least on the surface. In time, however, once he gained awareness of the charismatic persuasion power contained within him, he could usher forth as a fiendish tyrant worse than anything the world had yet seen. In my soul there was no denying this to be the solid truth. My nightmares continually reinforced these fears.

There would be grave consequences for protecting Varak and keeping him alive. A hefty penalty would be demanded by the powers that had chosen me. I understood that, but never in a thousand lifetimes would I have ever imagined how great that cost would be.

In addition to these dilemmas surrounding Varak, I grieved over Jacques' absence. The loss of his companionship made me ache inside. While I was happy that he and Matilda were going to have a child, he had been more like a father to me than a cousin and I selfishly suffered jealousy that his attentions and fatherly affections had turned elsewhere. In less than a year's time, I had lost my mother, Rose, and now Jacques. Off and on, Father seemed absent. Even though he traveled alongside me, his mind obsessed over other factors.

Father slept on the seat across from me in the coach. He had bundled a heavy blanket into a wad, pressed it against near the corner of his side window, and used it for a pillow. Across his lap was a thick wool rug he favored to use as a blanket. Madeline sat with her back in the other corner with her legs slightly pointed toward Father. She had wrapped a small woolen blanket around Varak and cradled him in her arms.

I sat on the seat across from them. Because of my height and width, I almost required the entire seat just to sit down. Neither of them could have squeezed in beside me had they wanted to. Sleeping comfortably along the journey had been nearly impossible for each of us.

The temperature inside the coach wasn't much warmer than the outside cold except we were protected from the bitter biting winds and snow. Our breath was visible when we exhaled, and I couldn't imagine how our coachman, Thomas, had been able to withstand the extreme wintery conditions seated near the top of the coach. Thomas wore two thick overcoats, heavy gloves, and double thick woolen britches, which possibly wasn't enough to keep him warm, but he had never complained one time.

The coach suddenly bounced, jarred us sharply, and creaked on what had been, until that moment, one of the smoothest roads we had traveled. The coach tilted to one side, so I slung my weight to the opposite side of my seat to counter it, which was possibly the only thing that prevented our coach from tipping over.

Thomas shouted at the horses, "Whoa!"

I pulled the curtain slightly aside and peered through the ice-covered window. Dusk was upon us, making the thick forest trees along the road's edge even more ominous. Uncertainty settled over me since we had stopped in such a foreboding place. Thomas had insisted we had enough daylight to make the next village before nightfall where we could find a small inn. But this unexpected delay was inevitable.

Strange misfortunes continued to plague us throughout this journey, and I had a difficult time shunning my suspicions that they kept occurring because of this child.

"What is it, son?" Father asked, arousing from his sleep. "Why have we stopped?"

I shook my head. "I don't rightly know."

Madeline gently rocked Varak in her arms. She smiled when I caught her gaze. The cute dimples at the edges of her narrow lips deepened. Her bright eyes sparkled, reminding me of Rose, and even though I ached inside, I couldn't resist smiling back. She had been kind and pleasant company during our trip, and I found her endearing like a lovesick fool in spite of our age difference.

The were-rat had chosen Madeline to accompany us to Freiburg to tend to Varak. She and Father had taken a liking toward one another, and at times the two acted like Varak was their own child, which disturbed me. It troubled me more that Father behaved that way since he knew *what* the child really was. She and Thomas didn't know because Father and I had sworn to maintain secrecy concerning the infant.

Father sat upright, pulled his curtain aside, and peered out the window at the growing darkness. "Well, boy, aren't you going out to see what's the matter?"

I reached for the door latch. "I suppose I am."

Stepping outside the coach, I was rewarded with a harsh welcome of cold wind whipping across my bearded face. I shuddered. Thomas stood in front of the horses. The hard thin layer of snow crunched beneath my feet as I approached him. "What's wrong?"

He pointed. "Bridge is blocked."

Rocks and snow had fallen onto the road and covered part of the bridge. The howling wind whistled across the narrow stream below. Most of the rocks didn't look too large or heavy, but clearing the path would take several hours. I walked to the roadblock and hefted one of the larger stones, tossing it aside.

"Forrest," he said. "It will be dark in less than a half hour. We should focus more on setting up camp and getting a fire started. We can worry about moving the rocks in the morning. From the looks of it, we might be better off finding an alternate route come morning."

I glanced back toward the coach and nodded. He was right. Getting a fire started was the most important thing. Once the night set in, the temperatures would plummet. At the back of the wagon, I lifted a trunk lid and took out several small dry logs. Deeper in the forest, owls hooted. The piercing howls of wolves echoed.

Before I turned with the firewood, something on the road caught my attention. Farther behind the coach I noticed a deep trench had been dug across the road, which seem odd. It appeared freshly dug.

Thomas stood near the rocky ledge, looking down. With all of the extra clothes he wore, he looked like a massive man, but underneath all the layers he was actually medium framed and thin like my father. I wondered why this man had owed Albert a favor. He had readily accepted this task of providing his horse and wagon to drive us halfway across Europe without ever questioning our intent or offering a single complaint.

The were-rat had sought seclusion and remained hidden underground because he couldn't risk being seen by mortals, and yet, these two people who traveled with us had somehow become indebted to him? Even though I was curious, I didn't ask. We all had our secrets.

I set the logs at the edge of the road and joined Thomas. He regarded me with nervous eyes, but only for a moment before he looked down again. The stream below wasn't large or fast flowing, so it seemed strange that it had divided the rocky outcrop in half with a several hundred foot gap over time. Water and wind weathered out gorges, ravines, and mountainsides, but usually those water currents were much stronger.

In the dimming daylight the view of the darkening cliffside was like the barrier that divided good from evil. I imagined dusk at this crag during the summer months was livelier with hundreds of bats swarming into the night on their hunt for insects. But, this winter night, the bats were dormant, silent.

The coachman removed a glove and broke away the snot icicles that had formed on his gray moustache and beard, ignoring the thin ice attached to his thick bushy eyebrows. He tried to hand comb his beard straighter before his nervous beady eyes glanced up at the narrow ridgeline that followed the road to the ravine where we stood.

"This might sound odd, Forrest, but this small avalanche didn't occur from nature. It's not by chance." His voice was a near whisper and shaky, but not from the cold.

"What do you mean?"

Thomas nodded toward the cliffside. "Somebody has intentionally blocked this roadway."

Glancing up, I could see that most of the debris had fallen from the peak of the ridge not too long ago since no fresh snow covered the surface. The fallen debris had not crumbled from the side of the rocks. The top edge was barren with several long smooth logs lying at the edge where it appeared someone had used them to dislodge the stones to make them tumble onto the road.

"Since it was almost dark," I said, "I don't know if you noticed or not, but there's also a trench dug across the road. That's what had made the coach nearly tip over right before you stopped the horses."

His bushy white eyebrows rose, and he stared back at the coach.

"Really? No, I didn't notice that, but I wondered why the coach rocked so hard."

Instinct caught my attention and I gave a shrewd stare toward the coach. "I think we'd best get back to the others and quickly."

"Why?"

I started running. "Either we're under attack or about to get robbed."

From the dark edge of the woods, two shadowy figures slinked toward the side of the coach and yanked open the side door. Madeline screamed.

"Forrest!" Father shouted. "Help us!"

CHAPTER 2

*M*ore frantic screams echoed from my father and Madeline. I raced faster while patting my coat pocket for a weapon, finding none. Every weapon I possessed was in my Hunter box inside the coach. It's nearly impossible to sleep with sharp stakes in your coat pocket without getting pricked whenever shifting from side-to-side and much safer to store them in the box.

Madeline shrieked. Someone dragged her from the side of the coach toward the forest, but she stubbornly resisted, planting her feet and pushing backwards. She clutched Varak in one arm while flailing her fist at the assailant gripping her elbow. Father dove out the side door and landed on her attacker's back, wrapping his arms tightly around the person's throat.

By the time I reached the coach, Varak had been pulled from Madeline's grasp by the other assailant who darted quickly into the thick dark forest.

Father held the other man in a chokehold and fought to prevent the young man from getting away. The man's panicked eyes peered at me for only a moment before my huge right fist struck him unconscious.

"Tie him up!" I shouted.

Without knowing the exact direction the other assailant had run, I rushed into the dark forest. The dense trees and underbrush made running nearly impossible, but I didn't slow my pace. Instead my broad body snapped dead branches as I ran headlong between the firs and pines. Thick bramble with sharp thorns fastened to my pants, ripping and tearing, but I ignored the pain.

Dusk faded, welcoming the darkness of night. The needled branches obscured visibility, so I chased after the crunching sounds several rows of trees over.

My mind raced almost as quickly as I ran. The roadblock had been deliberate, but these two weren't normal highwaymen. They had not blocked the road so they could rob us of our gold or valuables. Their goal had been to take Varak, and that alarmed me for several reasons.

How did they even know the child was with us? Who were they and *why* had they taken him? Did they know that he was a half-blood vampire?

If they didn't know Varak was a hybrid, they'd be easier to deal with once I caught them. But if they did know ... They held a more sinister agenda. They wanted him for his power and what he'd eventually become.

Branches snapped against my body. I kept running. My lungs ached from the cold night air, but I continued moving, with my hands out before me, shoving aside the bristled tree limbs. Suddenly I wondered about Varak's welfare. Surely whoever was carrying the child through this dense forest had already injured him by moving through these trees so quickly. I couldn't see any way the infant could escape injury.

The floor of the forest sloped downward. A huge log lay before me. How I knew in the depth of darkness other than whispered instinct was beyond me. I leapt over the log and landed where the gradient was even steeper. I tried to slow my descent but my boots skidded on the thick layers of ice-covered moss, causing my feet to slip out from under me. I fell hard, rolled, and slid down the steep hill. When I stopped sliding at the bottom, I didn't move. I simply lay there. I held my breath and stayed completely still, listening for footsteps.

No doubt my theatrical display of plummeting downhill reaching and grabbing for anything to slow my descent had silenced everything in the surrounding forest. If chipmunks could laugh, they were rolling over one another inside their tiny dens. At least none of my family or companions had witnessed it.

Without a light source in hand, and since the moon had not yet risen, I was practically blind. Never had I wished Jacques was at my side more than I did now so he could guide me with his night vision. That was a trait I truly coveted.

After several minutes of silence, the underbrush and dead leaves crunched about thirty feet away in what sounded like cautious foot-steps. I pushed myself up slightly and craned my neck, trying to detect the sound better. My hand rested upon a thick solid stick that I could use for a sturdy club. I took it and rose to my feet.

As much as I wanted no part in delivering Varak to the archbishop in Freiburg, I couldn't abandon the child with strangers who might have darker motives for taking him.

The slow footsteps crept through the trees, but instead of heading away from me, they moved toward me. I slipped my back against a wide tree trunk, held my breath, and waited, gripping the club tightly with both hands.

I had been in some dark eerie places before. Nothing was darker than a vampire's crypt at midnight, but standing deep inside this dark forest and not knowing what was approaching brought uneasiness to a new level. Footsteps pressed down leaves and brittle twigs, heading to the spot where I had abruptly stopped sliding down the hill. The person or *creature* sniffed the air, trying to find me I assumed, but the air was filled with the scent of earth, damp leaves, and moss, making it more difficult to pinpoint my exact location.

Because of the surrounding darkness, I still didn't know what I was about to confront. I tightened my grip on the thick tree branch and eased around the side of the tree, keeping my boots on the tree's massive roots to decrease the chance of making more noise. When I peered around the tree, green eyes glanced in my direction. Before the creature ran or attacked, I swung the branch low, narrowly grazing it.

A wicked growl escaped its mouth. It snarled and snapped at me.

What I had thought had taken the child and fled turned out to be a wolf. An angrier wolf since I had attacked it.

"Sorry," I whispered. "My mistake."

It snarled and growled, unforgivingly.

Instead of retreating, I advanced. I smashed the tree branch hard on the ground, inches away from the wolf. Realizing I was a bigger foe and not afraid of it, the wolf slowly turned and disappeared into the forest without any further confrontation. Thankfully, it was a wolf and *not* a werewolf. I stood there for a few minutes, listening and wondering where Varak was and who had taken him.

The forest remained eerily quiet except for my heavy breathing.

No more footsteps disturbed the forest floor while I listened. Finally after a half hour of waiting for some type of disruption, I decided to return to the coach. At least we had captured one of the assailants. He had answers to the questions burning in my mind, and he'd give me those answers, one way or another. Only, he didn't know it yet.

CHAPTER 3

By the time I fought my way back up the steep forest hillside, Thomas had a fire burning at the edge of the ridge. Father had set up a nice lean-to to block the cold wind while capturing the heat of the roaring fire. A bountiful stack of sticks and half-rotted logs lay near the tent, which seemed to be enough to keep the fire alive until daybreak. Wolves howled deeper in the forest.

Madeline sat inside the lean-to sobbing while my father wrapped his arms around her shoulders, trying to console her. Her closeness to the child was understandable since she had been the one to nurture him for the past month and a half. I wondered how much of her affection was due to her role, and how much came from the child luring her with his mesmerizing eyes.

I constantly felt his alluring power, which wasn't as strong as older vampires, but at least I was immune and able to resist his charms.

Near the fire Thomas had bound our attacker's hands behind his back and the man sat on the edge of the road. His ankles were also tied tightly together. When Thomas noticed me standing at the edge of the forest, he met me at the road.

"Did you get his name?" I asked.

Thomas shook his head. "No. He has just awakened. You hit him pretty hard."

I shrugged.

"I take it you lost his accomplice?" he asked.

"Yes."

"Why would they want the child?"

"That's what I plan to find out." I walked toward the bound man, carrying the large club I had found in the forest.

After I crossed the narrow road, the young man looked up at me with a slight sneer on his face. He looked to be in his early twenties. Shaggy black hair hung to his shoulders, and his beard was sparse. By his clothes he looked to be nothing more than an ordinary farmhand. His eyes weren't menacing like thieves I had encountered before, but some thieves were masters at playing innocent, often weaseling their ways out of blame.

"Why did you take the child?"

He scoffed and shook his head, softly laughing.

"Where is he?"

"In a place *you'll* never find him."

I brought the branch up over my head and then swung it downward, striking his leg hard. He screamed and wailed. I'm certain if his hands weren't tied behind his back, he'd have hugged his leg. He fought to do so in spite of his tight restraints. His sudden tears glistened in the fire's glow. He panted with sharp sobs and looked at me with fear in his eyes.

I examined the large stick and shook my head. "I can't be certain if that cracking sound was from this tree branch or a bone in your leg. But I'm going to ask you once more. The next time I will strike your head, not your leg. Now where's the infant?"

The man gulped air and whimpered. His defiance had disappeared and was replaced by intense fear. His voice became high-pitched and feminine when he replied, "In the forest."

I shook my head. "I'm aware of that. *Where* in the forest?"

He looked at me nervously but didn't want to offer an answer. I brought the club up again. He closed his eyes tightly and bit his lower quivering lip.

"Don't!" a woman said behind me. "I have the child. No need torturing my brother. It's not worth it. Here, take the infant."

I lowered the stick and turned to face her. The young woman stood with Varak in her arms. She must have left the forest when she realized we had retained her brother.

Her long black hair flowed down her shoulders and outlined her pale face. Under different circumstances, without my anger focused toward them for abducting Varak, I might have found her partially attractive and attempted a more cordial conversation. Deception and theft immediately alienated me from any person, making him or her an instant enemy.

She was extremely thin, even her face. She stood a few inches above five feet in height. For a couple of moments, I questioned whether she was the one I had chased into the trees. In my rush to aid Madeline, the culprit had seemed so much larger. My imagination had magnified the person.

However, unlike me, this young lady didn't have thorns stuck in her clothes or abrasions on her face from running through the tree branches. Of course, for all I knew, she probably had planned a quick route of escape ahead of time. If nothing else, she knew the forest much better than I. Or due to my desperation to find Varak, I might have run right past her if she had crouched down, waiting for her brother to join her.

My adrenaline waned, and the cuts on my legs and hands stung. I glared at her. "Why did you take the boy?"

Seeing the child, Madeline rushed from the lean-to and reached for Varak in sheer desperation. The girl readily handed him to her. Madeline hugged the child close and hummed as she walked back to the safety of the shelter.

The young lady glanced toward her brother. "Do you mind untying him? Hasn't Drake suffered enough? He's in quite a bit of pain."

"You answer my questions, and he's free to go."

The young man sobbed. His face creased from his agony, and he looked sick from the pain.

"We were offered a great deal of money to intercept you." Her demeanor was calm and her smile almost boastful. "And to take the child."

"Why? By whom?"

She shrugged.

I pointed toward the roadblock. "That was your doing?"

She shook her head. Her long black hair flowed from side to side like soft velvety ribbons. "His actually. Neither of us is strong enough to have done that. He did it for us."

"Why?"

She half smiled, somewhat proud. "As a distraction so we had a better chance to take the child. His plan worked."

"Don't provoke him, Ruby," Drake said, his face strained. He leaned back, propping himself on his restrained hands.

I said, "But there has to be a reason why he set you up to do this."

"All we know is that he has placed a bounty upon that baby," Ruby said. "He told us if we didn't want to do this, he had others who would. We had aimed to collect it."

My jaw tightened. "So you're willing to kidnap an infant for money?"

She appeared hurt by my accusation, even though it was the truth. "Times are hard. With winter upon us, we have no food and are hungry. The bounty is more money than we'd ever earn in a year working the fields. But we'd have never hurt the little boy."

"How do you know the man who hired you won't?" I asked.

Her eyes shifted back and forth while she thought. "I ... we really don't know. I'm sorry, but we never considered his purpose."

At least she was being more honest now. Perhaps her need for money had blinded her. Hunger caused people to do hasty things, and as frail as she looked, she was probably near starvation.

"Why does he want the child?"

"He didn't say exactly."

I shook my head. "It makes no sense why he'd hire the two of you instead of coming after us directly."

Her brother whined. "That's what we had asked him, too."

Thomas and Father came and stood beside me.

"And what was his reason?" I asked.

14

"That there'd be less complications if we or someone else did it instead of him."

Father glared at her. "How's that?"

Ruby's nervous eyes flicked from my father back to me. "He looked a lot like you."

I frowned. "In what way?"

"Other than him being much older and his face scarred, you're similar from a distance. The type of clothes you wear, the hat, and he said that he was a ... *Hunter*. Sounded quite odd the emphasis he had placed on that word since people *hunt* all kinds of animals in these forests. There's nothing unusual about that. But he insisted he didn't wish to fight against another Hunter."

Father gave me an uneasy glance. She was ignorant of what the man had meant, but I understood fully. I didn't like the idea of fighting another Hunter, either. Doing so went against everything the Chosen were ordained to do. We were to be allies with one another, not enemies. But I knew why he wanted Varak, which wasn't something he'd have told these two when he had offered the reward. He planned to kill the child. I held no doubts about that.

"Did he give you his name?" I asked.

Ruby stared at the ground, deep in thought. Her eyebrows rose, and she looked at me. "Philip."

"If you had succeeded in taking the baby, where would you have met to exchange?"

"In town. At the tavern."

"Which tavern?"

She smiled. "There's only one there."

I glanced at Father. "Can I borrow your knife?"

Father took it from its sheath and handed it to me.

I knelt beside Drake and cut through the knots of the restraints binding his hands and feet. He immediately reached for his leg, wincing.

Ruby stood beside him and offered to help pull him to his feet. At first he was hesitant, but finally he took her hand and she pulled. When he placed weight upon it, he cried out and shook his head.

"It's broken, Ruby," he said, lifting his foot off the ground and bracing against her for support.

"You *broke* his leg," she said, glaring at me.

I frowned back with a harsher stare. "Yes, *but* he's still alive. Had I been forced to hunt you down in the forest to get Varak, it might have been much worse for the both of you. You kidnapped a baby and you think you should go unscathed? In some cities a person could kill you for what you've done and never be charged for such an offense."

Ruby stood in stunned silence thinking about what I had said. She offered no further argument and helped her brother hobble closer to the fire.

Thomas shook his head and walked to the coach. Since it had been a while since we had eaten, I guessed he was going to prepare something for us to eat.

CHAPTER 4

*F*ather and I stood near the road. He looked at me with great concern. "Another Hunter wants Varak?"

"Seems so."

"What will you do?"

I sighed. "Continue on to Freiburg like I promised."

"You ... um ... don't think he'd try to kill you, do you?"

"It's possible," I said, trying to hide my nervousness.

"Does he want Varak so he can kill him?" Father asked.

"That'd be my guess."

"How would he even know about the child or where we are for that matter?"

I took Father by the elbow and walked farther away from the others so they couldn't hear our conversation. "In my heart I know what Varak will become. You know it too. I have no doubt about where his destiny ends. All of this was discussed with Albert, but none of us would do what needed to be done."

"You mean killing him?"

I nodded. "Even now, I cannot do something like that. I just can't. Because I'm essentially protecting Varak by taking him to the archbishop, another Hunter has been issued to do what we have not."

"And this Hunter will kill you if necessary so he can kill Varak?"

"I believe he will try."

Father's eyes hollowed. He shook his head. "Then give him the child, Forrest. Let the other Hunter perform his sworn duty."

"As much as I'd like to be done with this entire ordeal, handing the child over to another Hunter is the same as me breaking my promise."

He sighed. "Which is worth more? Your life or Varak's? We know what Varak will evolve into. By keeping your promise you've also put a mark upon your head."

I nodded. "Yes, I've thought about this a lot during the past few weeks while we've been traveling. I've struggled inside."

"See? Then do what's right. Your promise is a violation of your duties, isn't it?"

"That's what I fear. Since I've placed myself on the wrong side of my calling, a hefty price will be required of me. What exactly? I have no idea."

"Forrest, you should reconsider what you're doing. It's not safe to betray those who have granted such blessings to you."

The brightness of the moon shone over the ridgeline. Father's face was grim as he stared at me. His emotions stirred, but probably less deeply than my own. He looked away and turned to face the fire, watching Madeline. The longing in his eyes for her was obvious.

Sadness shadowed his voice. "Son, I'm certain you realize how much I covet the gift you have. At times, I've not been able to hide my jealousy."

"I know," I said softly.

"Other than your mother giving birth to you, nothing else would have been as great to me as being one of the Chosen. Only the two of you I have held in higher esteem, so don't forsake your calling."

"So, if you had been Chosen, you'd kill this infant?"

Father remained silent. He didn't look toward me.

"Father, you couldn't stake Bodi because he was a small boy. I don't fault you for that, but I've seen the way you and Madeline act with Varak. You nor I could harm him, in spite of the knowledge we have."

He sighed. "You're right, son. I couldn't either. But, if we manage to get Varak to Freiburg, I might lose you. That's not something I'm willing to sacrifice."

"You're not considering—"

"No, let me think on this for a while. There must be another solution."

"I hope so, but believe me, I've tried looking at every angle while we've traveled."

"We can sleep on it," Father said, glancing toward me. "Maybe we'll know better in the morning."

I shook my head. "We cannot wait here until morning. Not with this other Hunter wanting Varak."

He frowned. "What do you propose we do?"

"I'm clearing the road."

"Now? In the dark?"

I shrugged. "We'd be a lot farther east if this roadblock had not been set. Besides, I'm not left with any other choice. The more distance we put between us and Philip, the better."

"Why not meet with the Hunter and talk it out?"

"There's no negotiation over this matter, Father. I assure you."

"We need to find a way."

"Go warm yourself, Father, and get something to eat. Make sure the girl and her brother get plenty to eat, too. I'll move enough rocks where the wagon can pass, and we'll move on."

"During the night? It'd be safer for us to remain near the fire."

I didn't bother continuing the argument. I turned and started heaving aside the rocks. I understood Father was tired, and being scrunched on the narrow coach seat made his aching legs hurt even more. Sleeping was nearly impossible, especially for me. The coach was also cold, even if a pile of quilts was stacked upon us. The cold weather made his legs hurt worse.

After a few minutes of his silence, I paused and looked over my shoulder. He had already returned to the fireside where he held his hands close to the flames. The bright flames revealed the comfort on his face.

While I tossed more rocks, my mind delved to find understanding and reasoning for how Philip had learned about Varak so quickly. He was determined to obtain the child, and if his goal was to kill Varak, Philip had to be a seasoned Hunter. Age-wise I had recently turned nine-years-old, so I wasn't hardened to emotions like I'd eventually become. Since my childlike mind was still more compassionate, I viewed Varak as an infant and not a detrimental threat to the world—yet.

I *wanted* to believe what Albert had suggested. Having this child reared by a person of high moral standing might alter his future thirst for becoming an uncontrollable heartless tyrant. If there was even the slightest hope, and I had to admit, it was *very* slight, Varak deserved the chance to circumvent the expected destiny that lay before him. Like Hunters feared one of our own becoming a vampire, I imagined the fear a hybrid bestowed to the vampire hierarchies if he proclaimed himself an enemy of all vampires and sought to eradicate them. He could succeed without much of a challenge because he held the upper hand.

That slightest chance of hope was what I clung to at the moment, and yet, this Hunter knew where we were. How? The most probable reason was that his Hunter instinct had prompted him to act, but the more I thought about the situation, the less likely that seemed.

After all, Albert had mentioned that it was almost impossible for a Hunter to discern a hybrid, at least not until *after* its bloodlust had overtaken all sensibility and rationality, and he left behind a massacre for the Hunters to discover.

But Varak was a child and his powers had yet to mature, so he couldn't attract the attention of a Hunter. Other than my father and myself, the were-rat and his boys were the only ones who even knew about Varak being a half-blood. With the superstitions most Gypsies kept, it was unlikely Esmeralda would have even told those closest to her that the child was a half-blood vampire. I was fairly certain they never knew she had been turned into a vampire, so it was doubtful any of them had sent the Hunter after Varak since he was one of their descendants. They, like her, would seek to keep him alive. So that left Albert, the were-rat.

I found it difficult to believe Albert would have betrayed us and sent this Hunter after Varak. Had he done so to test my loyalty? Surely if this other Hunter approached me, he'd challenge me for the child and harshly rebuke me for not doing what was expected of a Hunter. If I refused to surrender the boy, Philip would go to any means necessary to get Varak, even kill me.

I didn't like the idea of fighting another Hunter, but faced with such a situation, I'd have no other option. For Varak to live, I needed to remain alive.

Then, the forewarning Albert had given dawned upon me. He had said that one day I'd be faced with the task of killing someone who wasn't an undead or a supernatural creature. I'd be forced to kill another human and the ordeal would forever taint me inside, breaking my resolve to remain pure and making me colder. The were-rat seemed determined to set all the proper elements into place, leaving me with no other choices but to follow through.

A rise of anger pulsed through me. I began throwing the rocks aside quicker. His betrayal cut deeply. I had trusted Albert, and he had stood with us to destroy Duke Raginwulf and the Gypsy witch, but he had done so probably more for his own advantageous needs rather than for London's or my own.

Now I wondered if Albert had been the one who had sent the vampire Trenton after me, nearly killing me, and then left the bounty money the following morning.

What was his purpose?

My mind raced.

Turning Varak over to the Archdiocese directly contradicted my duties as a Hunter. My disobedience wrought dangers that I now recognized. Albert might have sent this Hunter to pursue us, however, many more might be summoned to track me and slay the hybrid because of my disobedience to the Chosen.

While that might explain Philip's reasons for following us, it didn't explain *why* the Hunter needed to hire the brother and sister to kidnap the child. Neither had the fighting skills or ruthlessness to succeed. He had to have known that by looking at them. They were simply poor desperate farmhands who needed food more than money. And whom he was using for a greater advantage.

Ruby had mentioned the rockslide had been used for ... a *distraction*. I hurried to throw, roll, and hurl the last rocks off the road and bridge that allowed enough room for the coach to pass.

"Everyone get into the wagon!" I shouted.

Everyone around the fire paused and looked toward me with great alarm.

I ran toward them.

How could I have allowed myself to be misdirected again?

Father hobbled toward me. "What is it?"

"Get in the wagon. Thomas, get to the coachman seat. We need to get out of here. *Now.*"

"Son, what's going on?"

"The Hunter. He's here."

"What? Are you certain?"

I nodded and pointed at Madeline. "Get Varak into the coach. Hurry."

"Forrest," Father said. "You're acting like a madman."

I opened the coach door and grabbed my Hunter box. "Get into the wagon, Father. We don't have much time."

"What are you doing?" he asked.

"Father, get into the wagon." I dug through my box, grabbing my dagger, and the gun. "The Hunter's here."

Father frowned. "Here? He's nowhere around."

"He's been here the entire time. Now, let's move. Otherwise we might all be dead," I replied.

Thomas sat on the driver's seat and nervously grabbed the reins. I helped Madeline step up into the coach. Father kept looking around but made no attempt to get inside. Finally I grabbed him by the back of his coat and heaved him through the coach door.

"No need for that," he said, frowning.

After I placed what few weapons I could use to defend myself against a Hunter, I closed the Hunter box and slid it onto the seat.

Ruby stood beside Drake and offered her hand to help him stand.

I shook my head. "You two stay here."

"What?" She whined with a feel-sorry-for-me face. "You're going to leave us here and him with a broken leg?"

"Ask the man who hired you for help, if you need a way home. Besides, there's no room for the two of you in the coach." I nodded toward Thomas and pointed. "Head on across the bridge."

"You're not riding with us?" Thomas asked.

"No. I'm following along on foot to keep watch," I replied. "I will catch up with you."

"No need for that, Forrest," a man said. "Just hand over the child and you're free to go. We'll have no troubles or contentions between us."

I turned to see the Hunter behind me. He was a massive man, my equal in height and weight, if my assumptions were correct, but he was a lot older and more experienced at everything a Hunter knew. The scars on his face were visible even through his beard. His eyes were cold and his gaze was worse than any vampire's heartless stare, sending chills down my back. He had survived a lot of fights and his severe scars testified to that fact. It didn't take but a second's time to realize he wasn't a sensible person.

I shook my head. "I'm afraid I cannot allow that."

A wild grin crept across his face. It was the answer he had hoped to hear. He pulled a dagger from his belt. "Then your problems are just beginning."

CHAPTER 5

I never had to say another word to Thomas, nor did he hesitate, as our danger was evident. He leaned forward, cracked the whip above the horse's head, causing it to bolt ahead, pulling the coach forward toward the bridge. He then snapped the reins and yelled commands until the horse was running at full speed.

Philip faced me with his knife at his side. The ease at which he held the blade informed me that this was his weapon of choice and one he enjoyed using. His menacing gaze indicated he was eager to shed blood. Mine.

Although I held my dagger, it was with far less confidence. I frowned at him, attempting to be more intimidating, but my lack of scars was a fairly good indicator of my fighting inexperience. "So that's it? You're just going to attack another Hunter?"

His jaw tightened. "You were given a choice."

"Hunters don't kill other Hunters. There's already too few Hunters in this world without us killing one another."

With the number of vampires escalating, we needed more Hunters than what were in the world. Those of the Chosen were few. Many like my father coveted being tapped with such a calling, so much so that I had encountered self-appointed Hunters who foolishly hoped to make their fortunes slaying vampires but instead reaped early graves. Being a Hunter I could discern an actual Hunter. And Philip was definitely one.

He frowned. "Your actions contradict what you've said. The number of vampires has increased. But from what I understand, you've gone rogue and that child with you is a half-blood, which is far more dangerous than a legion of vampires. So you've proven yourself useless to our cause."

"Is that what Albert told you?" I asked.

Mentioning the name jolted him slightly, causing his eyes to widen slightly, but he rebounded quickly without replying.

I grinned. "That's what I thought. Hunter instinct didn't reveal to you what the baby is or his location. The were-rat sent you with the knowledge."

"Does it rightly matter where I got the information since you're one to ignore the dangers of what a half-blood could do if left to survive?"

"It does matter, actually."

Perplexed, Philip gave me an odd stare and chuckled. "Why?"

"Because Albert didn't want to kill the child, either. It was he who insisted we take the child to Freiburg's cathedral for the archbishop to rear. This was his idea, but for my father and I, it was a setup."

"So the were-rat duped you?" He shrugged.

"And you, too, apparently."

He ground his teeth. "The child still cannot be allowed to live. There isn't any need for blood to be shed between the two of us, Forrest. As you've already stated, Hunters shouldn't attack one another. Just let me do my duty. I'll be on my way and you can be on yours."

"No. I won't allow you to harm him."

"Why would you keep this child alive?"

"Because there is hope that his destined path can be altered."

Philip's brow narrowed. Fury set in his gaze. "You're a fool. You cannot coddle a poisonous asp and expect it to gradually acquire affection for you. Eventually it turns and bites you. Regardless of how well you have treated it, it is still deadly and will kill you without hesitation at the first opportunity that arises. A half-blood is no different."

"He is an infant—"

25

"Don't be blinded by the smallness of the vessel. It's the vile content, deep inside, which longs to come to the surface. It will only magnify and never lessen." He pointed his dagger at me. "You need to realize it is *not* human."

"He is half."

"Fool! Have you been mesmerized by its gaze? Has he charmed you into being his servant?"

"No," I replied. "I'm immune to—"

Philip nodded with a sly grin. "See? You've already felt his power. Upbringing will not lessen what he already is."

"Time will tell."

The Hunter lunged toward me and slashed his dagger. I recoiled but almost failed to avoid the blade. "Seems we're at a standstill when it comes to reasoning."

"There isn't any rationalization with you."

He came at me again. I watched his eyes, waiting for him to strike. He looked to the left, I reacted, but his hand made an underhand slice to the right. His eyes had deliberately tricked me. The sharp blade split open a long section of my thick coat sleeve, narrowly missing flesh. He took a quick step back and then shot forward again. This time I kept my eyes on his dagger, stepped slightly to the side, and gripped his wrist tightly. I yanked him in the direction he had thrust the blade, and pulled him off balance.

His feet fought to slow his momentum but he was unable to gain traction upon the icy edge of the road. He fell forward and rolled into the thick bramble.

I considered running to catch up with the coach, but I wasn't certain how fast this Hunter was. If he were swifter, he'd catch up and attack me from behind. Plus, I wasn't certain what other weapons he might have.

From the dark embankment he growled and rose. In the light of the campfire his eyes looked dark and sinister and nothing like I imagined an aged Hunter's eyes to appear. I worried if this was what I'd eventually look like after years of slaying vampires. His frigid gaze fastened upon me. Death gleamed in his eyes. Like I had felt power leap from aged vampires, a similar energy stirred around him, not necessarily evil, but not untainted either.

"You're a young Hunter, aren't you?" he asked, cocking a brow. He sensed my weaknesses compared to what power he yielded. "Naïve and trusting, that's why you won't kill the child."

He stepped from the embankment and walked slowly across the road toward me. His eyes regarded me in the same manner mine often viewed vampires and other undead creatures. He was enslaved to his need to kill. I was his enemy, only because I had chosen to hope Varak could somehow be redeemed. But I wasn't foolish. I knew my limitations. I wasn't strong enough to beat him. His rage overrode my strength. In a knife fight, he'd shred me open and watch me bleed to death. He held no compassion for me, no mercy.

I never expected to fight to the death with another Hunter. It wasn't something I had ever imagined until after I had taken Varak. I understood why I was Philip's enemy.

He leaned forward and rushed toward me with lightning speed. His blade was extended outward so he could plunge it into my gut, or change the angle quickly and slash me high or low. I wasn't certain how to defend his advance. Even though my blade was out, I was too worried about getting stabbed to consider a counterattack.

My mind focused on the blade and his swift advance. The blade shone in the fire's light. Before he was able to stab or slash, I attempted to run, but I tripped over my large feet and tumbled sideways. I pivoted, fighting my fall, but I had nothing to grab to correct my balance.

The Hunter turned slightly, trying to follow my accidental direction and slice me with the blade, but I fell outside his reach. His right boot caught my feet, tripping him. He hit the ground, growled out of frustration, and rolled around to get up. From behind Ruby swung the club and struck him in the back of the head hard, sending him to the ground unconscious. He dropped so fast the pain had never registered on his face.

She held the club overhead, staring down at Philip, waiting to see if he was going to try to get up again. Until this moment, I had completely forgot about her and Drake. After she was satisfied that he wasn't getting back up for a while, she lowered the club and with bewildered eyes, she stared at me. "Did he say that he wanted to *kill* that baby we had taken?"

I nodded.

"Why?"

"It's best you don't know."

"What's a half-blood? The baby looked normal to me," she said.

I ignored the question and nodded toward the Hunter. "Thanks for ..."

Ruby grinned. "Thanks for the food."

I took some of the longer twine that Drake had been tied with earlier before I had cut through the knots. I flipped Philip facedown and tied his wrists together tighter than normal, hoping he didn't possess the strength to snap the restraints. I didn't want him to get loose until someone happened upon him and cut him free.

"Ruby, you two don't need to be nearby when he awakens, but with Drake's leg, I can't see any quick way for you to get far."

"You regret breaking my leg now?" Drake asked.

I narrowed my gaze at him, and he swallowed hard. "Perhaps a little. But don't forget *why* I did what I did."

I reached into the Hunter's coat pockets and found his wallet and coin pouch. I tossed them to Ruby. She smiled. "When we first met him, he had a horse."

"Did he?"

She nodded.

"Then it's probably tied nearby. But I've never heard one." Tied horses grew impatient and usually protested with some type of nay or stomping of feet. "Wait here."

Drake scoffed. "Where do you think I'll go?"

I grinned. "Not far."

I jogged along the crude mountain pass road until a soft whinny caught my attention. Tied at the edge of the road was a dark mare. I untied her, swung up onto the saddle, and rode back to the campfire.

"You're taking it for yourself?" Ruby asked. "When my brother's injured?"

Swinging off the saddle, I shook my head. "No. I'm going to help Drake onto the saddle, and then you slide in front of him. Ride to your home, but not too quickly. You don't want Drake to fall off. You might not be able to get him on the horse again, or a fall might hurt his leg even worse."

Ruby tucked her long strands of hair behind her ears and offered a radiant smile. After helping them both onto the saddle, I searched the saddlebags and took all the Hunter's weapons stored inside.

"What kind of weapons are those?" she asked.

I shrugged. "Let's hope you never need to find out. Now, you two head on home."

"You just going to leave the Hunter there?"

"I'm sure someone will come along in the morning to free him."

"And if they don't?" she asked.

"I imagine he'll become quite cold after the fire dies down. Now go."

Ruby tapped the mare's sides softly. The horse began walking.

Once they were farther away, I searched through Philip's pockets and took any other Hunter weapons he had. I found his dagger on the ground and tossed it over the ravine and hoped it landed in the stream. Even if it didn't, I doubted he'd ever find it again. Other than Dominus I had encountered a few Hunters without contention but none had befriended me like Dominus, and I hated being on this one's bad side. Under the current conditions, there was no redeeming myself with Philip. I needed to catch up to the others, and we needed to put a lot of distance between this aged, mentally disturbed Hunter and us.

Traveling faster to Freiburg might help, but Philip already knew our destination. Albert had told him. Albert had mentioned that our paths would probably pass again. After his betrayal, to that I held no doubts. I definitely intended to seek the were-rat out in the future, but our meeting would not be pleasant. He had a lot of explaining to do.

Staring at Philip's face, I worried that I'd become what this man was, and that deeply disturbed me. I supposed even the righteous slayings of vampires and the undead affected a person's mind over time. Shoving a stake into the heart of a vampire was justified, but the subconscious could become suppressed from guilt since in appearance a vampire still looked like a human. Dominus had partly warned me, but I truly hoped to keep my sanity intact regardless of the number of vampires I slayed during my travels. While awake, slaying vampires was different than what can be projected in a nightmare where the mind doesn't necessarily distinguish the living from the undead.

As I hurried down the road toward the bridge, I thought about the issue at hand. Weighing both sides of the arguments, I was still torn in making a solid decision. There wasn't any accurate way to predict what was best. I had chosen mercy and hope for a child that might eventually possess neither in his regard for society.

CHAPTER 6

*A*fter I had crossed the bridge and rounded the next bend of the descending mountain road, I realized I might end up walking through the night before I ever caught up to my father and the others. But at least the moon shone brightly in the clear night sky.

Wolves howled in the wooded valley below.

The large oaks and maples on both sides of the road weren't tightly knit together like the pine and fir forest I had run through when I had searched for Varak. No thick underbrush and bramble weaved in-between the tree trunks, either. The moonlight cast odd shadows through the leafless canopy and at times, I could have sworn somebody was running from one tree to the other, following me.

Shoving my hands into my coat pockets, I gripped a stake in each gloved hand. While I was fairly certain Philip was still restrained, I didn't believe I was alone. Besides, Philip wasn't one who would hide amongst the trees. As angry as he'd be when he finally awoke, if he caught up to me, he'd be certain to make a direct attack. However, since Ruby and Drake had left on his horse, his journey on foot slowed him down quite a bit.

A part of me worried that leaving him bound and weaponless had not been the right thing to do. I didn't know what lurked in this mountainous area, but if a vampire came upon Philip, it wouldn't hesitate to drain the Hunter's blood or possibly turn him into one of the damned, creating something as bad as what Varak was. I cringed. It would be my fault and another iniquity against the Chosen, something that would ensure additional penance.

The Hunter had left me little choice though. He could kill me; I could kill him, or we surrendered the child to him to kill. None were outcomes I favored.

Crisp leaves smashed underfoot in the forest. When I stopped, the crunching sounds did as well. I picked up my pace, disliking the shadowy trees more and more by the second. As I walked, the footsteps followed.

The wind howled, slicing through the trees and causing me to tighten my coat near the collar and tip my hat forward. The frozen road crunched under the thudding of my heavy steps. Whoever or whatever was in the forest kept its distance and seemed to avoid being seen whenever I glanced toward the trees. Perhaps it followed me from its curiosity, and I was fine with that, as long as it never charged toward me to attack.

While watching the trees from the corner of my eye, my mind returned to Albert again. I couldn't make any sense out of why he had set us up. His actions surrounding Varak were sinister and hypocritical. Several times he had offered to turn *me* into a were-rat, but I had declined. I couldn't see that being the reason he'd sent the Hunter after us. If he were truly vindictive about my decision, he could have clawed or bitten me in the tunnels during our pursuit of the vampire or the Gypsy witch, but he had never made any such attempt. He seemed to honor my refusal without bitterness, which was why his underhanded betrayal angered me.

Something else troubled me now as I continued down the road. Thomas and Madeline. Albert had offered their services to me because these two owed him favors, but I wondered if that were true. After encountering a Hunter dead set on killing me for the baby, were these two we traveled with trustworthy or did they have ulterior motives?

The descending road arced toward the left. I partway jogged. I was about a mile from the small town we had intended to reach before the roadblock had slowed our pace.

To the right side of the widening road, the forest ended. A crude rock wall lined the edge of the road, perhaps to prevent a wagon or coach from slipping over the embankment during the icier times of the winter, but it also offered a nice overlook of the town below.

A flickering torch caught my attention. Parked farther down at the edge of the rock wall was our coach. Thomas stood in front of the horse with a bag of feed slipped over the horse's mouth. Frothy sweat dripped from the horse and steam rose off its body.

Thomas turned at the sound of my heavy footsteps. He gasped. I guessed his reaction was from how the brightness of the moon had obscured my shadow on the roadway, but I was wrong. It was what stood behind me that horrified him. The air grew even colder, making my next breath so painful that I expected it to be my last.

I sensed something behind me. Glancing over my shoulder, I swung around to the shadowed outline of a creature that made me flinch. My eyes adjusted enough for me to see more details. Its ears were pointed. The creature was nude. Its skin was ebony and hairless. Its bald head was dome shaped. The beady red eyes shimmered like flames and it had rows of sharp jagged teeth.

At first glance, I thought this was a ghoul. I grabbed the torch from the sconce on the coach.

"No, Forrest," Thomas said. "Don't. It's a plague-demon. If it touches you, you'll die within minutes."

Was this what had followed me through the forest?

The demon gnashed its teeth. I held the torch between it and me. Small bubbling pustules formed all over its skin, swelling and popping, leaking pus, and cycling through the little eruptions over and over.

"Fire won't hurt it," Thomas said.

"How do you know this?" I asked.

"Because it has come for me."

I stared at him over my shoulder. "What?"

He nodded. Fear shrouded his face. "Albert sent it."

"Albert?"

LEONARD D. HILLEY II

"Yes."

"He sent this demon after you? Why? To kill you?"

A look of utter gloom overshadowed his face. "I owed him a debt. One I could never repay. He offered me a challenge that either freed me of what I owed or I paid with my life. Either way, I didn't owe him anything afterwards."

"What was the deal?"

Thomas sighed. "If I could get you, your father, and the child to Freiburg before the plague-demon caught up to us, I kept my life and owed him nothing, provided I never returned to London."

"And after you died, we became essentially stranded?"

Thomas looked down. "Yes."

"Well, you're not dead yet."

"Let me accept my Fate, Forrest. Don't jeopardize your life for mine."

Perhaps this was why the entire time he had driven during the worst winter conditions he had never issued a complaint. It certainly explained his nervousness when we had come to the roadblock. His goal had been to stay ahead of the demon. But I didn't think this creature was able to pursue a horse and coach so quickly, even with our delay at the bridge.

"Thomas, I'm a Hunter. No need to sacrifice your life to it. There has to be ways to kill it."

I turned toward the demon and thrust the torch at it. It didn't move, nor did it show any fear of the fire. Its intense stare focused on Thomas and ignored me, not even regarding the torch or me as a threat.

"Fire isn't one of them, Hunter," a female said from the hillside above me. "I've been tracking him for hours through the woods. Don't you dare rob me of my kill!"

I glanced in her direction. Her silhouette showed her pull back the bowstring and fire. The arrow pierced into the back of the vile demon's head and disintegrated. Its black body stiffened. Red flames surfaced on its skin through its leaking pustules and the demon crumbled into a heap of ash.

She ran down the road toward us. Her hand dusted away the thick ash until a polished stone the size of a small grape became visible. She picked it up and examined it in my torch's flame. With a slight smile, she said, "An emerald this time."

"An emerald? From a demon?" Thomas asked with keen curiosity.

"Reward for my service. The last three had been sapphires."

"There were more?" Thomas asked.

She nodded.

He glanced toward me. "He mentioned only one."

"Albert cannot be taken at his word," I replied.

Thomas whispered, "I suppose not."

I held the torch above my head to look at the young lady. The bright flame revealed more of her. She had streaked her face with mud, which had dried and become cakey and was starting to crumble. Dead branches and weeds had been tucked into her oily braids. I supposed to help conceal her as she slinked through the trees and shrubs. In her disguise it was difficult to judge her true appearance.

Her odor, on the other hand, was ripe like soured sweat. I had seen fewer boys with less filth upon them after a day of labor in the muddy fields than what she had traipsed during her hunt for these demons. Of course, I had no idea how long she had been out on this particular hunt, either.

Around her neck hung a strange pair of goggles. The lenses were bulged and connected with a leather strap. She tucked the gem into a small pouch on her narrow belt. Then she took a wide mouthed jar from the small pack on her shoulders. After unscrewing the lid, she filled the jar with the smoldering ash and sealed it shut.

Her eyes glanced toward me. Her soft voice was more pleasant than I expected. "Thank you, Hunter, for not robbing me of my kill. Did you really think fire would affect a demon?"

"I had hoped."

She laughed in a wild high-pitched tone. "Demons come from the pits of Hell where they find comfort in the flames. You offered no real threat to him at all."

"We greatly appreciate your help ... Miss—" I said, looking at her.

"Penelope," she replied. "And you are, Hunter?"

"Forrest, and this is our coachman, Thomas."

She did a slight elegant curtsey in spite of her grimy exterior.

Thomas removed the feedbag from the horse's mouth. "We should get going, Forrest. If she's killed four of them, there's bound to be more."

I nodded.

"You need to take me along," Penelope said.

"We don't have enough room," I replied.

"That's gratitude for you. Leave me out in the cold after I saved your friend's life." She scrunched her nose.

"There's hardly room in the seat for me," I said.

She grinned. "Then it will be nice and cozy, eh? I don't mind. Really. As cold as it is, it will keep us warm until we reach our next destination."

I stood with a long awkward silence, which was broken by Thomas smacking my shoulder and laughing softly. "The two of you will manage quite splendidly, regardless of how little room you have."

My brow narrowed as I watched him climb up onto his seat.

"Besides," Penelope said, "more of these demons will appear. They seldom travel alone, but these seem determined in infecting whomever they've been sent after. Even though I've only encountered one at a time, I've killed four in the last half hour. They're coming after Thomas, aren't they?"

He nodded nervously.

"Interesting," she said.

"What?" I asked.

"With their dedicated determination, I would've assumed they had come after you since you're the Hunter. He's just a coachman."

"No, the demon wasn't my problem," I replied.

"He has another Hunter hunting him," Thomas said.

She cocked a brow and pursed her lips for a moment. "Really? Why?"

"It's a long explanation," I said.

"We have plenty of time." Her face beamed beneath the layer of dried mud. Bits of loose debris flaked off her skin.

I looked up at Thomas. "What exactly did you owe Albert?"

"Now isn't the time to discuss it, Forrest. Honestly, we need to be moving onward. I will drive through the night, if necessary, to prevent us from encountering any more demons."

Penelope nodded. "That's wiser than stopping along the way. Plague demons seldom appear during the day."

"So travel at night and sleep during the day?" I asked.

She shrugged. "Shouldn't be any different than what a Vampire Hunter does anyway, correct?"

"Depends upon the vampire," I replied. "I'd rather stake them in their crypts during the daylight hours whenever possible."

Thomas glanced over his shoulder to the road behind us and then he narrowed his gaze at me. "Please, Forrest, let's go."

"What about Madeline?" I asked. "Was she indebted to Albert as well?"

He shrugged. "I don't know. You need to ask her. Now get inside, so we can travel on."

Penelope smiled and opened the coach door. "Should I get in first?"

I shrugged. "Only if you want me to crush you by accident. It's probably safer if I get settled first."

She waited for me to squeeze inside the coach and seat myself before she climbed in. I slid over as far as I possibly could, and she fit beside me with more room than I had imagined she'd have. She placed her bow at our feet and yanked the door closed.

Father snored, and Madeline opened one eye momentarily before closing it and returning to sleep, if she had awakened at all. I doubted our presence had even registered with her. At least I hoped she was still deeply asleep because I wanted to learn more about the Demon-hunter without any interruptions from Madeline or Father.

CHAPTER 7

"*H*ow did you kill that demon?" I asked.

"You worry about slaying the vampires. Let *me* kill the demons."

"What's that hanging around your neck?"

"My spectacles? You like them?"

I nodded.

Penelope untied the leather strap and handed the odd glasses to me. "Take a look."

I placed the spectacles against my eyes and peered through the lenses. Immediately everything in the coach brightened as though we were in daylight or had several bright oil lanterns lit. The outer rim of the glasses was solid brass with thick brads fastening the goggles against the thick leather. On the right lens were crosshairs to zero in on a target. I pulled back the curtain and gazed outside. Everything was bright in the forest. I marveled and turned toward her. "Where did you get these?"

"I had a craftsman make them for me," she replied. "Since most demons are active during the night, I needed a better way to see in the darkness. No need to give them an advantage over me."

"I'd love to get a pair of those. Were they expensive?"

"I had to kill one Astaroth demon and two lesser abyssal demons to earn enough money to pay the metal crafter." She picked up her bow and pointed at a round lens. Brass protected the glass. "He also made this, so I can have almost pinpoint accuracy."

"Do all of the demons you've killed leave behind gems?"

Penelope shook her head. "No. An Astaroth is extremely rare to happen upon. They are seldom seen. It left me several large diamonds, which I sold to a gem crafter. The lessers each left large garnets of rare colors, so I fetched a good bit of money for those. But I have killed dozens of demons and not reaped a single gem or gold nugget. These plague demons have been consistent thus far, but I don't understand why. Of course I've never seen them travel alone or have a replacement emerge soon after I have killed one. They usually are sent in small numbers to infect an entire city."

"What did you kill it with?"

"You saw the arrow, didn't you?"

"I thought I had, but it must have dissolved when it struck the demon. The arrow wasn't there after the demon turned to ash. That's why I asked."

She smiled. "The arrow was consumed by the plague, which is a protective measure for these demons. But the poisoned arrow destroyed the disease, causing the demon to incinerate. These demons don't have blood. The plague oozes through their veins, keeping them alive until they gut themselves inside a group of people in a town or city and the disease is released. You kill the plague and they die. Fire can't hurt them, but the poison I use can."

"So you have a poison that destroys the plague? How'd you happen upon that?"

"A healer. But most folks would probably consider her a witch."

"I see. Is she in your town?"

She shook her head. "No. She lives in the forest. Deep in the forest. She doesn't like visitors."

"But she likes you?" I asked.

Penelope shrugged her narrow shoulders. "After she accidentally summoned a demon during one of her rituals, she sought me out. I killed the demon for her, and we sort of entered into a bartering exchange. She has ... *medicines* I need, and I trade her things she needs."

"Like what?"

"Witches need a vast array of ingredients for their incantations. Demon dust is obviously something easy for me to obtain. Vampire dust, on the other hand, I occasionally get whenever a Hunter is *kind* enough to allow me to go along on one of his kills."

I was still staring at her through the goggles. She batted her eyelids at me with a flirty smile, which might have worked better if she didn't have the cakey mud smeared across her face and the twigs and ferns tucked in her matted hair. A bath would have helped as well.

"I'm all out of vampire dust," I replied.

She rolled her eyes, sighed, and looked away. "Like *you'd* be carrying it on you to begin with."

I chuckled. "To be honest with you, our funds for our journey have almost depleted, so my father and I will probably seek to find a place where a reward is being offered to kill a vampire."

"Your father is a Hunter, too?"

I shook my head and whispered, "He hunts them, but he's not one of the Chosen."

She winked. "Ah, I see. I suppose he's sensitive about that?"

I nodded.

"I know a place," she said, looking toward me with a broad smile. "Where you could earn money for killing a vampire."

"Is it far from here?"

"We should reach it by daylight, depending upon which route your coachman decides to take. If any other plague demons are following us, they won't likely surface after the sun rises. It would give us enough time to find the lair. You kill the vampire, I get its dust, and then you return to get the money. Afterwards, your coachman heads to the next point of your destination. Where are you traveling to anyway?"

"Freiburg," I replied.

Her brow rose. "That far away?"

I nodded.

"Why?"

"The child Madeline's holding. We're taking him there."

"To the Archdiocese?"

"Yes."

Her eyes widened with excitement. "Would you mind if I traveled there with you?"

"Why?"

"I've heard about the beauty of the cathedral and the town. It's always been a place I've wanted to venture to. Since I do most of my traveling on foot, it's unlikely I'd ever get to go. So do you mind letting me ride along?"

"If you're not too crowded?"

Again her broad smile widened. It was cute in spite of her ... muddy cheeks. "Not at all. I have plenty of room right here beside you. You put off enough body heat to dispel the cold. Do you think the others will mind? My coming along?"

There was something about her that intrigued me. Maybe it was the softness of her voice or the look in her eyes when she stared at me, but I rather liked the thought of traveling with someone who was closer to my age. Besides, she had not only saved Thomas from the demon, she had ensured that I hadn't been infected by it. I didn't have much knowledge about demons. By having her with us, I could learn a lot from her.

Her eyes showed her eagerness for my answer. I smiled. "I don't think there will be any objections."

"Thanks." Penelope scrunched her nose and scooted against the doorframe. She tucked her arms tightly to her sides. "I hate that we're traveling through the night instead of stopping at an inn though."

"Why?"

As she closed her eyes, a grim smile formed on her face. "I'm embarrassed to say that I have developed quite a foul odor from tracking and killing those demons. I apologize. I didn't ... realize it until after getting inside these tight quarters beside you."

"I probably don't smell any better after my earlier run-ins." I thought about my plummet down the mossy hill and landing in all the half-frozen mud and debris, not to mention how much I had sweated from my nervous near-death encounter with Philip.

LEONARD D. HILLEY II

"I'm afraid it's much more different."

"Why is that?"

"You're a man, and well, men tend to sweat a lot, especially after a hard day's work. There's seldom a man in my village that you cannot smell far before you see him. Even deer musk isn't *that* bad." She grinned. "But a *lady* needs better cleanliness."

Lady? I almost scoffed, but watching her through the goggles, I read the sincerity on her face. The meekness in her voice caused me to view her in a different light. She was genuinely embarrassed. Based upon our first meeting and seeing her now, I couldn't ever imagine her in a frilly dress. It contradicted her rugged appearance. She had more dirt encrusted around her fingers and beneath her short fingernails than I did, and she still regarded herself as a lady, in spite of everything else. But like me, she took her calling seriously, and sometimes, that demanded us to step outside our normal boundaries.

A tear trickled from her eye and the cakey mud quickly claimed it.

I felt sadness for her. "You're amongst friends, so no need to fret."

She frowned and pointed toward my father and Madeline. "They're asleep. What would they fret over right now anyway?"

I shrugged with a teasing smile. "The less they'll complain."

She thrust a playful elbow into my ribs with a soft giggle so lovely I could have listened to her laugh for hours. I found myself attracted to her and liked her being close to me.

I turned slightly in the seat to see her without constantly straining my neck. "Whenever we reach this town you mentioned where the vampire is, we'll find an inn or a bathhouse."

Penelope didn't reply, so I decided to change the subject.

"How long have you been a Demon-hunter?"

"Eight years."

She had been killing demons for almost as long as I had been alive, and she didn't have any visible scars. "How old were you when you killed your first one?"

"Twelve, I think. It's hard to remember. How about you? How old were you when you killed your first vampire?"

I froze. I didn't wish to reveal my actual age to her. For some reason,

42

I thought she'd think less of me or treat me like a child. I frowned, pretending to be deep in thought. "Like you said, it is hard to remember, isn't it?"

Her thick dirty eyebrows rose. She remained skeptical for a few moments. "It can be."

"What prompted you to hunt demons? Few men your age would dare hunt down demons."

Penelope looked at me with a sense of pride glowing on her face. "Like Vampire Hunters, we're Chosen, too."

"I didn't realize that."

She smiled. "There are those who hunt demons without being Chosen, but they usually end up possessed or sacrificed. While I'm not exactly immune from being possessed, it's a lot harder for a demon to gain the control over me to enter my mind or body."

"I'm resistant to a vampire's compulsion, and even a master's. Thus far, anyway."

"I guess such abilities were deemed upon us so we can slay the demons and vampires. Otherwise, we'd become victims."

"How is it that you know so much about Vampire Hunters?"

Penelope folded her hands together and rested them on her lap. "My father was one of the Chosen."

"*Was?*"

Biting her lower lip, she turned toward the window, but she didn't attempt to move the curtain to peer outside. "I've not seen him in years, so ... I suppose he *might* still be alive."

"If it eases your mind any, the Hunters I know travel constantly, sometimes moving across the oceans and through many countries. The older ones become drifters. My guess is they do so to draw less attention to themselves or to protect their loved ones. Maybe he's traveling elsewhere?"

"Maybe. How long have you been a Hunter?"

"Less than a year."

She offered a bewildered stare. "How many kills?"

"Nearly a couple of dozen."

"Impressive. Where did you and the others depart in this coach?"

43

"London."

She looked stunned. "So tell me *why* you're taking the baby to Freiburg when there are other cathedrals along the way?"

That was a good question since I had discovered Albert had betrayed us. "I don't rightly know."

"And why take the child to a cathedral and *not* an orphanage?"

"The child's welfare could become greatly jeopardized in an orphanage."

Penelope looked at me and realized I was still looking at her through the spectacles. "You like those, huh?"

I nodded. "I like to see who I'm talking to."

"You're at the advantage then."

I lowered them. "Here, I'll give them—"

"No. I'll let you keep using them while we ride, but should we be forced to exit the coach due to a demon attack, I'll need them back." She smiled. "You can hold onto them but *only* if you answer a question for me. Deal?"

"Depends upon what information you're fishing for."

"Fair enough. I'd rather you tell me than for me to draw my own conclusions."

"That isn't a question," I said with a teasing smile.

Penelope stared at Varak, took a deep breath, and sighed. "This child must be of the utmost importance for a Hunter to escort … him? It's a boy?"

"Yes, and now I've answered your question."

She elbowed me slightly and shook her head. "That was *a* question, Forrest, but not *the* question."

I tsk'ed with my tongue. "You need to be more specific."

"The boy is very important for you—a Hunter—to be escorting him across several countries to get him to the Archdiocese. Why is he this important and *why* are you protecting him?"

"That's two questions. You said one."

"It was asked as a single question." Penelope gave a me a shrewd narrowing of the eyes and scrunched her nose.

I shook my head. "It had *two* whys. Which question do you wish to have answered?"

The expression on her face indicated that she knew I was teasing because I half expected her to hit me. Instead of being agitated, she grinned. "Fine. I'll rephrase the question. Why is he so important that you need to protect him? Anyone could deliver him to the Archdiocese."

I handed her the spectacles.

"You're not going to answer?" she asked.

I shook my head.

"Why not?"

"It's safer you don't know."

Her brow furrowed. "Phht. Really? I kill demons, Forrest, sometimes on a daily basis. You realize that, so whatever reasons you have for making this journey pales in comparison to what you *think* you're protecting me from. Unless you're hiding something else from me?"

I turned slightly on the seat.

She placed her hand onto the back of mine. "Your coachman said that another Hunter is hunting you. Is that really true?"

I nodded.

"Has he attacked you?"

"Yes. His intent was to kill me."

Penelope rubbed the back of my hand. "Because of this baby?"

I stared through the darkness to where the baby was cradled in Madeline's arm. Even though I couldn't see them without the aid of the spectacles, I sensed his presence. He wasn't quite a year old yet, and Madeline continued nursing him, but his aura was growing stronger. I wondered if Penelope could detect his power yet or not, or if Demon-hunters were even capable of sensing what Vampire Hunters could?

Varak definitely could influence others to do his bidding. He couldn't speak yet, but he commanded his persuasion in subtle unex-plained ways. His eyes were captivating, and Madeline had been endeared to him in the same manner as Esmeralda and the former wet-nurse had been. They were willing to fight and sacrifice their lives in order to save his. The same had occurred when Ruby had held the baby for less than an hour. Her knocking the other Hunter unconscious wasn't her idea. Varak had somehow indicated to her the threat this

45

Hunter presented to the child. Ruby was small and frail compared to the Hunter, and obeying his request for the reward would have outweighed her decision to attack the man. Had he not lost consciousness, he could have killed her in an instant.

Varak was already powerful and those unknowingly yielding themselves to him would never suspect he was inside their minds controlling their thoughts. It would be ludicrous for anyone to believe, except for me or any other Hunter. Even my father forgot what Varak truly was at times.

The things babies needed the most were food, shelter, and love. Of the three, love was the most important. Love shaped minds early, allowing a child to feel safe and sheltered. Babies couldn't ask to be loved. That came from the parents, but Varak was different. His real parents were dead. His life had already been threatened many times, and to survive long enough for him to reach adulthood, he needed dedicated, undying devotion. He already understood that his life was endangered. Such knowledge could only come from what he truly was—a half-blood.

Penelope had separated her spectacles into two separate lenses and placed one on my lap. Then she enveloped her tiny hand around the side of mine. I closed my hand gently around hers. "Did you hear my question, Forrest?"

I jerked around toward her. "I'm sorry. My mind was drifting."

"I thought maybe you were thinking about something else. It's late. You can stare through the goggle I handed you, if you wish to look at me while we talk." She placed hers to her eye and faced me. "I can see you now, too."

"You didn't break them, did you?"

"No. They fasten back together rather easily."

I placed the one to my eye. "What did you ask?"

"The hunter is after you about this baby. Why?"

"Penelope," I said softly.

"Forrest, since I'm traveling with you, I need to know *why* he's pursuing you over this child. I cannot think of any logical reason for him doing that. So let me know if me fighting alongside you against this

Hunter is worth even sacrificing my life, okay? That's fair enough, isn't it?"

I sighed and whispered close to her ear. "It is. And if you decide it's not worth it, we let you off at the next town."

She squeezed my hand and nuzzled closer so we spoke only in whispers. "Okay."

"Varak is a half-blood. He's half vampire and half human, considered by Hunters to be an abomination to the human population."

"A half-blood?" Her eyebrow above the goggle rose. "Are you certain? That's so rare most people regard it as only a legend."

"I wish that were the case, but it isn't," I replied.

"How are you certain?"

"We know Varak's origin. He's already capable of influencing those who are taking care of his needs."

"According to the legend, since you're a Hunter, you're supposed to … kill him but you don't intend to?"

"That sums it up," I replied. "So do you want us to let you off at the next town or do you still wish to go to Freiburg with us?"

"To be honest, I couldn't carry out those orders, either. I'm surprise any Hunter could. But, you know, I cannot recall in history where a half-blood has ever reigned, can you?"

I shook my head.

"Where is it written that all half-bloods are evil?"

"I don't know."

"Me, either. Does the archbishop know you're coming?" she asked.

"My guess is no. But we were given strict instructions *not* to tell him what Varak is. Madeline and the coachman *don't* know. Just my father and myself, and now you."

Her mouth came closer to my ear. Her whispered breath was hot when she spoke. Chill bumps prickled down my neck and back. I closed my eyes. My stomach felt odd because of her closeness. "I wish to continue to Freiburg with you, Forrest. You might be intimidating to a lot of people, but you seem to have a gentle heart. I like talking to you and don't mind sharing this seat with you at all. I hope you feel the same, too."

Before I replied, she softly pressed her lips to my cheek. I swallowed hard.

"It's late," she said. "If you don't mind, I'd like to get some sleep."

"Perfectly fine by me. I'm tired, too."

With the gentle rocking of the coach, it didn't take long for me to fall asleep. Dreams this night were more pleasant than any I had had in months.

CHAPTER 8

A sliver of light shone through the curtain where my shoulder had pushed it aside while I slept. The light caught my closed eyes perfectly, prompting me to awaken. I shifted slightly and discovered Penelope had snuggled against me during the night. Her face was nuzzled against my chest and her arm wrapped around my waist. Her hand clung to my side like she was hugging me, and my right hand rested on her back.

She breathed softly. The warmth of her embrace brought strange excitement to my chest and stomach that I didn't understand. I found comfort from her closeness and hoped she didn't awaken for hours. I didn't want her to stop holding me. I felt less alone and isolated with her pressed against me.

I glanced up and noticed Father staring intently at me. His eyes questioned without him uttering a single word. A slight grin crossed his lips.

"Where did she come from?" he asked softly.

I explained what had occurred while he was asleep.

"Plague demons?"

I nodded.

His brow furrowed. "This journey gets more livelier the farther we go."

"It's been eventful," I replied.

"And she's traveling with us?"

"Yes."

"To Freiburg?"

I nodded.

"She hunts demons?"

"Yes."

Varak stirred in Madeline's arms, causing her to awaken. She pulled a thin blanket to cover him while she let him nurse.

Father stared at Penelope for a few moments before his eyes shifted to look into mine again. "You reckon she ever bathes?"

Even though she was asleep I found myself offended by his question. My jaw tightened and I spoke in a low even tone. "She was trying to keep herself concealed while tracking demons through the forests. I imagine she doesn't always look like this, but you're free to ask her when she awakens."

"Son, I didn't mean that like it sounded."

I picked bits of dried fern sprigs and twigs from her tight braids with my left hand, trying not to disturb her sleep. She took a deep breath, raised her head slightly, and rubbed her cheek against my chest. Dried mud crumbled. Small pieces of dirt clods slid down my shirt and formed a tiny pile at the top of my belt.

Father said, "I just thought that demons could sense a human's presence, even in disguise."

"Something else you need to ask her. I don't know enough about demons to tell you."

"Perhaps she can train you."

"I'm willing to learn."

I peered down at her. Her brow furrowed, and she blinked several times before looking up into my eyes. I held my breath. Her hazel eyes were bright, almost sparkling and more beautiful than a priceless gemstone.

"You're stomach's growling," she said, easing up.

My hand eased off her back.

"He's always hungry," Father said.

She jolted up and glanced in his direction. I quickly introduced her to Madeline and Father.

After Penelope slid away from me, I suddenly felt cold without the warmth of her body next to mine. She lifted the curtain slightly and peered out. "We've reached the outskirts of a city with a large cathedral."

Thomas slowed the coach. I leaned beside her and peered out. Even with the coachman driving through the entire night, we were still days away—or *weeks* dependent upon the weather and terrain—from arriving at Freiburg. As magnificent as this cathedral was, this wasn't the Archdiocese.

He stopped the coach along a side street at a small inn. Once he tied the horse, Penelope opened the door and hurried out. I followed, but slightly slower since I had to maneuver my large frame through the narrow door. I turned and helped Father and Madeline climb down. She clutched Varak to her chest.

The overcast sky hinted of cold rain or snow and added a gloomy tint to this rundown set of buildings on the edge of the city.

"Where are we?" I asked.

Thomas rubbed his bloodshot eyes and grinned. "Strasbourg, France. We're less than a week from reaching Freiburg. If I can get a few quick hours of sleep while everyone eats, I'll push onward at noon."

I glanced toward Father. "Our funds are nearly depleted. Penelope says that she knows where we might obtain a decent reward to slay a vampire."

Father eyed her nervously.

She grinned, but with all the dirt and debris covering her, it wasn't exactly a reassuring smile.

"Is this true?" Father asked.

"Yes," she replied. She pointed toward a building across the street. "We need to talk to a man in that shop. The vampire isn't in this city. He's farther down the route, perhaps twenty miles from Freiburg."

"How do you know this?" I asked. "You said that you've never been close to Freiburg."

"I haven't. I know because … my father had made it his objective to slay that vampire. He had learned about the reward in that shop. He sent me a post after he visited here and set off to slay the vampire. That was the last I've ever seen or heard from him."

Father frowned and glanced at me. "Her father is a Vampire Hunter? One of the Chosen?"

She nodded. "He is."

"So what do we do if we visit the man offering the reward and the vampire's already been slain?"

"If that's true, then there's hope my father's still alive, provided he's the one who returned to claim the bounty. But if the vampire still preys upon the living it means he failed and is dead." Her desperate eyes flicked toward me. "I need to know, Forrest. I wasn't trying to be selfish or deceitful by traveling with you. Don't you understand?"

"Of course. If it were my father's life, I'd need to know, too."

"And should the vampire already be slain, I'll cover the cost of the trip," she said.

Father shook his head. "No, that's not necessary."

"I insist."

Penelope glanced at her appearance in a large storefront window and looked surprised by her reflection. She untied her braids and shook her head back and forth, sending a small shower of dust, dirt, and debris into the cold breeze. "I can't go into that shop or anywhere like this."

Thomas climbed into the coach, pulled the door shut behind him, and scrunched along one of the seats to sleep.

"I think Father and I can get enough scraped together so you can get cleaned up."

She shook her head and grinned. "No need, Forrest. I have gems I can sell or trade. I have money tucked away in my belt, too."

"Breakfast?" I asked Father.

He nodded.

Penelope patted Madeline's arm and looked at Varak for a moment. "Would you like to bathe with the baby, too? I will pay."

A kind smile broadened on Madeline's face. She looked relieved and her eyes moistened, nearing tears. "Thank you, young lady. That's generous of you."

It had been several days since we had the luxury of staying in an inn, partly due to the unpredictable weather and also due to our depleting funds.

I looked at Penelope and pointed. "When you two are finished, we'll be in that bakery at the corner. Come eat with us."

Penelope gave me a slight, blushful smile. She nodded and turned quickly to the inn door.

After Madeline followed Penelope into the inn, Father and I walked to the small bakery. The aroma of fresh bread and pastries wafted down the narrow street. We ordered several types of pastries, coffee, cheese, and fresh goat milk. Surprisingly the stacks of food weren't as expensive as I expected.

"Will Thomas be safe left alone?" Father asked.

"According to Penelope, most demons won't materialize in the daylight, but we won't stop here too long."

Father stared at the stacks of pastries and cheese at the center of our table. "I don't know. Your appetite has increased a lot since London, and you're not a fast eater."

I chuckled. "I like to enjoy the food, well most of it. There have been some rough meals along the way."

He winced and his expression was comical. "Some rough ale, too, son. I really think the one farmer gave us horse piss."

"None of that, today," I said, sipping the hot coffee. "If we have enough money, perhaps we should see about baths, too?"

Father shrugged. "Get one if you must. Wanting to impress her?"

"Penelope?"

"Yes." He took a huge bite of an apple tart.

I blushed. "I don't like being dirty all the time."

"It doesn't matter to the undead. They have foul odors of their own."

"I know, but I don't want to *blend* in with them."

He grinned and shook his head.

"What?"

"She's struck you pretty hard already, eh?"

"I wouldn't say that—"

Father downed a glass of milk. "Neither of you can hide your interest for one another. Your eyes give it away, and so do hers."

"You think she's interested in me?"

Father rested his elbows on the table, grabbed another hunk of cheese, and smiled with pride. "Of course she is. What girl wouldn't be interested in you? You're more handsome than I, tall and muscular like a Roman statue, and have a soft demeanor in spite of your size. She likes you ... *a lot.*"

"But her age—"

Father sighed. "Let's settle something in your mind right now while it's just you and I alone. Okay?"

I shrugged.

"Forget about the calendar years for your age from this day forward. Since you're one of the Chosen, clearly a man in size, and have been gifted with knowledge from each vampire you have slain, you're *not* a boy anymore. Sure, you will make the occasional mistakes that a child will make, but overall, you're not a lad. Your body and mind have matured into manhood, skipping the awkward stages. It was beyond your control, but face it, son, you're every bit a man. I've seen men my age act younger and more irresponsible than you. But one thing I know for certain, you don't think like a child. You haven't for quite some time."

Hearing those words come from my father meant the world to me. My chest swelled with pride. My eyes heated with tears, but I resisted their flow. I smiled. "I appreciate that, Father."

"I cannot deny the truth, so why should you?"

I stared at the food on my plate.

"What's wrong?"

"What you said is true, about me growing older so quickly, but ... it gets all awkward when I'm close to her. My stomach gets nervous. My hands and underarms sweat. I get these odd feelings inside and don't know what to say or do. I think she'll laugh at me."

Father grinned. "Every man and woman goes through those emotions and that awkwardness. It's part of maturation. But this much

I've learned, and take it to heart. Tell her how you feel, even if it seems awkward, even if you're uncertain of how she feels. The awkwardness is magnified in your mind more so than what she actually sees. A woman seeks sincerity. But the longer you resist telling her, the less she'll believe you're interested in her, and she'll turn her attention elsewhere."

"But what if she doesn't feel the same way?"

"At least you'd know, right? But the two of you were quite *cozy* this morning."

I chuckled nervously. My face heated, and I imagined it was bright red. "We weren't that way when we fell asleep. I awoke with her burrowed against my chest. Maybe she got cold?"

Father laughed heartily, causing the others seated around us to look in our direction. Nearly a minute passed before his laughter ceased. His eyes dripped tears, and he wiped them away. "Sorry. I'm not laughing at you. But trust me on this, son. If she didn't feel safe around you and didn't have any interest in you, I don't care *how* cold it was, she'd have still placed as much distance between the two of you as possible. Not even a thread of her clothing would have touched yours."

I sipped my coffee but refused to make eye contact, thinking about Penelope.

"You still don't believe me, do you?"

I didn't know what to say, but I still held my doubts.

"You have doubts," he said, as if reading my thoughts.

"How do you know?"

"I've been there. Every man goes through these feelings. But watch her eyes, her smile, and how she acts when she's near you. The best advice I can give you, is for you to take that chance to tell her how you feel. Don't think about rejection. If that happens, the next time you talk to a woman you're interested in, telling her how you feel will become easier."

I stared at my father in silence. Since Jacques had headed to America, Father had stepped back into his rightful place as the man who could offer me the sound advice that I needed. Not only that, he hadn't taken a drink of any ale or spirits since the last time he had gotten drunk. I'm not certain what Jacques had said when he had scolded Father, but I didn't think that was the reason behind his devoted sobriety. I believe he did it because it bettered him and strengthened our relationship. Maybe he also thought about how Momma would feel if she saw him lost in his stupors. Whatever had changed him inside, I was just thankful it had occurred.

Father said, "You always point toward Fate. She's a Demon-hunter, the daughter of a Vampire Hunter. Perhaps Fate has purposely crossed your paths. Have you considered that yet?"

I frowned at the suggestion, but until that moment, I hadn't thought about such a possibility.

Before I replied, he nodded toward the door. I glanced over my shoulder and saw Penelope through the glass. My heart raced. A lump formed in my throat, and for nearly half a minute I had stopped breathing. I glanced toward Father and his face was frozen by a stunned expression. Neither of us recognized this to be the same Demon-hunter that we had parted with nearly an hour earlier.

Father cleared his throat, nearly choking on whatever he had been chewing. "Just remember what I told you."

CHAPTER 9

*P*enelope walked through the door, saw me, and blushed with a nervous smile. While she and I had talked for a couple of hours during the night, I found myself at a loss for words like I was staring at someone I'd never met.

Her curly brown hair, still partially damp, had been combed and spilled across her shoulders. She wasn't wearing a dress, nor did I think she would, being as we were about to find out if the bounty on the vampire remained valid. No traces of mud were on her face or in her hair.

She wore a new pair of dark leather pants, a brown undershirt, and a dark leather vest. Where she had found a place to buy these clothes on such short notice was beyond me. She walked toward our table and offered a flattered grin, even though I hadn't said a single word. Perhaps my speechless expression and gaping mouth impressed her with how overwhelmed I was by her beauty. I didn't know what to say or how to act. I was stunned.

Father's chair scooted back, and he rose to his feet. His hand smacked the back of my elbow. I glanced to him to see his frown and head nod for me to rise and pull out a chair for her. I did so quickly, nearly knocking my own chair over while halfway tripping over my feet to grab the back of the chair beside mine. She noticed my immense nervousness and bit her lower lip while watching my clumsy display, but she seemed adulated.

I pulled her chair back, allowing her to lower onto her seat while moving the chair closer to the table. Her hair and skin smelled of sweet roses.

"Thank you, Forrest," she said softly.

I barely heard her words, simply taking in her radiance, and without realizing it, I said aloud, "You're so beautiful."

The silence afterwards hung for what seemed an eternity. Her cheeks reddened, even though she had freshly powdered them before her arrival. Her wide smile grew even wider, and she tilted her head slightly so she could see me, but her nervous glances toward my awestruck gaze were brief, volleying back and forth from my eyes to the table and back again.

I wanted to speak but my dry throat had constricted. My chest hurt and I wondered if my breathing would ever return to a normal rate. I stood there unable to take my eyes off her.

Father lowered himself back into his chair. He motioned with a nod and his eyes for me to return to my chair instead of standing beside her like a gawking fool. Believe me, it was implied, without him ever saying a word. His gazes, frowns, and expressions held their own vocabulary that I had learned since birth. Momma had had fewer but each was easily interpreted.

My face and neck felt like they were on fire; no doubt redder than the ripest autumn apple. I kept clearing my throat, trying to get the muscles to relax.

Father mercifully broke the silence. "Where is Madeline?"

Penelope took a quick breath, still smiling, and said, "I rented a room for half a day. She didn't want to take Varak out into the cold after she had bathed him. She asked that we bring her some food back."

Father rose and stacked several items onto a napkin. He glanced toward me while choosing a few more pastries, probably for Thomas. My eyes pleaded for him not to leave, but his giddy smile implied that he took slight pleasure in my discomfort. "You two take your time and enjoy breakfast. After you eat and talk to the man offering the bounty, let me know what our plans for the rest of the day are. No sense in me slowing you down."

He hobbled toward the door and opened it.

Penelope turned slightly in her chair. "The room is—"

Father paused at the door. "I'll ask at the desk. No hurries."

The door closed.

A thousand thoughts rushed through my mind, but none aided me in what I should say or do. How was I supposed to act? I rubbed my sweaty hands on my pants, trying to find the words. Nothing coherent surfaced.

She and I exchanged several nervous glances at one another. The quiet expounded. I wondered what had changed since we had parted earlier? Inside the coach we had talked about a lot of things but now, complete silence. I was confused. We were both the same people, but her beauty captivated me. I suppose I feared I'd do something foolish to alter her feelings toward me. I was afraid of making stupid childish mistakes.

Father had said that she liked me. I liked her. Both of us could do nothing except exchange silent stares. Her eyes still looked at me with interest like she had in the coach, and her repeated smiles awaited me to start conversation.

I took a deep breath and shook my head. I was a Vampire Hunter and had killed zombies, ghouls, and vampires, and yet, I couldn't express my thoughts to the most beautiful young lady I'd ever met? I had even come close to death a couple of times, and here I sat more frightened than ever. I chastised myself for being a coward.

Timidly she sat, looking at the food and her teacup, but she hadn't reached for a single thing.

"Here," I finally said, grabbing one of the apple tarts and setting it on her plate. "Those are really good."

Her eyes met mine, and she smiled. "Thank you."

I lifted the tea decanter and filled her cup with steaming hot tea.

Penelope eyed the apple tart on her plate. Without looking at me, she said, "Did you really mean what you said earlier as you were seating me?"

My stomach tensed. I swallowed hard. Yes, I had meant the words, but I hadn't meant to blurt them out. Nothing had escaped my lips any truer than what I had told her. I wiped my hands again. Sweat beaded on my brow.

I glanced at her. Her hopeful eyes stared at me, and her folded hands shook slightly, making me realize that she was just as nervous inside as I was, and asking the question had been difficult for her to even ask.

Father's words came to mind. *Tell her how you feel, even if it seems awkward, even if you're uncertain of how she feels.*

"The words rushed out without me realizing it," I said, almost apologetically.

Penelope broke our gaze and stared at the table.

"But," I said, "if I could clarify something since I just blurted that out earlier? You *are* the *most beautiful* lady I've ever seen. That's why I cannot take my eyes off of you."

I couldn't believe I had gotten the words out without stuttering or mumbling or *dying*. Perspiration welled beneath my arms, down my back, and down my chest. A lump rose in my throat. My heartbeat pulsed in my ears. The rest of the dining room seemed invisible. I even felt dizzy. When folks joked that *love hurt*, I now understood partially why. I was close to passing out for telling a woman how pretty she was. I was afraid to know how much worse it got from there.

She studied my face for several moments. A smile curled her lips. "No one's ever said those words to me before."

"Ever?"

She shrugged. "Other than my mother and father? No. But it's *expected* from them."

I sighed. "But it's true. You are beautiful."

Penelope bit into the tart, chewed, and nodded her approval. "I'm surprised I didn't frightened you off when we first met, but at least now I don't reek of that awful sweat and all the mud is gone, too."

I smiled. "I never complained, did I?"

She leaned closer to me and stared into my eyes with a deepness no one had ever shown me. I didn't want to look away, and oddly I didn't feel uncomfortable. I imagined that my eyes reflected the same emotions as hers. Her gaze was the same as Jacques' had been for Matilda and her for him. They had fallen in love, and I suspected I had already fallen for Penelope. I stared at her narrow lips longer than I should have. There was the briefest of moments when I almost leaned forward to kiss her. But instead I realized where we were, in a public place where such was frowned upon, so I fought the urge and resisted. I smiled and placed my hand atop hers and squeezed. Our fingers entwined a few seconds later.

I sipped more coffee while she ate, and we kept holding hands. My appetite had decided to vanish, which was a rarity considering how hungry I had been when Father and I had entered the bakery. My former nervousness when she had entered had also waned, but my uncertainty and doubts arose.

I thought about Rose and how I had profusely argued with myself to not have strong feelings toward her, and *why* we could never proceed beyond simple friendship. Of course the argument had been all mine and my justification for not ever falling in love. Nothing had ever been verbally exchanged between Rose and I because I had made certain the conversation never occurred. The situation was part of the reason why I had left Romania in the first place. Being a Hunter, I knew my biggest weakness was the ones closest to my heart. The same had been true for my father, and I was convinced it held true for me as well.

Vampires were heartless masters of torturing the mind over the physical body. They could kill an adversary easily, but driving a man to absolute insanity before killing him was an even greater reward. They thrived on such authority. Father had nearly been destroyed after Momma had been murdered. He still suffered from losing her. I had personally witnessed the torment ripping him apart, which had made abandoning Rose easier at the time.

And yet, my feelings for Penelope were far stronger than any stirrings I had ever held for Rose. What my father had expressed was most likely correct. Due to the intellect I was gaining from the minds of vampires I had slain, my mind had matured. I was no longer a child. I

LEONARD D. HILLEY II

viewed the possibility of love slightly different than I had only a few months prior. Without the intellect adhering to my rationality, I doubted I'd even talk to Penelope, much less be holding her hand.

Father had mentioned Fate being what brought Penelope and I together. Could that be true? Possibly. And if so, since she hunted demons and I hunted vampires, we made a nearly invincible team.

Other than exchanging smiles and glances, we finished our breakfast and I paid the tab. She grabbed her coat off the rack near the door and slipped it on. I had been so caught up in her appearance, I didn't remember her taking it off. Outside the door we turned our attention to the shop across the square.

Dark clouds loomed overhead. Beads of sleet bounced off my hat, the street, and the awnings. The cold morning breeze whistled as the buildings sliced its strength.

She squeezed my hand and smiled up at me.

"You ready?" I asked.

Penelope offered a slight nod and pulled a hood over her head. Together we walked through the nearly silent square to the shop.

CHAPTER 10

I reached to open the shop door, and she pulled my hand, shaking her head.

"Are you okay?" I asked.

Sadness came to her eyes. She took a deep breath, closed her eyes, and released it. When she opened her eyes, tears shimmered. "I thought I could do this ... Forrest, what if my father failed? What if he's dead?"

"Then we kill this vampire," I replied with boldness and slight anger in my voice. I took her hand into both of mine.

Penelope read the determination in my eyes and nodded. When it came to slaying a vampire, I had been successful each time thus far, but if this vampire had killed her father, I swore that I'd find and slay it. I would end its existence for the pain it had caused her.

I opened the shop door and allowed her to enter first. The shop smelled of various incenses. Smoke drifted in tiny spirals from brass canisters. Stacks of silk cloth in various colors were piled on one table. Another table was covered with dried ginseng roots, turnips, potatoes, and truffles. Dried flowers and herbs hung from the rafters. Fishing nets and supplies hung on one wall. Hats for men and women were on another table. The shop contained a hodgepodge of items without focusing upon any specific wares.

An elderly stooped man and I assumed his aged wife stood behind the counter. No other customers were in the shop, but the day was still early. From the look of the nearly abandoned, rundown section of town, business probably stayed slow.

"Excuse me," Penelope said. "But I was wondering if the bounty for the vampire in the Black Forest is still unclaimed?"

The elderly man adjusted his wire-rimmed glasses and the wrinkles around his eyes deepened as he peered at her. "Lorcan? Is that the vampire you're speaking of?"

She nodded.

He made an odd smile, showing his yellowed teeth. "Yes! It is, actually. Several Hunters have sought directions and information to the Black Forest, but none have ever returned to claim the bounty."

She stiffened. Her voice broke when she spoke. "I see."

The man stared at her for a few moments. He pressed his glasses firmer against his nose, squinting. "You look familiar, young lady. Have you been in our shop before?"

She shook her head. "No."

He turned toward his wife. "She looks familiar, doesn't she Abigail?"

Abigail nervously looked up from her needlework, glancing a brief moment in our direction. She nodded and looked down at her needle. Her voice was rough and scratchy when she spoke. "Yes, Karl. She does."

Karl rubbed his chin and shook his head. "My old mind can't keep my memories straight. I could swear you've been here before."

"No, but my father was here a few … years ago."

"Oh?"

"Yes. Wilbur Hastens."

"One second," Karl said in a shaky voice. His aged fingers shook as he thumbed through some papers in a drawer. He licked his thumb and pulled up one document and held it close to his face to read it. After he lowered it, he nodded. "He sought the reward for the same vampire you seek."

Penelope glanced back at me with tears in her eyes. I stepped beside her and wrapped my arm across her shoulder. She turned and buried her face against my chest. Her hands clenched my shirt and formed tight fists around the material.

"I'm so sorry," he said. He studied her for a few moments, as if he was trying to figure out why she was crying. After failing to make the connection, he glanced toward me with what sounded like a complete repeat of his pitch to entice people to collect the bounty. "A lot of Hunters have sought to kill this vampire but not one has ever returned to collect the bounty. But, the good news is that the bounty has more than doubled."

"Good news?" I asked with a firm frown.

Karl looked at Penelope still confused, and then to my angered gaze. "Forgive me. I … I shouldn't have worded it like that. But, you're a Hunter, too, aren't you?"

I nodded.

"There's another bounty for a vampire in a cemetery nearby, if you're interested in a quicker reward? Granted, the reward to slay Adnet is about a fourth of what Lorcan's is, but it's less than a half hour's walk on foot. Isn't that correct, Abigail?"

She nodded but didn't look in our direction. She stuck the long needle into the thick cloth. "Less than a half hour. Not far."

My jaw tightened. Anger swelled inside of me, not toward the old man, but for Penelope's loss and her pain. She sobbed against my chest. "Give me the information for both of them."

"Certainly," the old man replied with a shrewd grin. "Give me a few minutes to write out the directions for both Lorcan and Adnet. And in the adjoining room, I have wares a Hunter like yourself might be interested in."

I held her close, rubbed her shoulders, and rested my chin atop her head. "Just because your father never returned for the bounty doesn't mean he's dead. Perhaps he was sidetracked or changed his mind."

"If he changed his mind, he'd have returned home before now."

"Maybe, but lots of things happen when one travels abroad. Cling to the hope that he's still alive for now. Until we have proof otherwise, no need to abandon the likelihood of him being amongst the living."

She squeezed me tightly and then released me. She patted my

muscled stomach with her hand and formed a tight smile as she looked up at me.

"Care to see what wares he has?" I asked.

"Sure."

We walked into the adjoining room to find three small tables layered with various weapons used to slay vampires. There were stakes made from different types of wood and in assorted sizes. Other items were tacked to the wall as well. The first weapon on the wall that caught my attention was a polished wooden crossbow. I took it off the large nail and stared down the sight to check the straightness of the flight groove. Pure perfection. Great attention had gone into every detail of its design. The wood grain was nearly black, which made it almost invisible in the dark. Power pulsed from the wood into my hands with a slight tingling sensation, causing me to examine it even more closely.

"That's a nice bow," she said, running her fingers down the dark wood. "Do you prefer a crossbow over a regular bow?"

"My mentor had one and let me use it. I've never shot a short bow like yours. For me these are easier to maneuver and require less time to aim. I think I'll buy this one." Without stating it aloud, I believed I was meant to find and purchase this crossbow, even though I didn't understand why. But I never argued with my Hunter's intellect.

I found a dusty wooden crate beneath one table. It was filled with empty, corked globe-shaped bottles that I liked to fill with garlic juice and toss at vampires. Since such an attack only worked if the bottle shattered, I needed to restock the ones I had destroyed and fill these to use later. I counted out eight and placed them into a small empty crate. On a table with garlands of garlic cloves were small bottles labeled: Holy Water. I took a half dozen bottles of holy water, the biggest garland of garlic, and placed them in with the empty bottles.

"I'm set. Do you see anything you want?" I asked. "Since we are hunting vampires and not demons, do you have any stakes?"

Penelope shook her head. "I've never hunted vampires, but wouldn't a wooden arrow through the heart work?"

"Yes, but you might consider having a few stakes for backup in case something happens to your bow. Vampires move faster than a mortal's eye can track, and vampires tend to be somewhat cautious in their approach if you're holding a stake."

She grabbed several wooden stakes off the table and practiced downward motions with each in her right hand until she found a couple that suited her.

We returned to the old man at the counter. He had two pieces of yellow parchment in his hand. On the top parchment he had drawn the map to find Adnet's lair at the cemetery. It looked like a simple run to the crypt, stake the vampire, and return for the reward. In and out. Such arrangements are ideal but rare, and drew immediate skepticism on my part.

"Why hasn't anyone slain this vampire yet?" I asked.

"A few have tried and failed."

"Why? What do you know about Adnet?"

The old man adjusted his glasses and then rubbed the stubble on his chin. "No one rightly knows. He settled in the cemetery after the last war. None of those who have entered the cemetery have ever made it to his crypt."

"Were they actual Hunters?" I asked.

He shook his head. "Very few Hunters visit the outskirts of the city. As you have probably noticed most of the buildings here are empty or rundown. We're still recovering from the war. Most of the residents packed up and moved away. Some refuse to leave. It's their homes, but labor ... finding a trade, tis hard here. People get desperate and are willing to do almost anything to make money. That includes risking their lives to slay a vampire."

"So Adnet killed them?"

"We don't know. A few returned and swore the cemetery is haunted. Right, Abigail?"

She paused with her needlework, nodded, and said, "Haunted."

I placed the crate of supplies and the crossbow on the counter. "I'd like to buy these."

He rummaged through the crate, counting out the items, and then he looked at the crossbow. He held it up, admiring it. "Fine crossbow. I almost hate to part with it."

"Why?" I asked.

"This one came from an Irish weapon-maker living in Bucharest, at least that's how the story goes. Finest craftsman I've even seen."

I frowned, staring at the crossbow. "His name?"

"Roy, I think." He scratched his wrinkled forehead and nodded. "Yes, Roy."

Rose's father? No wonder I had felt a connection with the weapon. He fashioned all types of weapons exclusively for Hunters. This one shouldn't have been in a shop for sale though. A Hunter would never have parted with it. "How did you get it?"

He closed his eyes for several moments while rubbing his chin. "Let me think. If I recall correctly, a peddler brought it in. He was having difficulty selling door to door with all the empty houses, of course, and decided to ask if I'd buy any of his supplies. When I saw the crossbow, I figured I'd eventually sell it to a Hunter. And if I didn't, it was worth far more than the modest price he had asked."

I nodded. "So how much for all of this?"

He adjusted his glasses, and pointed at each item, counting again. Finally he gave me the price, which I thought was too modest, given the bow's quality, but with our money almost gone, I couldn't have offered more if I had wanted. After paying him, I barely had enough to buy one meal to split between all of us. We had no choice but to slay the local vampire.

The old man smiled. "Can I help you with anything else?"

I pointed to the goggles tethered around Penelope's neck. "Do you happen to have any goggles like these?"

His brows rose with interest when he noticed them. He leaned partway across the counter, squinting. Penelope stepped closer for him to see. His lower lip tightened over his upper one while he thought. Finally, he shook his head. "No, I've not seen anything like that, but in our kind of business here, we get odds and ends all the time. I never know from one week to the next what a traveler might bring in to trade."

"Okay, thanks."

"Anything else?" he asked.

"What should we bring back as proof we've slain these vampires?" I asked.

Karl frowned. His brow furrowed deeply. "What do you usually turn in as proof?"

"If you know what types of jewelry he wears, that's usually something. Or we can bring back his ashes."

"I don't know if Adnet wears any jewelry, but if he does, that will suffice."

I shrugged.

"If there's any other way I can help you?" he said.

"Do you happen to have a garlic press?" I asked.

He nodded. "Sure. Follow me."

CHAPTER 11

My eyes stung and my throat itched after pressing enough garlic to fill three of the globe bottles with garlic juice. Penelope and I reeked of garlic. If anything, neither of us needed to worry about vampires trying to bite us anytime soon. However, I feared the odor would alert the slumbering vampire before we could get close enough to stake him. Overall, I was just glad it hadn't been onions we'd pressed.

Once she and I stepped outside the shop into the cold, she asked, "Have you seen that crossbow before?"

"No."

"Do you know the craftsman?"

"He crafted my Hunter box and carved some of my stakes."

"So it's a good bow?"

"If he made it, it'd be one of the best a Hunter could get."

Penelope smiled. "Then that's good for you."

I nodded.

The ominous sky was dark with thick gray clouds that hung lower than normal. For a moment I was reminded of the blizzard sky on the late afternoon when I had encountered my first vampire. It wasn't something I'd ever forget, and I supposed I'd be reminded of it with each winter storm that arose.

A few snowflakes floated along with the twirling breeze. The old buildings looked abandoned, even though we knew several that were not. The old shops reflected the depressive spirit of those who continued to reside here. The aftereffects of any war left scars, and it often took decades, sometimes generations, before the townspeople fully recovered. It was a common scene throughout the unrest in Europe, and one that I had grown tired of seeing, but the wars weren't about to lessen. In fact, I feared they'd become far worse.

Midway across the square, Penelope took our rolled map from the small crate I was carrying. After unrolling it, she studied it while we walked toward the inn. "Do you think this graveyard is haunted?"

I laughed softly. "Have you ever seen a ghost?"

She gave me a serious side-glance. "Would you laugh at me if I said that I have?"

I stopped and looked at her. "No, I would never laugh at you. Have you seen one?"

Penelope gave a reassured smile before she nodded. "A few actually. You never have?"

I turned and started walking. "I've felt the coldness of one's presence, but as far as actually seeing one? No. I don't deny their existence though."

"I'd worry about you if you did," she said, playfully crinkling her nose at me.

"Why?"

"You kill vampires and I kill demons. We both know zombies, ghouls, and were-creatures exist, so why not ghosts?"

"Don't forget magic."

She grinned and her eyes sparkled. "That, too."

"Pixies and fairies?" I gave a sly grin.

"And leprechauns, too. Especially if you're a wee bit Irish."

I was glad to see her smile again. I had hurt inside when I watched her cry. I wanted to make her aches go away.

I placed the crate beneath my left arm and pulled open the inn door, allowing her to walk through first. I followed her down the narrow hall until she stopped outside a door and unlocked it.

Father sat in an old rocker with a quilt covering him from the neck down. He was snoring. Madeline sat with her back against the head-board of the bed. Varak was cradled in her arms. The child was alert and staring around the room. When he heard us enter, he sat upright, watching us.

Penelope glanced toward Varak and stared at him for several seconds before turning toward me. She visibly shivered, leaning closer to me as I set the crate onto a small round table. "His eyes …"

I nodded.

"Wake your father and let's head to the cemetery," she whispered. "I'm not very comfortable being near the child."

"I told you."

I crossed the room and gently shook my father's shoulder. Alarmed, his eyes popped open. He took a deep breath and put his hand over his heart. "Heavens, son, I didn't even hear you come in."

"Sorry," I said, grinning.

"So did you get the directions to find a vampire?" he asked.

"For two different ones," I replied.

"Two?"

Penelope nodded. "One is nearby, and the other one is on the way to Freiburg in the Black Forest."

"We could use the extra money," he said. "Since our party keeps growing."

"Don't worry," she said. "I'll earn my keep."

Father smiled. "I wasn't implying that you are a burden to us, but we still need to eat and find lodging whenever the weather's unfavorable."

"I know," she replied with a narrow smile. "But I refuse to expect others' charity."

"She makes more than we do, Father, and she doesn't even *collect* bounties."

Penelope laughed softly.

Father folded the quilt and placed it onto the rocker's seat. He came to the table where she had placed the map and studied it for a few moments. He frowned with confusion. "What's the catch?"

"What do you mean?"

"It seems *too* ... easy?"

Penelope laughed. "The old man said that the cemetery is haunted."

"Don't tell me that you two believe that?"

I shrugged. "We won't know until we get there."

"Did he indicate how far we needed to travel to get there?"

"Less than a half hour on foot," I said.

"In this cold?" Father asked with wide eyes.

"You don't have to go. Penelope and I can probably handle it."

"No," he replied in a gruff tone. "I'll manage."

I imagined his legs still ached from the cramped seating arrangement in the coach and the cold weather would make them hurt even more. "We could get Thomas to drive us out there, but he was up all night and intends to head on to Freiburg once he awakens," I replied.

"Do we even have enough time to walk there and back by noon?"

"Not if we keep standing around talking, Father."

He pointed his finger at me and shook it, before giving way to a grin. Then he noticed the crossbow on the table. He picked it up and studied it. His eyebrows rose, and he stared at me. "If I had to wager, son, I'd say Roy carved this himself."

I nodded.

Penelope looked impressed. "Just by looking at it, you know who made it?"

Father smiled. "He's a master woodworker and craftsman. None better. Where'd you happen upon this, son?"

"Bought it from the man who drew the two maps."

"I see." He stared at me with sudden uneasiness.

I knew what he was thinking without even asking. Roy had gifted my Hunter box to me, refusing to accept anything in return since he considered his craftsmanship the most suitable donation to aid the Chosen in their pursuit of slaying vampires. A disease cursed him from setting foot in the sunlight, so he housed himself underground where he diligently worked on weapons for Hunters to eradicate the undead.

Most likely, Roy had gifted this crossbow to a Hunter. Since the Hunter no longer possessed it, he was probably dead.

Father put on his overcoat and limped toward the door. "Madeline, we will return as quickly as possible."

She nodded. "Be careful."

Penelope walked to the bedside and handed her an opal. "In case we don't get back before the noon hour to checkout, give this gem to the keeper as payment. It's more than enough to compensate for the rest of the day, if necessary."

"Thank you."

"Barter for some food, too," she said with a sly smile.

I met Father at the door. "I need to get my Hunter box from the coach."

He patted his pockets and his lips formed a snarl from his frustration. "I left my cross and stakes in the coach, too."

We hurried out of the inn. When we reached the coach, I twisted the handle downward as quietly as possible, hoping not to awaken Thomas. The door creaked slightly as I pulled it outward. I reached inside, grabbed the handle of my box, and pulled it to me without scraping the floor.

After I stepped aside, Father leaned inside the coach and patted under the seat until he found his silver cross and his bundled stakes. He picked up Penelope's pack and bow and turned to hand them to her. She smiled as she took them. Several feathered ends of arrows protruded from the top of the pack.

The wind whistled softly through the barren trees at what appeared to have been a park, possibly before the war. I carried my box to a round, frozen water fountain and set the box on the icy brick wall. When I unlatched the clasps, Penelope was standing at my side. I never heard her approach.

I put the fresh bottles of garlic juice into the box. The garlic odor lofted.

She reached into my box and took out a bottle of blessed salt. "This stuff works on vampires, too?"

I shrugged. "I've never used it. Supposedly a salt barrier can drive a vampire to insanity since they must count every grain. Sounds farfetched to me."

"Some vampires are insane to begin with," she said. "I've heard older women talk about how fairies have to count the grains, too."

"Don't tell me you've seen fairies," I said.

"No, but I'm hopeful." She leaned against me, bumping against my ribcage with her shoulder. "By drawing the proper symbols inside a circle of salt, I can trap a demon."

"That works?"

Penelope shrugged. "It's supposed to. I've not tried it yet, but the healer told me how and drew the diagram for me."

"This is the same healer that *accidentally* summoned a demon during one of her rituals?"

She nodded.

"With such a dreadful error in her incantation, I don't know that I'd trust her drawing to trap a demon. It might agitate it more."

A slight giggle escaped her lips. "I see your point. I've only killed demons from a distance, which I consider much safer and keeps me scar free. Besides, it takes a lot of salt to draw the circle and the symbols."

I pulled six short narrow arrows from the box, examining the sharpened tips by pressing my thumb against them. All seemed sturdy.

"You were already carrying arrows without a crossbow?" she asked.

"Only because these are *unique*."

"Oh? In what way, dear Hunter." She beamed a playful smile at me, clasping her hands together at her chest and swaying toward me. Her dramatic actions reminded me of a play Father and I had watched before leaving London. It appeared she had seen the same one, but her feigned actions were better than the actors we had seen.

I gave her an odd look.

"What?"

"Theater?"

She laughed. "Sorry. I can get silly when I feel nervous."

"*You're* nervous?"

"I've never helped slay a vampire before. But why are those arrows unique?"

I explained the enchanted shrubbery in London and how the Gypsy witch had blessed them to attack and stake vampires.

"And you plan to use those in the crossbow against this vampire?"

"I'm hopeful," I said with a grin.

Father held the map and faced south where only frames of buildings remained. Burnt skeletons of once thriving trees displayed the sorrow of their deaths when whatever troops had come through scorching the terrain. The old cobblestone road was covered by dried weeds and bramble and was barely visible.

Father lowered the map and pointed. "We follow the old road to find the cemetery."

I snapped the latches shut on my box and hefted it, grabbing the loaded crossbow in my other hand. "I'm ready."

Penelope nodded and followed behind me. We walked past Father, and he took up the rear.

We didn't walk long before the remnants of the old road eroded into broken rocks, large holes, and thicker thorny bramble. Dry brittle strands of ivy threaded together overhead forming a thick canopy of vines and dead leaves, deepening the shadowy gloom that shrouded the path into near darkness. Between the heavily overcast sky and the darkened trees, one would believe it was dusk, even though we had yet to reach the noon hour.

Although I didn't express my sudden concern, I recalled what Jacques had told me almost a year earlier about how a vampire can move during the day provided the sun was somehow fully blocked. Some vampires were even capable of controlling mists and fog, as I had learned in London. The elements of the weather and our surroundings were more than favorable for this vampire to emerge from hiding and attack us before we even reached the cemetery or his lair.

However, worse things loomed that none of us had even considered.

CHAPTER 12

*T*he closer to the cemetery we walked, the worse the terrain became. No longer were the thin vines draped, connecting overhead and between the trees, but giant thick thorns capable of impaling a man grew on black treelike branches that spiraled around one another to form a wicked tunnel. Such could have only been brought to life by the curse of a vindictive witch.

An oppressive cloud of misery overshadowed me, draining me of hope and driving me toward despair. Whispers taunted me, drawing me toward one of the sharpened thorns, trying to persuade me to ram my chest against it and pierce my heart. I resisted, but the mental image of one of these black thorns staked through my heart while a widening pool of blood spread beneath my suspended body looked terrifyingly realistic. I wanted to think of pleasant thoughts, memories, anything except such a grueling death, but my mind was frozen upon this depiction of an unpleasant fate.

After a few seconds, I took another step into the narrowing tunnel. The pattern of the interwoven branches, thorns, and the never-ending spiral was mesmerizing, making me dizzy. I shook my head, trying to steady my next step, hopeful that I didn't fall against one of the sharp thorns. Because of the thickness of the coiled vines and the countless thorn tips, no alternate path existed. A small child couldn't press through the sides of this deadly tunnel wall. It was either continue forward or turn back. But my mind pressed me to go forward. Chattering whispers buzzed near my ears, as annoying as mosquitoes seeking blood, and urged me to sacrifice my life's blood, but offering no reason for such martyrdom.

Whatever sensation was pricking at my mind, was trying to overwhelm and control me, but a vampire wasn't causing it, I was certain of that, since none had ever been able to compel me. This tunnel had been formed by magic. I detected it, and it was far darker than any spells I had encountered before. Once I realized what was beckoning me to end my life, I was better able to resist.

I reached into my pocket and found the blessed protective talisman Matilda had given me in London. I rubbed it between my thumb and forefinger. Energy tingled against my skin. The evil whispering chants lessened but didn't completely dissolve.

A hand grabbed my elbow and tugged. I spun around.

Penelope stood, looking at me. "You feel the overpowering darkness, too?"

I nodded. The feeling was everywhere.

"Close your eyes," she said.

I did. Sharp pellets struck my face and bounced off my leather hat like sleet. I opened my eyes. She held out a handful of the blessed salt.

"What are you doing?" I asked.

"The salt should break the oppressive spell that's overshadowing us. Hold out your hand." She poured some of the salt into my hand. "Eat it."

I placed the salt on my tongue and let it dissolve. The uneasiness cocooned around me, and the whispers suddenly dispelled.

Penelope hurried to my father and placed salt on his tongue. After his eyes indicated he was aware of his surroundings, she returned to me. "Forrest, the cemetery isn't haunted like the people have told the old man. They walked into this oppressive wall of anguish. But whoever placed the curse here didn't do it to keep people out. It's here to keep the vampire trapped inside the cemetery."

"Even without the overpowering spell of gloom, I doubt he'd chance coming through these thorns. He could easily stake himself."

"I think that's the intent," Father whispered. "Some of the dreadful thoughts that came to mind ... I've had better nightmares and drunken hallucinations."

"I agree." I glanced to each of them. "Are you ready to continue or should we turn back?"

Father sighed. "My head's clear now. I'm ready."

"You?" I asked her.

"Of course. I realized what was happening before either of you."

I leaned toward her, pressed my cheek against hers, and whispered, "Thank you."

She turned her face slightly and kissed my cheek. "You're welcome. But we're not in the cemetery yet. Who knows what else lies ahead."

"Always the pessimist, aren't you?" I said with an even smile.

"When it comes to vampires and demons, it's better to be cautious than carefree."

"That's true."

I turned back toward the path. Since the other Hunter had threatened my life, I couldn't shake the feeling of the price I'd have to pay for keeping Varak alive. And with what had just happened, I feared this was only the beginning. I wanted to turn back, but we needed the bounty for this vampire. It would take weeks of menial labor to earn a fraction of the reward money. With plague demons after Thomas, and the Hunter or *Hunters* searching for me, we didn't have time to sacrifice. We needed to reach Freiburg quickly.

CHAPTER 13

$\mathcal{T}$he strange whispering vanished, at least for me, but the dark tunnel narrowed. I took each step more cautiously, watching the shallow shadow recesses and expecting something to lash out and attack or latch onto my leg and pull me into the thorns. I attempted to make my body smaller, which made walking more difficult.

While the narrowing tunnel was dark, we didn't need a lantern to see our way. Occasionally shreds of clothing or leather hung from the tips of the thorns where others had passed too closely. I wondered how many had braved the steps this far into the passageway. Like Karl had said, desperate people were willing to put their lives on the line when they lacked food or if they had hungry children.

The thorn-encrusted tunnel twisted in a slight curve toward the right. It seemed we had walked forever, and still we had not seen the first tombstone. The tunnel had come into existence long after the cemetery had been established because no one in their right mind would have troubled themselves to travel through here to bury the dead. But the longer we walked, the more I wondered if this tunnel even ended at a cemetery. Like Father and I had questioned the shortness of the map, the route to the cemetery had seemed too easy on paper.

Nothing Karl had told us or drawn even indicated this winding, dangerous path.

I stopped and faced Penelope and Father. "You two okay?"

They nodded.

"You want to turn back?" I asked.

Penelope glanced to my Father.

He shrugged. "I'm not tired, if *that's* what you're implying."

"No, Father, that's not why I'm asking. We've moved at such a slow pace that none of us should be weary. I'm wondering if we missed something before we got into this passageway."

"You think there's another way into the cemetery?" she asked.

"The winding branches forming this tunnel aren't an accident," I said.

Penelope nodded. "I told you they are here to keep the vampire inside the cemetery and prevent him from escaping."

"I agree. But that means someone is using magic to keep this vampire as a prisoner. But why?"

"Maybe," Father said. "But if he cannot get out to feed, he might be withered inside his crypt and unable to defend himself. An easy kill and easy money."

"If collecting the bounty for this vampire was *easy*, why hasn't anyone claimed it yet?"

"The people got frightened and ran out?" Father suggested.

"Possibly some of them did, but I've noticed some shredded clothing on the thorns. Some of those people might have made it into the cemetery to face a hungry vampire. They wouldn't have escaped death."

"Doesn't seem anyone died along the path," Father said. "No skeletons."

"Unless their bodies were dragged into the cemetery?"

"I don't know, Forrest," Penelope said. "While the thorns certainly could keep a vampire trapped, they are also an obvious deterrent to keep humans out. According to Karl, most of them fled and told him and his wife that the place was haunted."

"With those horrid voices whispering in my head," Father said, "I'd think so, too, if we hadn't discover it was a spell. Let's go a little ways farther, son. If we don't reach the cemetery, we turn back and pack the coach."

I nodded.

I turned, holding the crossbow as if I intended to fire. Other than the magic looming around us, I expected something else to appear. "Do you sense any demons, Penelope?"

"I haven't yet."

"Could a witch's magic mask their presence?"

She was silent for several moments while we crept deeper into the dark passageway. "I've never heard of it, but I imagine if the witch held dark intentions and was powerful enough, she might be able to control one. I know the healer summoned one."

"Do you have weapons to use at close range, if a demon emerges?"

"Yes." She slid her arm through her bow and knelt to look through her pack. She pulled out a dagger. Runic symbols were engraved into the handle and the blade. "This is the best demon killer I have besides my bow. Of course, holy water can work, depending upon the type of demon. Bibles can work, too. Crosses, if you know the proper scriptures."

"I'm at a loss there," I said.

She cocked a brow at me and opened her mouth, but I shook my head and interrupted her.

"Let's not discuss it now. I spend too much time explaining my views about religion and that is sacred to me. The important question right now is, 'do *you* know the proper scriptures?'"

Penelope nodded. "I do, but I'm surprised you don't. Strange how many of the same weapons work against demons and vampires."

"I know. Let's go."

The tunnel curved back to the left and straightened. Ahead of us light filtered through, where I guessed the exit to this long thorny passageway finally ended. I almost let out a huge sigh of relief when a loud sound echoed from behind us.

"Get out of my head!" the deep harsh voice bellowed.

"Son?" Father said. "Hurry!"

Penelope pushed her hand against my back. "Someone's coming."

I glanced over my shoulder but didn't see anyone in the dark tunnel. But whoever was approaching continued cursing, growling, and he was getting closer. By my guess, he was probably around the bend of the tunnel, but who or what he was, or even his intentions; there wasn't any way for us to know.

As we approached the faint light, the tunnel widened. I hurried my steps into a slight jog. At the end of the winding branches a rusted gate stood as the last obstacle. I pushed it open, and the hinges whined.

The soil on the other side of the gate was gray. Aged tombstones, some broken, tilted, or shattered, were clustered beneath dark leafless trees forking wicked branches toward the overcast sky. Some of the other tombstones were fashioned with little cherubs or stone vases. Scattered across the graveyard were three stone crypts larger than most cottages. Large menacing statues shaped like angels or hooded clerics held stone swords and daggers as if protectors of the dead, or the undead. Knowing a vampire resided inside one of the three stone crypts made me leery, but it wasn't dark enough for him to emerge.

I tugged my chained watch from an inner pocket and checked the time. It was three hours until noon. If ever I needed an old Hunter's intellect to bless me, it was now. The vampire slept inside one of these crypts or possibly even a grave, but I didn't expect any hints to be given to me. Hunters received guidance but we were never given full knowledge about everything. We were expected to hunt, which was why we were chosen, but being pressed for time, I selfishly desired a pinpointed location. I shook my head. It wasn't happening. My spiritual Hunter advisors were eerily silent.

Surveying the graveyard, looking for the slightest clue, I said, "We made it through."

The voice inside the tunnel shrieked with agony. I shoved the gate closed, but it wouldn't prevent anyone else from opening it.

"But we're not alone," Penelope said.

"Probably another Hunter wanting to get the reward before we do," Father said through tight lips.

"Someone help me!" the man in the tunnel shouted. "The vines are wrapping me up!"

I turned and grabbed the gate.

Penelope placed her hand atop mine and shook her head. "No, Forrest. It's probably a trap. You go back in there, and it might be a demon who wants to kill you."

"But can't you tell if it's a demon?" I asked.

Her eyes widened. "Not always. Some use such convincing disguises it's hard to discern whether they are humans or not. And besides that, the magic shrouding the tunnel has a distorting influence. While your intention is to help the person, if he's actually human, the magic could distort your appearance to him, making him believe you're a demon or monster. He might kill you when you try to free him."

Father glanced at me. "It could be worse than that."

"How?"

"There might not be anyone else in the tunnel at all. Think about the enchanted hedges. The spell over them was to yank the vampire into the hedgerow and stab him until a branch staked through his heart. I don't know what nightmarish visions you two suffered when we first walked into the thorns, but those voices want blood. They crave blood."

"I got that impression, too," I whispered.

"It makes sense," Penelope said.

"Why?" I asked.

"Dark magic by a witch with a dark soul," she replied. "The ones who practice black magic need to offer blood in their sacrifices. Perhaps blood feeds the wicked wall."

I told them about how the voices had tried to convince me to impale myself.

Father swallowed hard. His brow furrowed. "Mine was worse. The voices ... they wanted me to shove each of you into the giant thorns. I'd have never done it. I'd have impaled myself first, but having those thoughts haunts me."

"Those thick plants need blood," Penelope said.

"No skeletal remains on the path though," I said.

"But there were remnants of clothes," she replied. "The vines might have ways of pulling the bodies into the wall and dissolving them as food, leaving no trace of its victims."

"The only thing that saved us was the salt?" I asked.

"For now," she replied.

I took in the information, biting my lower lip. "Then let's find this vampire, slay him, and get out of here. But, we stick close to one another."

Father pointed toward the closest tree line. "I don't think there's another exit out of the cemetery."

He was right. The cemetery was a large circle surrounding by towering rows of thorny vines like the tunnel but these formed a wall by connecting to the outer perimeter trees. There wasn't any way to cross through them. The only good thing about the enclosure was it made an excellent wind barrier, and the temperature seemed warmer than back at the edge of the city.

"We have three crypts, Father. Which should we check first?" I asked.

He frowned. "Why are you asking me? Don't you know?"

"I don't. But you've hunted vampires longer than I have. I was curious as to what clues you'd look for in determining where he might be."

Father ran his hand through his beard, eyeing each crypt. "While I'm not certain, I'd go to the farthest first."

"Why?"

He shrugged. "Given how he's apparently imprisoned in the cemetery, that crypt is the farthest from the entrance, which intimidates those with lesser fortitude."

Made sense to me. "All right. Stick close. We need to keep check on the entrance in case it is a human hoping to slay the vampire and get the bounty. We don't want to accidentally kill someone who isn't an undead."

Penelope placed her hand on my forearm. Her eyes narrowed as she glanced across the cemetery.

"What is it?" I asked.

"Something evil."

"A demon?"

"Not necessarily. But I sense it. Do you?"

I scanned the areas around the crypts and the tall tombstones, seeing nothing. I didn't sense anything out of the ordinary. No forewarnings pricked at my mind. I shook my head.

"Sorry I cannot be of more help," she said. "I think whatever spell holds the thorny barriers in place has affected my psychic sensors."

"I'm still having problems from it, too," I replied. "But I'm under the impression that once someone gets inside the cemetery, they're not meant to leave. Let's keep going, but we need to stay alert. If you're sensing an evil presence, I believe we're going to find it. Soon."

At the path that led to a crossroads was the first large angelic statue with magnificent feathered wings. It must have been at least ten feet tall. In its right hand it thrust a long sword upward, as if leading a charge into a great battle. The smooth face beckoned peace while the sword shouted war. Its left hand was empty with its palm held upward. It had held something at one point in time.

I shuffled my feet at the statue's base to move aside leaves. My foot tapped a solid object. I stooped and brushed aside the leaves. On the ground was an open book carved from stone that this angel must have held. I assumed the book was supposed to be the Holy Bible, but I didn't open the subject for debate.

"Let's go," I said.

We causally made our way to the crossroads where another statue stood. Unlike the angelic representative, this sculpture exhibited evil. The face was featureless, except for the catlike eyes that receded into its head. A hooded cloak draped over the forehead almost covering the eyes from view. A long robe covered its body. Both hands extended forward, frozen in cupped formations, but no weapon was in its hands. On the ground was the massive stone scythe that had somehow been dislodged from its stone grip.

Crows cawed from the perimeter trees.

I glanced at the dark statue's eyes. I couldn't imagine anyone having the bravery to enter this cemetery at night. These statues were intimidating enough in the daylight. Shrouded in complete darkness? Even I would hesitate further investigation.

Beyond the center of the crossroads, the rock-covered path was buried beneath thick layers of dry leaves, but we didn't need to follow the road to reach the crypts. However we couldn't cross the cemetery *without* making noise. I kicked my way through the leaves while Penelope and Father crunched them underfoot. My boot struck something and it rolled across a rock-covered grave. It was a hat. A Hunter's hat.

Penelope rushed to it and picked it up. She examined it and looked inside. When her eyes met mine, her lower lip trembled.

"What's wrong?"

"It's my father's," she replied.

"You're sure?"

She nodded. Tears tugged at the edges of her eyes. I lowered my Hunter box to the ground and rushed to her. I wrapped an arm around her and squeezed her tightly.

I whispered, "It doesn't mean he's dead. It's only his hat."

Penelope pulled back, her chest heaving as she fought her building sobs. She took several deep breaths, trying to calm herself. "You're right. Besides, I can't lose my self-control here, not when there's a vampire nearby."

She wrapped her arms around my neck and hugged me tightly.

"Forrest," Father said with urgency rising in his voice.

Still hugging Penelope, I saw the creature, raised the crossbow and fired before he finished his warning. The arrow plunged through the ghoul's head, causing it to stagger for a few moments before it dropped backwards on the ground. It wasn't dead. Only fire completely destroyed a ghoul, at least in my experiences. They were the creepiest creatures I had ever fought and without fire, you couldn't kill them. Hack them into a thousand pieces and each piece crawled, moved, trying to find a living creature to kill and devour, even after they weren't physically able to do so. A strange sound erupted from its odd mouth like nothing I'd ever heard before. It sprang to its feet and turned until it located us. Its long pointy tongue hung from its mouth, dripping drool. At the edge of the closest crypt were three more with wide crazed eyes focused on us. I should have known not to shoot it because where there's one ghoul, there's generally a few more. Sometimes, a whole lot more.

They were diabolical creatures, and now we knew what Penelope had sensed. I wasn't sure how we were going to escape or kill them.

CHAPTER 14

"You ever fight a ghoul?" I asked Penelope.

She shook her head, staring at them with frightened awe. "I've only read about them, and my father … He told me stories about them. I doubt they were true."

"Unlike zombies, they have enough intelligence to hunt and kill humans. Fire's the only thing that will destroy them."

"Can we outrun them?" she asked.

"I can't," Father said.

The ghoul with the arrow stuck in its head pointed at me, jumped and squealed. The other three rushed toward us with strange gurgling sounds rattling from their oversized mouths. They snarled and ran on all fours.

"Father, grab my box."

He gave me a perplexed stare. "Don't jest with me in a time like this."

"Grab it!"

Father grabbed the handle tightly and glared at me. I stooped, slung him partway over my left shoulder while he held onto the box, and then I ran toward the crypt near the center of the cemetery.

"Penelope, run to that crypt over there," I said, nodding toward it.

She sprinted ahead of me.

"Forrest! Put me down," he said.

"Do you want to live or get eaten alive by those things?"

"Never mind. Run! The damned things are running toward us like wild dogs."

Penelope tripped over a small grave marker hidden under the leaves. She hit the ground hard and groaned, grabbing her ankle. As I neared her, she attempted to push herself up. She looked toward me and her face twisted from the pain. I flung the crossbow to my left hand, reached down and grabbed the pack secured on her back, lifting it and her off the ground without a pause in step.

Few times in my early years was I ever thankful for my abnormally large size and incredible strength, and this was one of those occasions. I ran full speed with Father propped over my shoulder while carrying Penelope like a baggage trunk in my right hand. My feet clopped like a Clydesdale on pavement as I hurried to the crypt. A few months ago, I would have probably tripped over my huge feet, trying to run, but Jacques had convinced me to keep practicing my running, which I had done, a lot, and it had helped.

I glanced toward the crypt, but kept my attention focused more on the leaf-covered ground because I didn't want to fall like she had. I couldn't imagine how bad that would be for Father should I topple forward, and he crashed to the hard ground. Physically, he was in bad enough shape without any added injuries.

"Hurry, Forrest," Father said, slapping my lower back with his free hand, as if his encouragement could make me run any faster. Maybe in the panic, he thought I *was* a Clydesdale? "They're getting closer."

I rounded toward the other side of the crypt, lowered Penelope to the ground, and Father dropped my Hunter box. "Prepare yourself, Father."

"What?"

I brought him over my shoulder, cradled him in my arms, and then slung him into the air. He frantically waved his arms before he landed on the top of the roof. "What the Hell, son? Are you *trying* to kill me?"

I reached for Penelope's waist.

She shook her head defiantly, trying to back away. "Oh, no. Don't you dare!"

I grabbed her and boosted her up where Father could reach her hands and pull her onto the roof.

"I see where your affections lie, son! Throw your decrepit old father into the air like a bundle of tied straw, but *she—*"

"There isn't time for arguments," I said, grabbing my box off the ground.

"What about you, Forrest?" she asked, reaching a hand downward.

"Not even the two of you can possibly pull me up there. Just keep your voices down and don't draw attention to yourselves."

Father gave me a worried look, but said nothing.

The four ghouls came around the corner of the crypt toward me, their long wet tongues swaying and dribbling viscous foamy spittle. Their strange yellow eyes turned blacker than ink. Their mouths elongated, and they flexed their hands, pointing their claws.

I turned to run and a fifth ghoul stood blocking my path. This ghoul was shorter than the others, but not any less deadly. Faint purplish blood vessels pulsed on its ashen gray face. The large eyes resembled globs of black tar enveloped beneath an oozy sheen. Its ears were pointed back, reminding me of the plague demon. It hissed and ran its long rough tongue across its jagged yellow teeth.

"Forrest," Penelope gasped, obviously as shocked to see this one as I was. I had only counted four, but there could be a dozen more.

There was madness in this creature's eyes. Raspy sounds echoed in its throat. It gnashed its teeth and growled. I swung my Hunter box with all my strength, smacking it square in the side of its head. The impact crushed its skull with a sick crunching sound, pivoted its head sideways, and sent the ghoul rolling across the leaves. Although it was injured, it wasn't dead. I carried the arc with the momentum and careened the box around at the ones behind me, hoping to incapacitate them for a few minutes. I only struck two of them, which caused the other two to scramble from my reach. I ran.

Ghouls were cowardly in some respects, which was why they traveled in packs and tended to hunt solitary victims. If their intended terrified victim was injured and scrambling for his life, a pack of ghouls became bolder and pursued.

Glancing back over my shoulder, I noticed the ghouls clambering together into a group. None of them seemed to notice that Father and Penelope were on the roof of the crypt, which was good. I had put some distance between me and the five ghouls, but I didn't have any idea where to go.

Without a substantial amount of help, I didn't have any chance of pulling myself up to one of the rooftops. None of the trees had lower branches I could climb, and since the ghouls could see me inside this small cemetery, they wouldn't easily stop their pursuit despite their injuries.

I wanted to slink to the side of the crypt, out of view, but I needed to be in a position where I could keep an eye on the ghouls. If they crept up behind me while I wasn't aware of their location, I'd die quickly. No doubts about that.

Father had said that they were pursuing us like a pack of wild dogs, and that was true. They also held the same type of mentality. Ghouls were stronger in groups, quick to rip and tear a human apart. I'd never seen a solitary ghoul. They actually relied upon one another. Because of this, I should have delayed my initial attack when I had shot the first one until after we had located where the rest of the group was.

The one thing I knew best about the ghouls was how much I absolutely despised them.

I dropped to my knees and opened my box. I considered using my pistol, but I didn't want to waste silver bullets on something they wouldn't actually kill. I had stove matches and flint, but no flammable liquids. Starting a fire out in the open would only frighten them away until the fire burned out, and I needed a large fire capable of consuming them. Such was the dilemma.

The five ghouls moved in unison at a slow gait like hunting dogs on the scent of birds, ready to flush a covey out of hiding. They remained low, on all fours, sniffing the air, making strange guttural sounds, and they used large tombstones to hide behind as they peered around.

Closing my box of hunting tools, I left it on the ground. With the tip of my dagger, I pricked my finger and squeezed several drops of blood onto the corner of the box. I smeared the blood across the box with my thumb and grabbed my crossbow before rushing toward the nearest crypt. When I reached the wall, I glanced to see their location. They scrambled across the ground to my box; almost apelike in how they carried themselves. They sniffed the box and clawed at it with their long sharp nails. They obviously smelled the blood. One tried chewing on a corner of the box but didn't seem happy with the taste. A couple of the ghouls found my smeared blood and licked at the box hungrily, smacking at the others when they attempted to nudge their way closer. They gnashed and growled at one another, but I doubted their bickering would last long since there was little blood to fight over.

I made my way around the far side of the crypt. A protective iron fence ran alongside the building, approximately four feet away from the wall. It was a safeguard to prevent people from plummeting over the edge onto the carved rock stairs that led down to an iron gate below. The set of stairs led to a lower level where a casket was probably stored, and I contemplated heading down. At the bottom of the stairs a large pile of leaves, at least knee-deep, had collected over time from the wind blowing them through the fence.

It appeared to be a good fire source, but how could I set a trap?

An old iron gate secured the sepulcher. It could be locked, but I doubted it would be. Of course as corroded as the gate was, it could be wielded shut by the thick rust.

If I could get inside the crypt, kick in enough leaves, and get the ghouls lured inside ... Phht. The ghouls would follow me regardless of anything else. I didn't need to worry about that. I was more concerned about getting cornered inside by the ghouls. I didn't like the odds of fighting against five ghouls inside a tight space. But what choice did I have? The entire cemetery was magically sealed inside the thickly coiled thorny vines. One could only run so long around the circular graveyard before suffering exhaustion and falling victim to these ungodly creatures or the vampire, if one resided in the cemetery.

That was the first moment such a thought had dawned on me. Did the vampire we had come to slay actually exist?

Hoarse gurgling sounds echoed softly from the other side of the crypt. The ghouls were coming for me. I had gifted them with the taste of blood and now they wanted more. A strange sound echoed farther away, like the scraping of a sharp object being dragged along a stone. A few seconds later, the sound occurred again, but at a different location in the cemetery, and then at another spot. The rough scraping noises reverberated faster, making an ear-piercing painful sound. I had no idea what was responsible for those noises, but the ghouls had not made them and seemed to have ignored them.

I hurried to the bottom of the steps. Grabbing the gate, I was alarmed by how close their growls were overhead. They were trying to squeeze their heads through the iron bars of the fence. Ghouls were smarter than zombies, but not overly intelligent. Their hunger controlled them more and desperation set in their eyes as they peered down at me. Nothing registered in their minds that they could have simply followed the fence until they found the stairs. Instead, they sought to get *through* the iron bars.

I pushed the small iron gate open. It didn't budge. I yanked on it and shook it hard. Bits of rust cascaded off the bars. The hinges squeaked. The ghouls lunged at the fence above, reaching through the bars with their long pale arms, and swiping their claws uselessly. I was thankful they had not figured out how to follow the fence to get to the stairs.

I shoved the gate, pushing my weight against it. It moved slightly where the latch connected but still resisted. The ghouls growled louder, sometimes moaning from their anticipation. I was a big enough meal to satiate all of their hunger, provided they reached me, but I was just outside their reach.

"Forrest!" Penelope yelled. "Are you okay?"

All five ghouls stiffened and turned toward the direction of her voice.

Well, I was. I cringed, shook my head, and grumbled.

The ghouls scurried along the fence, tugging the bars as they moved. When they reached the end of the fence, one noticed the stairs and hobbled down two of the steps. Its long winding tongue curled. It bore sharp jagged teeth. Instead of a growl, it seemed to purr for a moment with contentment and a sense of accomplishment.

I took a step back from the gate and kicked the door latch hard. The gate swung inward with screeching hinges. I raked the leaves inside the door with the side of my boot, as many as I could. I glanced up the steps. The five ghouls descended. Their black eyes grew wider and more menacing, possessed by their insatiable hunger.

They turned their heads slightly and their jaws popped loudly. Their mouths were larger and their jaws came unhinged so they could take larger bites and rip the flesh from my bones. Coldness rushed through me, and suddenly the thought of being impaled by one of the massive sharp thorns in the passageway had seemed a much better fate than how I pictured myself dying now.

CHAPTER 15

$\mathcal{I}$ rushed into the crypt, kicking more leaves into a huge pile near the door. In hindsight, I don't know why I had thought this would be a good plan. Leaf debris was a quick burst of heat and fire, rapidly escalating and plummeting in strength almost as fast. The rising flames poised a greater chance of causing the ghouls to flee rather than harming them. I needed a longer lasting fuel for the fire to destroy the ghouls. There wasn't anything useable inside the crypt. The entire sepulcher was made from stone. No wooden rafters. Even the coffin was carved out of stone.

The first ghoul charged through the door without hesitation. I side-stepped and cupped my huge hand around the back of its hairless head, lifting it into the air. I turned and smashed its face against the stone wall. Bones crunched. Its forehead sunk inward and bits of shattered teeth showered down. It yelped. I flung it hard against the opposite wall and it collapsed to the cold floor.

I pulled my dagger as the next two dashed toward me. I kicked the one to my left, knocking it out the door into the other two. The other ghoul leapt into the air and landed on my chest. Its rotten breath reeked of death and decay. It opened its large mouth wide enough to take off my head. I staggered backwards, trying to avoid its mouth, especially the teeth, when I noticed it had raised its clawed hand into the air. It swung, aiming for my throat, hoping—I guessed—to gash open my tenderest flesh to spill the greatest amount of blood.

Before it flailed downward, I toppled, falling fast to the hard floor. I rammed my dagger into its gut as I hit the floor. It squealed in pain. I grabbed it by the throat and squeezed, pushing the dagger deeper. Black blood leaked over my hand. It gurgled for a moment and desperately raked its claws across my arm. The thickness of my coat prevented a deep gash, but it had cut me. The scent of my blood invited the other three to rush inside the tight quarters.

I yanked my dagger free and flung the ghoul toward its three companions, missing, but I rolled and pushed myself to my feet. The ghoul I had smashed against the wall writhed on the floor. It wasn't dead but at least it wasn't a threat *yet*.

I moved to the other side of the stone coffin and faced the four ghouls. I pushed the coffin lid aside. The coffin was empty. It was a shame the vampire wasn't lying asleep or dormant inside. I had once executed a vampire with the indiscriminate help of hungry ghouls who had torn him and his offspring apart. It would have been good to use this vampire as a distraction while I escaped the crypt. That wasn't an option though.

The ghouls formed a semi-circle, facing me, and slowly moved inward to trap me in the corner. I could have run for the narrow door, but not without at least two of them latching onto me with their sharp claws and trying to bite me. With the large number of sharp teeth each ghoul had, it didn't take but a few strong bites to cause rapid blood loss for a victim. The slightest bite, however, could infect the person and curse him or her to slowly transform into a ghoul. These were other reasons why I hated encountering and killing ghouls and another situation where I missed Jacques. Werewolves were resistant to most undead infections. I was not. So even though I greatly outsized them, I couldn't risk one sinking its teeth into me. And besides that, I needed to survive so I could get Penelope and Father down off the roof. I believed it would take the three of us together to get through the tunnel safely.

I hefted the stone coffin lid upright and held it so the long narrow side was horizontal, and I used it as a shield. The stone lid was heavier than I estimated, and I strained to carry it. My arms and back ached.

The ghouls seemed confused with me holding it. Fighting the burning sensation of fatigue building in my biceps, forearms, and my hands, I growled with ferocity. The noise partially startled them for a moment, perhaps they thought I was transforming into some sort of beast, but I took the opportunity of their hesitation to rush at them. With the lid I pushed two of the ghouls across the floor and smashed them against the wall. The other two were too swift to get pinned or trapped. One leapt over the lid while the other scurried underneath.

I left the heavy coffin lid against the wall with the two ghouls struggling unsuccessfully to get the weight off of them. I turned quickly to face the escaped ghouls. One of the two still had the arrow protruding from its head. I grabbed the arrow shaft, pulled, and swung the ghoul into the air. It bounced off the far wall and dropped beside its injured companion.

The last standing ghoul leapt onto my back, growling and slashing. I winced as the claws cut through my overcoat. I tried to reach over my shoulder, but the wicked creature stayed outside of my reach and refused to let go. Fiery lines of pain surfaced where its claws had penetrated through the leather material and into my flesh. I had never heard an instance where the claws spread the ghoul infection, but I supposed it was possible. Something for me to worry about later.

A second before I would have rammed my back against the wall in an attempt to crush the ghoul, a line of brightness cut through the shadows. Air *whooshed* past my head, the ghoul fell slack, and dropped to the floor. A fiery arrow smoldered in its head. Smoke drifted from its ears, nose, and mouth. Its body twitched and spasmed before growing stiff. I glanced toward the door. Penelope flashed a broad smile. "Can't let you have all of the fun."

"Where's Father?"

"Still on the roof. I had to jump. I needed to know you were okay."

I winced, rolled my shoulders, and turned my back toward her so she could inspect the lacerations.

"You have a lot of cuts but none are deep or look severe."

I sighed. "What about disease from their claws?"

"I don't know."

"We need to get out of here," I said. "But I don't want to leave these creatures alive, just in case others come to the cemetery seeking to slay the vampire. I had thought about using the leaves to start a fire, but it might not be hot enough to kill them."

"They're not getting around too good right now."

"They'll recover, given time."

The two beneath the coffin lid were trapped between the lid and the wall. The two against the other wall were panting and sprawled out on the floor, but neither made any attempt to crawl. The one she had shot with the flaming arrow wasn't moving. If anything the fire had obliterated its brain, but I doubted its body wouldn't eventually try to become mobile again.

"I have an idea," I said.

"What?"

I carefully grabbed the brain-dead ghoul by one foot and tossed it into the empty coffin, and then I grabbed the two against the far wall and placed them inside as well. I hurried to the heavy stone lid. "When I lift this, throw them into that coffin, too."

She nervously glanced to the ghouls and then to me.

"Both are probably suffering from broken bones, but be quick and make certain you don't get bitten. Are you ready?"

Penelope pursed her lips. "Ready? Forrest, you could ask me that a hundred years from now and I still wouldn't be *ready* to touch one of them."

I gave her an even stare as I reached for the lid. "They're hideous creatures. I agree. But leaving them where they can recover and kill again isn't something any Hunter should do."

She nodded. We were both obligated to tasks neither of us enjoyed.

I heaved the stone lid, and she grabbed each ghoul by one foot and dragged them like burlap bags of sand. She put them into the coffin, and I slid the lid across until it was flush with all sides.

I arched and stretched my back, and groaned with some relief.

"You think they can slide the top aside to escape?" she asked.

I gave a slight shrug. "I doubt they can budge it."

"Will they die?"

"All but one."

Penelope gave an incredulous stare. "They'll eat one another?"

"That would be my guess. They cannibalize whenever there's no other choice."

Panic widened her eyes. "And there's five of them in this cemetery, which is closed off from the rest of the town. They don't appear to be lacking for food."

I nodded. "For ghouls, they looked quite healthy, if one can measure such a thing, which means a lot of people have come into this cemetery on a fairly regular basis."

"My father?" She closed her eyes and clenched tight fists.

"He's a Hunter with intellect. There's a good chance he found a way to escape."

"I hope so."

"Sometimes, hope is all we have."

Outside the scraping stone sound echoed again.

"What is that?" I asked.

"I'm not sure. Your father and I heard it earlier."

"You didn't see what made it?"

She shook her head. "We should help your father down and find where that vampire is. It's obvious he wasn't in here."

"What if there isn't a vampire in this cemetery?" I asked.

"You don't think there is?"

"I'm not certain, but I'm beginning to wonder."

"Why?"

"The whole place seems like a giant trap," I replied.

"For what purpose?"

"I don't know, but these ghouls patrolled the cemetery. The thorny giant vines make a quick escape almost impossible."

"Are you proposing that we leave without looking for the vampire?"

I shook my head. "No, we need to collect the bounty if he is here. A quick search should tell us."

I scooped up a huge pile of leaves in my arms and covered the lid of the coffin.

"What are you doing?"

I grabbed another armful of leaves and piled them around the coffin. "Roasting the ghouls."

"That will work?"

"It won't hurt to try. With enough leaves burning around the stone coffin, it will be like a brick oven, magnifying and trapping the heat inside. They should cook."

"Provided they don't escape?"

"They fear fire. Even if they slid the lid over a little, they'd see the flames and scrunch away into a corner. But I don't think they have the strength to move the lid."

Penelope gathered a lot of the leaves and piled them on top of the lid. When the leaves completely covered the coffin, I struck a long match against the stone wall and lit leaves at each corner of the coffin.

The fire rose.

I grabbed my crossbow and walked to the door with her. Once we stepped outside the door, I yanked the small iron gate back into place. The latch clicked shut. I picked up a thick piece of iron that had fallen from the overhead fence and bent it around the small gate and the bar where the latch had been welded. Even if the ghouls survived the fire and pried the lid off the coffin, they'd never get through the gate.

The stone-scraping sounds reverberated again, only faster and closer. She and I exchanged glances.

"Forrest!" Father yelled. "Come quick! I need your help!"

CHAPTER 16

*P*enelope and I came up the steps to discover what was making the sounds. She limped slightly.

"Are you okay?" I asked.

"I'll be fine."

"You hurt yourself coming off the roof?"

She shook her head. "No, it was when I tripped and fell earlier, but dropping from the roof didn't help it any."

The rough scraping sounds came from near the crypt where Father was. At first I didn't see what was making the noise, until I saw what appeared to be large statues moving, but they weren't statues at all. They were living creatures made out of stone.

Three gargoyles.

There was that moment of disbelief when I questioned if I was walking in a nightmare. Seeing these things made me stand silent. Captivated, I found myself admiring how these gargoyles moved effortlessly, being as heavy as they had to be.

Penelope placed her hand on mine. "When I said that I sensed evil earlier, it wasn't the ghouls but it definitely is associated with them."

The stone creatures were half my size but probably four times my weight. Each step or movement they made produced a stone-raking-stone sound. Their wings rose and shifted as they walked, helping them keep their balance. Due to their weight and size, they weren't fast movers. At least they didn't seem to be.

Father edged himself higher on the roof until he noticed us. He waved us toward him with desperation.

All three gargoyles were slate gray like the tombstones and the crypt buildings. They had noticed Father and were approaching his building.

I glanced at Penelope. "What do you know about gargoyles?"

She shook her head. "Only that they're not *supposed* to be alive."

"These apparently are."

"I see that, too."

"How do you kill something made from stone?"

"You cannot kill stone since it isn't alive."

Good point. "But something has brought them to life."

She nodded. "Some type of magic or they might actually be demons trapped inside the stones."

"Then these are more your type for slaying rather than mine."

"No, I'm seeing them for the first time like you."

Father glared at me. "You two going to stand there and gawk or help me down before they kill me?"

"Be patient, Father. They are stiff and slow and barely moving. You're probably safer being on the roof than for us to get you down."

The smallest gargoyle squatted, stretched its wings, and propelled itself into the air. It landed with a thunderous crash on the rooftop not far from where Father stood. The vibrations from its landing caused Father to stumble. He grabbed the ledge and peered back at its demonic face.

I was stunned. These stone creatures had seemed sluggish, and I had underestimated their agility and speed.

"Do you mind mulling through your theory again, son?" he said. "Don't take too long thinking about it because this thing is going to flatten me."

Father edged his way to the corner of the roof. He was about to jump. I can't say that I blamed him, but doing so would probably kill him.

I ran toward the building. The other two gargoyles noticed me and stamped their feet in rapid succession, making an incredibly loud noise while shaking the ground. If their actions were meant to frighten me, they were partly successful. However, I was more frightened about Father jumping and killing himself than I was for what danger I was placing myself into to rescue him.

"Hold on!" I said.

He made an odd face. "To *what* exactly?"

"Patience," I replied, rushing toward the side of the crypt.

"She left me about five minutes ago, son. Don't think she's coming back anytime soon, either."

"Jump!"

Father looked at me questionably. I still wasn't quite close enough to catch him, but by my estimate I'd be under him before he reached the ground. He glanced over his shoulder. The gargoyle wobbled in its gait toward him. It widened its muscular stone arms like it wanted to hug him, but he and I both knew it was going to embrace him and crush him to death.

He jumped.

I caught him with both arms as I ran. I didn't stop running, trying to put as much distance between them and I as I could.

"Forr—rrest!" Penelope said.

The two gargoyles that had been stamping their feet were flying overhead. While I was not completely certain, it seemed they had been ramping up speed to get into the air. They weren't after me though. They were circling over her.

She hobbled and winced with each step. She had twisted her ankle worse than she had let on. One of the gargoyles swooped downward. She dove toward a tall obelisk gravestone and flung her arms over her face. The gargoyle dipped and careened, trying to miss the pointed tombstone, but the tip pierced through its thin stone wing, cracking it. The slight splintering cracks didn't shatter the wing but caused the beast to tug the wing inward, and it dropped hard to its side.

Its heavy impact sank the creature several inches into the ground. It pushed with its massive left stone hand to lift itself, but only rocked back and forth like a tortoise stuck on its back. It appeared it needed both hands to upright itself, but its weight was pinning down its other arm.

Penelope pulled herself to her feet and placed her back against the tombstone. The grounded gargoyle snorted and puffed like an angry bull, still trying to right itself to get at her. The one in the air circled and was in a downward glide, coming straight at her.

"Go help her, son," Father said. "I'll hide behind a tree since I don't have any idea how to fight something like that."

I put him down. "I don't know either."

"Well, one of us better come up with something or we're all dead."

Penelope watched the gliding gargoyle. With her back pressed against the tombstone, she clung to it, watching—I supposed—to see what it was going to do. While she stood there, I ran back toward the crossroads.

"What are you doing?" Father shouted.

I sprinted to the dark robed statue and leaned down to pick up the stone scythe. The weapon was heavy, almost too heavy for me to get my fingers beneath it and pry it off the ground. After I lifted it and wrapped my arms around the section where the curved blade attached to the handle, I drug it down the road toward Penelope.

The gargoyle widened its wings and circled around, gliding in at a lower descent the second time. The clawed toes on its feet spread out and lengthened.

"Run, Penelope," I said, huffing. I hefted the scythe and leaned forward, pressing each step firmly down and pushing off with my feet.

Penelope glanced toward me and then looked at the gargoyle. It descended fast. I kept rushing toward her, but at the speed it was dropping, if she waited any longer, she was dead.

The gargoyle aimed at her with its feet, but she rolled out of the way. The winged beast snorted, tried to pull itself upward, but due to its weight, it crashed to the ground. It maintained its balance after running a few steps and turned.

Penelope crawled toward me. I ran past her, lifting the long scythe and propping it against my shoulder. The gargoyle stood about ten feet in height. It turned toward me, sensing my approach. Its hideous bat-like face contorted. Orange flames blazed behind its eyes. Even with my weapon in hand, the creature held no obvious fear of me. I brought down the scythe and balanced it in both hands, and then I swung my entire body around to get the most momentum for the stone weapon as I could. It didn't help.

The long curved blade made of stone, cracked and crumbled when it struck the gargoyle. It hissed and stomped its way toward me. The ground shook beneath my feet. I took a step back when it lunged to grip me with both of its huge clawed hands. Wrapping the stone handle in my arms, I used it like one would use a battering ram against a door, and struck the creature in the center of the chest. A gurgling sound echoed inside its throat that I assumed could be nothing other than sheer laughter.

I tried to back away, but it grasped the stone handle in its thick hands and yanked. I released the handle or otherwise, it would have pulled me into its reach. It slammed the handle on the ground and it shattered into a dozen pieces. I examined the fragments, but nothing seemed useful enough a weapon for me to claim.

"Forrest," Penelope said in a nervous whisper. "The other one is approaching."

So we had two gargoyles approaching and neither she nor I had weapons to defend ourselves. The third gargoyle continued struggling on the ground, trying to roll free of the small crater it had created when it had crashed to the ground.

"Any suggestions?" I asked.

"I'd say run, but we're limited to where."

I nodded and picked up a stone fragment from the handle. I lobbed it hard at the bat-faced gargoyle in front of me. The fragment struck and disintegrated into a puff of dust. The creature's brow tightened and its mouth widened, revealing a double row of teeth set inside its jaws.

I had seen gargoyles atop buildings in many of the countries I had traveled through. Each one was crafted with unique faces, resembling what the artist believed a demon might look like. These were no different, except they were *alive*. Gargoyles were believed to be guardians to frighten off evil spirits, but these seemed to be possessed by some unseen power, and not one I believed to befriend or protect humans from.

The gargoyle hissed, flexed its massive wings, and rushed toward me. I attempted to step to the side, but it caught my arm. As heavy as these creatures were, I never anticipated one rushing that fast toward me. It held me firmly in its tight painful grip.

"Forrest!" Penelope exclaimed, covering her mouth with her hand.

I gripped the creature's thick stone finger and tried to pry them apart or at least loosen its grip, but I didn't possess enough strength. I pulled back and placed my feet against its chest, pushing and pulling and yanking. Nope. It had me.

It leaned closer, pressing its face to mine. It snorted and chuffed with breath like brimstone. With its free hand it wrapped its fingers around my throat and tightened. Immediately I couldn't breathe. It had cut off my windpipe and if it tightened anymore, it could pop my head from my shoulders.

The world was growing dim. Blackness was covering my vision. In desperation, I swung a hard fist into its face, not certain where the strike might land, but I wasn't going to die without at least trying to fight.

I hit its nose. It leveled a harsh frown. Those eyes blazed with angry flames. Penelope had picked up part of the scythe blade that still had a curved edge and she slashed at its stone wings. Its eyes widened and it turned toward her. The distraction was enough for it to loosen its grip, but it didn't release me. I took several deep breaths.

My ears rang, but faintly I heard stone striking stone. She was still trying to do some sort of damage to the gargoyle but from my angle I couldn't tell if she was having any success.

I placed one hand on the forefinger of the beast and the other on its thumb. Using all the strength I had, I couldn't pull his fingers any wider apart. Penelope groaned and grunted, striking the winged beast over and over, making a dull *thwacking* noise with each hit. She didn't seem to be hurting it any, but she was annoying the hell out of it.

It formed a fist with its free hand and swung around hard and fast.

Its fist narrowly missed her, but its long draping wings sliced through the air toward her. She fell backwards, crashing to the ground. If she had waited another second, it would have removed her head from her shoulders. It turned and tried to stomp her. While on her back, she used her elbows and pushed with her feet to crawl awkwardly away, just barely keeping herself outside of its reach. Panic and helplessness claimed her face.

It swung to the side, using the long trail of its wing to strike at her. For a stone creature it definitely held unpredictable tactics. She kept crawling, scooting away, but the gargoyle refused to allow her escape. It stomped one foot after the other, trying to flatten her, but fortunately she stayed one step ahead of it.

With my fist I struck the side of the gargoyle's face again and again. My flailing went unnoticed by the creature as its determination to kill her controlled it. It clutched me closer to its chest without any thought that it was still holding me. I reached for the chiseled crevices between its chest and neck, hoping to find a handhold to get more leverage and pry myself free.

My fingers caught in a small narrow groove of the stone chain that was carved around its neck. I grabbed hold, pulled, and one of the links cracked and fell loose. A gem about the size of my fist glowed inside the hole. I struck my fist against the opening several times. Bits of dust and rock chunks cascaded from the opening. I hit the gem once more and it slipped from the opening and landed on the ground.

It craned its neck around and peered at me. Its mouth widened momentarily, revealing its large teeth. A deep intake of air rushed through its mouth. I anticipated a nasty roar or growl, but instead, the creature dismantled at every joint, dropping to the ground in a series of pieces. The fingers clamped around my neck released me and dropped at my feet.

I rubbed my neck and gulped air. When most of the dizziness passed, I walked to Penelope. I offered my hand and helped her to her feet.

"What happened to it?" she asked.

I shook my head. "When I dislodged that gem, it fell apart."

She brushed herself off.

Glancing around, I said, "Where's the other one?"

She shrugged and frowned, gazing across the cemetery. "I don't know. How can something that large move so quickly?"

"I have no idea."

I took the piece of scythe from her and hurried to the gargoyle still stuck on the ground. I walked around so I could see its face. It snarled and swiped at me with its clawed hand but I remained outside of its reach. A chain necklace wrapped around its neck, too.

Father picked up the glowing yellow gem from the disassembled gargoyle and rejoined us. I was trying to get past the gargoyles claws to strike the necklace on its chest. "Careful, Forrest."

"Did you see where the other gargoyle went?" I asked.

"No." A winged shadow passed overhead. He looked to the sky. "Ah, it's in the air."

I stepped toward the angered gargoyle and waited for it to swing at me. After it did, I lunged inward and struck the necklace hard. The chain cracked but held in place, not allowing me to dislodge the gem. I shook my head in frustration. I glanced toward Penelope and Father. "I don't think this one's getting up anytime soon. While the other one is in flight, we should at least examine the other two crypts for the vampire."

Father nodded. "And then what?"

"We head out through the passageway. I can't see how this can get much worse."

"Hunter!" the deep voice beckoned from near the large angelic statue. It was Philip. Another person stood beside him. Philip shoved the man to his knees and placed a knife to the man's throat. "Your coachman refuses to tell me where the child is. Tell me where the boy is and your coachman lives."

CHAPTER 17

"*D*on't tell him, Forrest," Thomas said in a solemn tone. "You know my destiny. And we're already running behind schedule."

I glanced at my watch. It was after eleven a.m. I had never intended to spend this much time at the cemetery. Of course, when you're fighting to survive, time escapes at a rapid pace, not exactly begging one's attention.

"Is this what you've been reduced to, Philip?" I asked. "Blackmail and killing innocent people? That's not the true heart of a Hunter."

Blood dripped from Philip's arm that hung to his side. His fatigued face revealed that he had been injured. By the thorns? Had Philip been the one who had cried out from inside the passageway? He blinked hard and shook his head for several seconds. I wondered if his vision was blurred. He staggered slightly, found his balance, and pressed the dagger against Thomas' neck. Thomas stiffened. The whites of his eyes revealed his fear of death. Regardless of the coachman's bravery, he didn't really want to die.

Philip glared at me. His scars seemed more prominent than before. He spoke through gritted teeth. "To save humanity from that child's eventual wrath, I'll do whatever's necessary."

"Hunters don't kill Hunters." I walked toward him, placing my hand on my dagger.

"Forrest!" Father said in a harsh whisper. "Just tell him where Varak is. Let's be done with this."

I frowned at him and shook my head. Penelope seemed to agree with Father and nodded toward me with pleading eyes. The child had even made her uneasy.

The darkness in Philip's gaze consumed him. He was beyond reason. He might have been a good Hunter at one time in his life, but his obsession to kill Varak was akin to pure hate-filled evil. That's when I wondered if he truly wanted to kill the child, or did he have an ulterior motive? Did he want to use the child to gain power and influence over others, which was something else that went against a Hunter's credo?

My mind had sorted through a lot of issues during the past few weeks. I held no doubt that killing undead creatures might eventually tarnish a good Hunter's soul. But what if more than that had occurred with Philip? What if a Hunter killed an insane vampire that had been without any rationality at all? Hunters absorbed a good portion of a vampire's memories without any assurance that the memory impressions received would benefit the Hunter. Was it possible to absorb the madness of a mentally disturbed vampire and those mental persuasions overrode the rationality and competency an adept Hunter once had?

Dominus had probably killed as many vampires as Philip, possibly even more, but had shown none of the alterations Philip was exhibiting. Although I had no way to know, I had to assume at this particular moment that Philip was being controlled by something other than what we Hunters claimed our allegiance to.

Thomas had done nothing to provoke Philip, and yet the Hunter held a knife at the coachman's throat. Even if I agreed with Father and wanted to get rid of the child, Philip wouldn't be the one I'd hand him over to. I wasn't sure what he'd do.

"What's your answer, Hunter?" Philip asked.

Before I could reply, the gargoyle swooped down from behind Philip and thrashed its talons into the Hunter's back, knocking him forward before yanking him upward. Thomas dove aside, rolled, and slowly rose to his feet, uncertain of what had happened. Once he realized he had been spared, he hurried to us.

The gargoyle arced its wings slightly to the right in an attempt to miss an oversized tombstone, but with the added weight of the Hunter, it failed to rise any higher. Instead, it dropped Philip near the robed statue at the crossroads and landed abruptly on the other side of him.

The Hunter rolled several times and when he stopped, he wasn't conscious, but for a few moments, I thought he was dead. The gargoyle turned. Its heavy feet thudded as it walked. Its interest was keenly directed at the unmoving Hunter.

Even with all the threats Philip had made, I couldn't allow his fate to end here, but the four of us weren't a match against this gargoyle. It had been sheer luck that I had found a way to destroy the other one.

I glanced at Thomas. "Are you okay?"

He nodded.

"We can't allow it to kill Philip," I said, looking at Father and Penelope.

Father gave me a perplexed stare. "You cannot be serious?"

"He's a fellow Hunter," I replied.

"One who wishes to kill all of us," Father said. "Especially you, I might add."

"I'm aware of that."

"What do you propose?" she asked.

"Distract the gargoyle. Thomas and I will pull Philip to safety."

Thomas shook his head. "I will do no such thing, Forrest. This madman dragged me through the most horrible tunnel and put a knife to my throat. I'd rather face the plague demons Albert has sent after me than to offer any aid to that man."

I shrugged. "I can't say I blame you."

Penelope threw a fist-sized rock and hit the gargoyle in the back of the head. It stopped its approach toward the Hunter and craned its neck around. The next rock struck its flat nose, exploding into a cloud of dust. It growled, widening its mouth, and flexed its wings while forming huge fists.

The gargoyle roared and marched toward her with heavy steps. She took several steps backwards and winced each time she put her right foot down. Father wrapped his arm with hers to keep her from having to place her weight upon her weak ankle.

"We distracted it, Forrest," Father said. "I have no idea what you plan to do, but you need to do something *fast*."

The stone creature's face contorted with the most evil hideous expressions I've ever seen. It hurried toward Father and Penelope, neither of which were able to outrun it.

What had I been thinking?

I hadn't been. I had been reacting without considering they were placing their lives into jeopardy to spare the Hunter.

Father hobbled, using what strength he could offer to help support her weight. They moved across the leafier section of the cemetery, but the gargoyle didn't even need to rush to shorten the distance between them.

She and Father were nearing one of the crypts, but not quickly enough. The gargoyle bellowed deeply, something that sounded like a note of triumph mixed with rolling laughter. It kicked a large swath of leaves out of its path as it strode closer. The ground shook slightly from its awkward steps.

I scanned the area around me, trying to figure out what I could use for a weapon. The stone scythe hadn't helped earlier with the other gargoyle, and if a gem kept this one together like the other one, I knew I'd never survive a hand-to-hand fight with it. One stern punch from it would prove fatal.

Father and Penelope reached the wall of the crypt and turned to look at me. The gargoyle's right foot stomped hard on the top of a leaf-covered grave. Its enormous weight crushed through the grave plot and sunk. The creature toppled forward and landed facedown. Its huge wings fanned with fury, and it pushed with its hands to stand, but due to its excessive mass it appeared to be unable to get up.

I motioned them to keep moving, and I ran toward the angelic statue, found the large stone book on the ground and picked it up.

While she and Father hurried farther away from the gargoyle, I carried the book and walked upon the gargoyle's back between its wings. It fought to pry its foot free from the sinkhole but it was wedged tightly in the ground. I lifted the book over my head and brought it down, hammering the top of its head.

It roared, shuffling its wings, rocking back and forth. I almost lost my balance, but I brought up the book and struck its head again and again. The solid stone book chiseled at the back of its head, chipping away bits of the skull until larger fractures appeared. Several more hammered thrusts dislodged thick hand-sized chunks of stone. I kept striking and expected the stone book to shatter, but it didn't. After finally busting its head to pieces, the creature stopped moving altogether.

I dropped the heavy book and sighed. My shoulders slumped. I lowered myself and sat upon the gargoyle's back, panting. Aches ran through my body. Every abrasion, bruise, and cut magnified, but at least we were all alive.

Father and Penelope limped to me.

Thomas came up and patted my shoulder, smiling.

"After I catch my breath," I said. "I'll crush the other gargoyle."

Father looked at me with a sense of pride and smiled. Penelope leaned her head against my chest and wrapped her arms around me. Enjoying her warmth and closeness, I embraced her, resting my chin atop her head.

"Thomas," I said. "See if you can dislodge the gem on this beast's chest."

He nodded.

AFTER SEVERAL MINUTES of holding Penelope and catching my breath, I slipped away, took the book, and decapitated the other gargoyle. We collected the three large gems that had somehow functioned like their hearts and placed them inside her pack. A search of the other two crypts proved fruitless.

No vampire.

Father frowned with disgust and leaned his back against the crypt wall. "No vampire? So why the ruse of offering a reward? Nothing but undead creatures and gargoyles."

I walked to where Philip lay unconscious on the ground. Blood leaked from his nose and mouth. His back had been flayed open where the gargoyle's huge talons had slashed into him, but if he were like me, I expected he'd heal fast and survive. He still had not awakened. With how he had been staggering and shaking his head *before* the gargoyle attacked him, I wondered if the thorns that had snagged him were also poisonous.

"What do we do with him?" Penelope asked.

I shrugged. "He's breathing but there isn't any way we can carry him through the thorny passageway. It was difficult enough keeping our own awareness of our surroundings."

Thomas nodded. "I thought I was going to die in that tunnel. I almost did. The vines lashed out at us but I managed to avoid them. One vine wrapped around his arm and tried to pull him into them."

"That's why his arm is bleeding?"

"Yes. I made it to the end of the tunnel, but he somehow freed himself and caught up to me before I stepped into the cemetery."

I knelt beside the Hunter and examined his wrists. Dark bruises encircled them from where I had restrained him with the ropes. As raw as his skin was and the deepness of the surrounding bruising, he must had fought against the tight ropes until he finally broke free. But he wasn't healing.

"If you leave him here, son, he's going to keep coming for you."

I flicked my gaze toward him. His haunted expression detailed his concern for my wellbeing. "I don't know about that. None of his previous injuries are healing, and I think the vines must have poisoned or weakened him. I'm not going to kill him, but I don't have any rope to tie him, either."

Penelope fished through her pack until she brought out a tied bundle of rope. "I do."

She handed me the rope. Father shook his head. "Let me do it this time, son. I can guarantee he won't get free of my knots. I've worked on ships before you were born. A sailor has to learn a vast variations of knots."

I handed him the rope and chuckled. "We don't want him to lie here and starve to death."

Father brought the Hunter's huge hands around behind his back. He frowned. "I don't want him killing you, either. If you still refuse to hand over the child, he's not going to give up his pursuit."

"He's right, Forrest," Penelope said.

"None of us can predict the future. We don't actually know what Varak will become, but I'm not certain this Hunter has been telling us the truth."

"Why do you say that?" she asked.

"It's just a feeling that came over me when he threatened to kill Thomas."

"Hunter instinct?" Father asked.

"Could be," I said with a shrug.

Father finished tying the knots and strained to stand. I extended my hand toward him, he took it, and I pulled him to his feet. He shook his head. "I can't believe there wasn't a vampire here."

"Other than us digging up the graves, we've checked all the possible places. But if the vampire was actually in the ground, the dirt on the surface would be fresh and loose. No new graves have been dug here in a long time."

Thomas nodded.

"So no bounty?" Father said with disappointment.

I smiled. "We have the gems from the gargoyles. I say we return to that shop and find out what's really happening."

"You think they'll buy these gems?" he asked.

"I don't believe they expect us to return." I grabbed my Hunter box and my crossbow.

Penelope picked up her father's hat and held it close to her chest while she scanned the cemetery one last time. Her eyes didn't moisten with tears, but her jaw tightened with determination. The bright sparkles in her eyes were ablaze. She glanced toward me with a slight smile, reaching for my hand. I took it and we walked side by side to the tunnel entrance. We each had a lot of burning questions that we intended to find the answers for.

CHAPTER 18

*T*he four of us made our way through the tunnel unscathed. The oddest thing about our exit was how the thorny vines retreated from us. Some of the climbers had wilted. Shed thorns had fallen to the path as well like leaves after the first frost. The large magical vine seemed to be dying. The whispering sounds that had plagued my mind before were now silent.

Father wore his anger on his face. He didn't have to verbally express *why* he was angry. It had to do with the fake bounty when he knew we needed the funds for traveling. He had been that way when I was growing up. If ever he was shorted in a trade that was when he grew the most hostile. He pinched pennies, but when you lived in a war-torn country that's under government oppression, you kept a watchful eye over every single cent because it was necessary to survive. A thief was a chief enemy, regardless of the sum he had stolen.

Father's hostility finally got the better of him. "Why would they do this, Forrest?"

"They are the only ones who can tell us the exact reason for what they've done. But my speculation is that they were sending gullible bounty hunters to feed the gargoyles and ghouls. And if that's the case, I don't understand why they'd do that."

"It could explain why all the people on the outskirts have vanished," Penelope said.

The wind whipped and whistled through the trees as we passed beneath them. Our coach was within sight. A man dressed in a drab suit stood admiring the horse. Unlike the others we had met in this rundown section of town, he appeared to have better fortune and possibly a fair amount of money.

"Can I help you?" I asked when we came closer.

He turned with a start and his eyes widened for a moment. "Ah, I am looking over this fine horse and coach. The elderly couple at the shop across the square offered to sell them to me at such a reasonable price. How old would you say this horse is?"

Thomas stepped to the horse, placed a hand on the bridle, and glared at the stranger. "This horse is *not* for sale, sir. Neither is the coach."

The man was taken back. "They clearly expressed that it is and so is the coach. Don't attempt to move in and swoop up the offer."

"The couple is mistaken," I said. "The horse and coach belong to this man. We've traveled with him for weeks."

The man turned with a fierce glare. "What scheme are the lot of you working here? They suggested the price, and I *shall* meet their offer."

"They cannot sale what they do not rightfully own," I said, stepping up to the man and staring down at him.

He studied me for a few minutes and took a couple of steps back. "Then why would they make such an offer?"

"They're deceitful people," Father said.

"If there's any schemes, it's been on their part. We plan to find out what they're doing," I said. "I suggest you move along."

He opened his mouth to reply but noticed my harsh frown and nodded, turning quickly away.

I placed my Hunter box inside the coach and loaded the crossbow. Father stood beside me with a look of concern. "Father, stay here with Thomas. Penelope and I will go to the shop."

"Stay? But I want to go with you."

"Thomas might need your help in case that man comes back."

"It's doubtful he'll return. You scared him quite good. I think I should accompany the two of you. I want answers."

"We all do."

"But we put our lives on the line and were betrayed."

"I know."

Father shook his head with a scoured expression on his face. "Very well, but if you're not back in a quarter of the hour, I'm coming to make certain the two of you are okay."

I smiled.

Penelope placed her father's Hunter hat upon her head and grinned. Her long wavy hair flowed to her shoulders and some strands covered her eyes.

"Suits you," I said, brushing her hair from her eyes.

She wrapped her right arm around my left and pressed against me to keep weight off her hurt ankle while we walked. "Is your father always so overly concerned about you like that?"

I offered a shrug and chuckled. "He's my father."

"He treats you like a little child sometimes."

I could only nod.

She shook her head. "My father sent me into the dark woods to hunt by myself when I was ten years old. He taught me to be independent and allowed me to work out my problems, not that you're *not* independent or—"

I smiled down at her. "We lost Momma not even a year ago. He has a difficult time … letting go."

Sadness came to her eyes, and she looked at the cobblestone. "I'm sorry, but I didn't mean you're not independent."

"It's okay. I understand what you were trying to say."

"You've been quite resourceful in keeping us alive," she said with a broad smile.

I squeezed her hand.

Once we reached the outside of the shop, I pulled the three gems from her pack and dropped them inside my coat pocket. I turned the doorknob with my left hand and held the crossbow to my side so it wasn't noticeable when we first entered.

The door hinges creaked as the door widened. Karl looked up from what he was working on at the counter. His wrinkled brow rose, and he adjusted his glasses, looking again in sheer disbelief. He glanced toward his wife who was sewing a piece of cloth to a quilt. "Abigail, we have company."

"Who?" she asked with a near growl.

"The Hunter," he said nervously.

"Which Hunter?"

He whispered, "The one who was here earlier."

"I told you something was wrong," she said in a stern whisper.

Karl forced a smile in an attempt to hide his nervousness. "Can we sell you more wares? Or—"

I leveled the crossbow and aimed at his head, walking straight for him. "No, we want to know *why* you sent us after a vampire that doesn't exist."

His face reddened. Sweat beaded his brow. His feeble hands shook. "Whatever do you mean?"

"You offered us a bounty to kill a vampire in the local cemetery, remember? No vampire was there," I said.

"Maybe you didn't follow the map's directions properly," Abigail said with a harsh scratchy voice. She coughed up phlegm and spit on the floor. "Do you even *know* what a cemetery is?"

"We followed the directions perfectly," Penelope said, raising her bow at the woman. She studied the old woman more closely than the previous time we had visited.

"How dare you raise a weapon at me!" the old woman hissed. "Come into our shop, threatening our lives. It's not our fault you probably got lost, or perhaps you're both seeking money without actually having to kill a vampire. We've had cowards do that before."

"How long have you been deceiving folks and sending them to their deaths?" I asked. "How many people have died?"

"You know not whom you're messing with," Abigail said, rising from her chair and pointing her crooked finger at me. Her voice strained. "Be on your way before you soon find out."

Karl became uncomfortable, swallowed hard, and tugged at his shirt collar.

I balanced the crossbow and placed my finger on the trigger. "Why did you offer to sell our horse and coach to a man?"

Karl paled. Sweat beads trickled down his aged brow.

My jaw tightened and I took a step closer. "You didn't expect to see us return, did you?"

His Adam's apple bulged. His breath grew more ragged.

"And what about the bow I'm holding? The man who crafted it was an acquaintance of mine. He builds weapons for Vampire Hunters. The only way you'd have this weapon is if that Hunter is dead. We Hunters never part with any weapon Roy makes for us. True justice for the Hunter would be for me to pull the trigger and fire an arrow through your head. That'd square up the deal nicely."

Karl shook his head. His trembling hands slammed onto the countertop, so he wouldn't fall.

"I've warned you Hunter," Abigail said. "Put down your weapon or your doom falls upon you."

I chuckled. I didn't know why the threat coming from a tiny bent woman had seemed so funny, but I suddenly burst into laughter.

"Only fools laugh before their demise," she said. "And you're an enormous fool."

I stood across the counter from him, reached into my pocket, and brought out the three gems, setting them on the counter. Karl looked at them and his eyes narrowed. He glanced toward his wife. "He killed them."

Abigail stepped out from behind the quilting table. Her eyes fastened upon the gems. "What?"

"He killed the protectors." Karl's voice still sounded old and weary, but it flowed with a tinge of surprise and hope.

"How?" she asked.

I glanced toward her. "We were at the cemetery, as you now can see."

"You will suffer for this, Hunter," she said with a scowl.

"Like the other victims?"

"Worse."

"How could you betray Hunters who are trying to protect cities and villages from the undead scourge?" I asked. I raised the crossbow and turned toward Abigail.

Penelope tapped the hat on her head. "What became of my father?"

An odd smile curled on Abigail's lips. She flashed her teeth. "Like the two of you, he managed to escape the cemetery."

"Did you kill him?" she asked, pulling the bowstring back.

The old woman sneered. "And what if I—"

Karl shook his head and waved his hands, stepping between Abigail and Penelope. "No. No, we didn't. He headed south. Please, don't shoot her."

"Don't grovel like a whiny little child, Karl. Show some backbone. The charade's over. They've no doubt discovered the ghouls and fled."

"The ghouls are dead," I said. "We killed them."

"You lie!"

I smiled evenly. "We stuffed them inside a coffin and roasted them."

The old woman's eyes hollowed. Her face drew slack. Her lower jaw trembled and her mouth moved but no words came out.

I grabbed Karl by the collar and yanked him toward me. "It was all one big trap, wasn't it? Lure in Hunters or your own neighbors to collect a bounty for a vampire that didn't exist, just so you can feed the ghouls and gargoyles?"

"My children," Abigail said in a pitiful small voice. Her eyes were vacant. "You *killed* my children."

"They were ghouls," Penelope replied.

Karl's eyes moistened with tears. "Yes, now. But once they had been Abigail's children before ghouls infected them during the last war. She couldn't kill them, even though they had become these vile creatures, but she ... *we* couldn't keep them in our home, you understand. They'd have infected us, too. But we couldn't let them roam the streets. There'd be a mass infestation within a few weeks. So we bound them to the cemetery, gave them protectors—"

"But they needed food," I said. "So you set an elegant trap to snare unsuspecting humans and Hunters?"

"Yes-s-s," Abigail said. Her eyes darkened and shifted toward us.

"Forrest," Penelope said. "Maybe we should work our way back toward the door?"

"Why?"

"Just a feeling," she said, scrunching her nose.

"What type of feeling?"

"I suppose like when you get your instinct premonitions. Please, Forrest, step aside. She's a demon."

CHAPTER 19

The old woman glanced toward me. Her dark eyes widened. I sensed evil permeating around her, dark and spiteful. Her venomous voice grew raspier. "You killed my children."

"They were already dead," Penelope said, keeping her aim on the old woman. "*Undead.*"

"The magical thorn barrier. How'd you accomplish that?" I asked Karl. "That was part of the snare. Who created it?"

His eyes grew fearful. He shook his head.

Abigail pushed herself to Karl's side. "When it comes to protecting my children, there's no limit to what I'd do."

Penelope lowered her bow and tugged my coat.

"What?" I said, glancing over my shoulder.

"Maybe you should step back now?" she said. "Since *I'm* the Demon-hunter."

"She doesn't *look* like a—"

Abigail's skin tightened on her face, splitting at her scalp and around her nose and ears. The illusion of what had been an old woman was actually something far worse. Her tongue lengthened, quite like a ghoul, but her eyes flickered like hot molten metal. She peeled her skin from her face, revealing scaly green skin like a snake.

"How?" I asked. My curiosity mesmerized me. I knew about shifters and Were creatures, but how did a woman become a demon?

Karl's eyes pleaded for help. "It wasn't my doing, Hunter. She's the one. I didn't have a choice."

"Forrest, move!" Penelope shouted.

I stepped back and tried to pull Karl with me, but the demon wrapped her arms around him. Her strange tongue darted out and licked the side of his face, leaving a slick trail of viscous drool. She opened her mouth, revealing her jagged teeth and reared her head back. She was going to bite his throat. The old man trembled, closed his eyes, and screamed. He tried the wipe the saliva from his face where his skin was blistering.

Penelope fired an arrow, striking the demon in the throat. It rammed its sharply clawed hand through Karl's back before releasing him and spinning around to flee. She clutched at the arrow.

Karl dropped to his knees, wept, and convulsed with pain. Blood soaked through the back of his shirt.

Penelope pulled her dagger and ran after the demon. She chased the demon past the quilting table where it grabbed sharp shears and turned, slashing wildly. Penelope dodged to the side to avoid getting cut. The demon pulled the shears close to its side. Penelope didn't give the demon a chance for another attack. She lopped the dagger through the air, striking dead center of its throat.

Black blood dripped from its neck. It clutched the hilt, tugged, but failed to pull out the blade. It dropped to its knees. Panting through its open mouth, its eyes bore at her, and gurgling sounds rose in its throat. It uselessly tried to speak, but the dagger and arrow had severed those abilities. Using both hands, it gripped the hilt and slowly extracted the blade. Blood gushed out.

The demon sat for a few moments longer before dropping facedown on the floor. I kept my bow trained on it, just in case it bolted up to attack again. Some creatures were quite successful at faking their deaths as I had learned once before in a difficult situation. From that day forward, I made certain what I had intended to kill was actually dead before I turned my back on it.

Penelope walked to the demon and picked her dagger up off the floor. After kicking it several times, she joined me as I knelt beside Karl. He jerked in pain. His head tilted upward, and he looked to find me.

I glanced at Penelope. "How did she turn into a demon?"

"She was half demon," Karl sputtered. Blood and spittle frothed in his mouth. He wheezed. "But she had the ability to present herself as either one whenever she wished."

"Half demon?" I asked. "Were the ghouls really her children?"

Karl's eyes dimmed. He was losing blood, but I believed she might have poisoned him with her claws. "She adopted them, *after* they became ghouls."

"Why?"

He coughed. More blood dripped from the sides of his mouth. "For pets."

"And the vampire bounty?"

"Her doing. The demon part of her hated humans but loved the undead ghouls. She chose them over our own people. The biggest reason most of this part of the city has vacated wasn't because they had moved away." He coughed violently. "She had beguiled most of them into going to the cemetery."

"What about the thorns?" I asked.

Karl gasped, taking shallower breaths. "She foolishly bargained with a greater demon to fashion the vines to captivate humans into sacrificing themselves. I'm surprised you … got past them. Those … sacrificed, offered … blood, not only to her and the plants, but to the greater … demon she had summoned for … help."

Penelope squatted down. "Why did you stay with her?"

Karl opened his eyes. A slight smile showed on his bloody lips. "It wasn't love or devotion, as you can see. She didn't hesitate to kill me, did she?"

"You're not dead yet," I said.

His body spasmed. "There's nothing capable of mending me. I've lived … a full life. Not a life of freedom but it does no good to complain at this point. Sorry for the deception. Look … in the top drawer behind the counter. There's … money to … compensate you for ridding my life of her agony and destroying her. It's more money than the faux reward … covers other bounty, too."

"What about the vampire in the Black Forest?" I asked. "Is that a misdirection, too?"

"No, Hunter," he said weakly. His eyes dimmed, starting to glaze. "He's very real and quite dangerous. One of the strongest … masters alive."

Penelope leaned closer to him. "Is my father still alive?"

"Last I had heard, yes. He headed south. When he learned of our deceit, he never returned. Peace to you." He lowered his head and became still.

"He's dead," she said.

I rose. "Are you certain the demon is? She didn't dissolve into ash."

"Not all demons do. The plague ones did because the arrows kill the plague, which causes them to self-combust. And she's part human, so—"

I walked behind the counter and opened the top drawer. Neat stacks of polished gold and silver coins filled half of the drawer. Some were German coins and others French or Spanish. On the coins being worth far more than the bounties offered, Karl had not lied. I found a medium sized drawstring bag and stuck all the coins inside, and then I tied it shut. We now had enough money to travel extensively without worry.

I felt guilty in a way for taking the coins, but since Karl and Abigail had betrayed us, and they were now dead, I didn't consider it robbery by any means. However, I was still bound by the contract, and my honor, to kill the vampire in the Black Forest. Since we'd cut directly through the forest to get to the Archdiocese, it wasn't out of our way.

I dropped the hefty bag of coins into my coat pocket. Penelope knelt beside the demon. It was making odd grunting sounds. Was the demon still alive and had attacked her?

I rushed from behind the counter to where she was. Her arm moved like she was using a handsaw. Before I reached her, she stood and held the demon's head in her hand.

"The demon is dead," she said with a sly grin.

"You mean that it wasn't?"

"You wanted me to make certain."

I'd yet met a creature that could survive without its head. Ghouls were an exception; only decapitated ghouls weren't really capable of inflicting much harm to a human, unless the human was foolish enough to pick its body up. The hand of a ghoul was still capable of strangling a person to death, but that required someone placing the hand to his throat. Appendages couldn't hunt for prey and were unnerving to behold.

Penelope chunked the demon head to the floor.

"So you get no reward for killing that one?" I asked.

"It's half human, so the only way I would have been compensated for killing her was if she had a bounty placed on her by another. As far as I know, no one has posted a reward."

"In a way, Karl paid us, but I never knew such a possibility existed where a demon and human produced a child."

She wiped the blood off her dagger on the quilt Abigail had been sewing. "The child you're protecting is half vampire and half human. If that's possible, why couldn't there be a hybrid between human and demon?"

She made a logical point. I had just never considered it.

Penelope smiled. "In fact, offspring between humans and demons is probably more common than we even know."

"Why?"

"Some demons are seductive and easily tempt humans into relationships, at least for a while, until they produce children."

I shook my head. "I've heard of exorcisms performed by priests, supposedly the priests cast out demons. But all the demons I've seen have been in physical form. How does a demon possess a human?"

Penelope sheathed her dagger. "They can't. Those *aren't* demons. Those are evil spirits. Huge difference and a dangerous feat to perform. Not my calling or duty. I will never attempt to drive one out."

I frowned. "But priests ... do they really excise them?"

"Not like they think they do. Most people who have been possessed die when the evil spirit leaves the body. It rips and tears its way out, causing as much damage as it can. They want to inflict pain. They thrive on it."

"But only priests can do that?"

She shook her head. "Priests have the person bound when they begin their exorcisms. It's not because these clergy are holy that the spirits tear out of the human body. Most likely the priest has agitated and annoyed the spirit until its rage can no longer be controlled. All the more reason they kill the ones they possess. If ever you're in the room where someone is trying to excise these spirits, run."

"Why?"

"They will seek another host," she replied. "But generally *not* a priest. What a lot of people don't know is almost as many priests get killed as those who have spirits cast out of them."

"Because the priest is supposed to be holy?"

She shook her head. "Revenge. They turn their aggression toward the priests and kill them. Then they will seek another human that's close by. That's why you don't want to be the only other person in the room. It's actually safer if the spirit stays in its host."

"Won't the possessed person kill others?"

"Not always, but if the spirit is actually detected, measures can be taken to prevent evil deeds."

"Like what?"

Her face became grim. "Asylums, unfortunately, are often filled with those who suffer possession."

"Won't the spirits simply leave the host and pursue someone not locked away?"

"They're content inside the people's body because they can torment their minds endlessly without fear of the host killing himself."

"So those aren't demons?" I asked.

"No."

"Good to know. Let's go back into the room where I got the vials. I'd like to get more supplies from the room where I found this bow, and then we need to hurry."

She nodded.

CHAPTER 20

*A*fter rummaging through the various weapons and equipment, we returned to the counter half expecting Abigail to have somehow arisen even though she had been decapitated. However, she and Karl were still dead and their bodies had not been disturbed. As strange as it sounded, I felt like we were being watched. The atmosphere thickened and became colder. The chill in the air was suddenly disrupted by a wisp of air that slithered past me, brushing my face.

Penelope stood still near the quilt. Her eyes became troubled.

"What's wrong?" I asked.

"Do you sense it?"

"I felt it, actually."

She glanced toward me with apprehension. She eased her way toward the quilting table, peeled back the quilt in progress, and found a pentagram drawn in faded blood. Beside this was a leather-covered spellbook. She took the book and slipped into her coat pocket.

"You sure that's a good idea?" I asked.

Penelope shrugged. "I think the *healer* I trade with will like this."

She took the bottle of blessed salt from her pocket and sprinkled salt over the pentagram. The tabletop burst into flames. She tried to put out the fire with the quilt, but the flames shot even higher.

"I think we'd best get out of here. Fast," she said.

No argument from me. I grabbed the large crate filled with glass vials, dried herbs, and wooden stakes I had packed in the supply room. Penelope had found a quiver filled with arrows and slung it over her shoulder. She took new bowstrings and a leather pouch to tie around her waist. We hurried to the door and exited.

Father was halfway across the square coming toward us. "Well?"

"It's a long story," I said. "One that will help pass the time once we start traveling again."

"Money?" he asked.

I nodded. "Lots of it."

"Then we should head into the city to get supplies before we cross the Rhine."

A hot whooshing sound hissed behind us. The fire shot through the chimney and crawled across the wooden shingled roof.

"You set the place on fire?" Father asked with a stern frown.

I shook my head. "No, sir."

"What do you call that?"

"No denying it's fire, Father, but we didn't start it."

Penelope said, "The woman had some sort of protection spell hanging, I suppose, so when they died the shop went up in flames."

"You killed them? Son, we needed the money, but—"

"Again, it's a long story. One we can tell on the way *out* of the city. But we did nothing except defend ourselves."

"Ah, very well," he replied.

"Still it's best we leave before we are actually accused of burning the shop down."

THOMAS DROVE the coach into the city. The architecture of the cathedral was the most spectacular building I had ever seen, holding me in awe of its beauty and its haunting carved statues and gargoyles. These intimidating stone creatures overlooked the streets and were mirrored images of the ones in the cemetery, but thankfully, *not* alive. Of course, that was merely speculation on my part, and I was about to climb the towers to see for myself.

After Father and I bought essential food items that could be stored in the storage compartment of the coach, Thomas drove across the Rhine River. Dependent upon the terrain and weather we should reach Freiburg in as little as a week. But that didn't take into account how long it would take for us to seek out the vampire inside the Black Forest and slay him.

Penelope and I told Father what had happened with the shopkeepers. He sat stunned and in disbelief, but never argued that we had done anything inappropriate. He did offer the occasional question to draw out more information, but he, like me, had never heard of someone who was half demon and half human. The thought alarmed him, and he was less cordial with Madeline and kept more distance from Varak, even though the child had taken quite a liking toward him.

For me, I could never get past looking at the child's strange sky-blue eyes that often seemed to be trying to search into my mind and look into my soul. The strange aura that surrounded him brought chills to me, and I constantly reminded myself that getting the child to the Archdiocese was my responsibility.

With daylight hours fading she suggested that she and I nap until after the sunset, just in case more plague demons tried to kill Thomas. As long as the coach kept moving, it was unlikely we'd have to protect him, but with a week more to travel, we'd have to find a place to stop. The horse needed to eat, drink, and rest. At least we had gold and silver coins to find a decent place to stay during the night and hopefully one with a stable.

CHAPTER 21

The first two nights that we had stopped in a town or village, no plague demons had come to attack and kill Thomas. Penelope and I had stood watch. I wondered if she had killed all of the ones Albert the Were-rat had sent, or if this was an attempt to get us to let our guard down.

Penelope had suggested that perhaps when we had crossed the Rhine, the demons somehow were not permitted to pass over the water or had lost their ability to track Thomas. While it was a hopeful thought, I still didn't think it was the last we'd encounter those demons.

As the third morning arrived, she and I were exhausted. The thick overcast morning indicated snowstorms were fast approaching. Thomas decided to get an early departure for the day in case the weather made the roads impassable. I didn't mind so long as Penelope and I were allowed to sleep.

Staying up throughout each night had not been the only reason I felt overly exhausted. My disturbing nightmares prevented me from restful sleep. The closer we got to our destination where we'd encounter the vampire, the worse the dreams became. I held the impression that he knew we were coming for him, and he *didn't* fear us. In fact, he was eager for our arrival.

Dreams of blood and slaughter caused my heart to race. At times, these visions seemed to be the vampire's vivid memories being displayed into my mind, as though he was boasting of his prowess, and indicating with an arrogant dominance that I was incapable of slaying him. Seeing these things disturbed me on a deeper level. He was trying to get inside my mind, and I suppose, in a way, he *had* because I had never received memories from a living vampire. I received portions of the memories of a vampire I had slain, soon after it was turned to ash, but for this vampire to prick his way into my mind from such a far distance was frighteningly impressive.

The only thing that had prevented me from rising in screaming fits was Penelope's arm draped across my chest. I sensed her warmth and closeness, even in the depths of these horrid nightmares, and a part of me knew the dreams weren't real. However, during my waking hours, my mind recalled and dwelt upon some of the worst incidents in those dreams. I wondered if these were premonitions.

Several times I had wanted to share these nightmares with my father. Perhaps I should have, but I expected his advice would be to avoid slaying the vampire at all. In many ways, realizing the power this vampire held, not entering his lair was the most solid suggestion for me to take since he *knew* we were coming.

Penelope and I slept for the better part of the third day while we traveled. When Father awoke me, the temperature had plummeted and the coach was moving at an abnormally slow place.

"Is something wrong?" I asked Father, rubbing my eyes. Penelope slept with her head against my chest. The peaceful look on her face made me not want to awaken her. I wondered how a lady who killed wicked demons rested so well. She half smiled in her sleep. Even though I'd rather leave her sleeping, I gently shook her. She pulled away, opening her eyes. I glanced at Father. "Why are we traveling so slow?"

"Weather's getting worse," he replied.

I slid aside the curtain and tried to scrap away the thin layer of ice that had formed on the inside of the glass. The dimming brightness of the day had not completely disappeared, but the sun was shrouded by thick grayness. The fir tree branches were bent harshly, covered by several inches of snow. From what I could tell, the only reason our horse could still pull the coach was due to the groove other carriages ahead of us had cut through the deepening snow. With the giant wet flakes dropping, the entire road would soon disappear beneath a blanket of white.

Two feet of snow or more covered the edges of the road. The forest on both sides of the road was so thickly coated that even the needles and bark of the trees gleamed white. No browns or greens were visible.

Penelope shivered, pulled the heavy rug we used as a blanket up over us, and pressed against me for additional warmth.

"Father, rap on the top of the carriage to get Thomas' attention. We need to stop at the first possible place. We'll freeze to death if we get stranded on the trail."

He nodded, turned, and hammered his fist three times.

Thomas stopped the coach.

A few seconds later, he opened the door. Outside he shook himself, knocking off several inches of snow from his hat and shoulders. He peered down the darkening road before glancing at me nervously. "Yes? Daylight is fleeting."

"I didn't mean for you to stop," I said.

He shook more snow from his heavy coat and broke away icicles on his moustache and beard. He tapped his hat against his fist to shatter a thin layer of ice and raked it off. His face glowed cherry red. "Sorry, but with this howling wind, I'd never hear a word you said from out here."

"Any idea how far from a town or village we are?"

"There's a clearing ahead, Forrest. Looks like maybe a village or small city perhaps."

"You think it's a place where we can stop? We can't go much farther. It's far too cold for you to keep driving."

He nodded. "Yes, frightfully cold out here. I'm stopping there anyway. That had been my plan all along. Demons or not, if that snow keeps falling at the rate it is, the ol' horse won't be able to keep pulling. I'm surprised he's lasted this long."

Thomas slammed the door shut and returned to the box seat.

Madeline wrapped Varak in another blanket and then covered both of them with a thick wool blanket. When the door had opened, what little heat we had generated amongst ourselves had been sucked out. I hoped the clearing ahead was a village where we could find an inn to spend the night.

About a quarter of an hour later, the coach wheels rattled when we reached the cobblestone street. Without knowing whether our accommodations would be mediocre or lavish, I didn't really care so long as we were able to get out of the extreme cold.

Exiting the coach, we stood inside a dark recess beneath the arch of a massive wall. The rock building looked to be an old castle and the long wall went for as far as I could see. Mortar between some rocks was cracked and pieces of the wall had shifted over time. Along the adjoining walls, awnings covered narrow walkways. And the archway where we stood was also shielded from the wind. Glass boxes shielded the flames of the gaslight streetlamps.

Snow continued to fall but not as heavily as it had been along the road. In some areas of the sky, the evening stars twinkled. The worst part of the storm seemed to have passed.

I watched the lingering snowflakes pelt softly, quietly, and like I'd always noticed during heavy snow there was a different type of silence when the snow began forming drifts. It seemed nature slept, seeking shelter and warmth in places where the snow couldn't penetrate.

Deep in the forests several wolves broke the silence with long wailful howls. Madeline turned toward the forest with a start, holding Varak a bit tighter.

Several watchtowers with pointed gothic gables were in view and spires rose off other buildings in the near distance. Some of the smaller houses had round tower roofs and others polygonal dormers. The angles prevented the heavy snow from staying on the roofs. The place didn't seem to be a large village but more a cluster of tall houses and buildings displaying gothic architecture.

Two men dressed in long dark overcoats and dark hats retrieved what little baggage we had. They looked like brothers and stood around my height. They were broad in the shoulders with long arms and very large hands. Their faces were extremely thin, making their delicate skin hug their skulls in a firm outline. One offered to take my Hunter box from me, but I shook my head and held it tight in hand. Two more men came and took the horse by its bridle and led it through an open door to what I suspected was the stables. These two men were almost identical to the others, and not a one had spoken a word of greeting to us.

Two rotund women with bunt gray hair offered meek greetings from a door beneath the awning and motioned us to follow them inside. Their smiles enhanced their chubby cheeks. Of all the inns Father and I had stayed at during our journeys, this was perhaps the most unusual. We glanced toward one another with uncertainty and were reluctant to readily obey. Father glanced toward me since I was the largest I suppose, but he hugged himself for warmth as did Thomas. It was foolish to stay out in the horrible cold any longer. This was a place for lodging. I took the initiative and headed toward the door.

After we stepped inside to a large room where a fire burned inside a wide hearth, they closed the door. They showed us where to remove our coats, hats, and boots near the door. I shed my thick overcoat and hung it on a large peg at the side of the door. Thomas and Father did the same. We hung our hats closer to the fire where they'd dry. I set my Hunter box and crossbow beneath my hanging coat where they were partially hidden.

The low ceilings kept the heat of the roaring fire concentrated around us, and made it difficult to breathe. A few minutes earlier, I had nearly gone numb from being inside the cold coach, and now sweat rolled off my body. Not that I was complaining. I could tell by the smile on my father's face that he was more than satisfied being surrounded by such warmth. Cold weather was his nemesis ever since he had suffered horrible injuries to his legs.

Over the fire a black pot bubbled with a fine aroma lofting into the room. Finely polished chairs with plush pillows were set beside small reading tables and one roll top desk. All were hand-carved from maple.

Beveled dark paneling covered the walls and the ceiling. The lit candles at each table flickered, reflected off the polished wood. A hand-carved cuckoo clock hung on the wall with such detail. One cherished the artwork more than an object that depicted the proper time of day. I walked closer and observed it. Strange as it seemed, the clock looked familiar to me. The little carved people were joining hands, dressed in lederhosen near a painted stream where a carved bear peered into the water, looking at the fish.

"Gorgeous," Penelope whispered, standing beside me with a broad smile.

I nodded.

This room was more elegant and larger than the cottage I had grown up in. Several single cots were lined against the wall, covered with designed quilts. A strange sensation came over me, and everything held familiarity like I'd been here before. I became dizzy, my stomach nauseous, so I placed my hand against the wall to steady myself. The feeling passed a few seconds later.

Penelope placed her hands on my arm. "You okay?"

"Yes. Fine."

One of the women smiled at Penelope and Madeline. "This way, ladies."

Penelope gave me a strange glance. I shrugged.

The woman noticed her concern. "I imagine after your long journey, you'd like to bathe and change into fresh clothes?"

Penelope smiled and nodded graciously.

A fine dressed gentleman stepped through another side door and motioned us to follow him. The extraordinarily thin man led us to a large room filled with hot humid steam so thick it looked like fog. He walked with stiff posture. "My name is Jensen, and I've been asked by your host to make certain everything is to your satisfaction. Have you need of anything, do not hesitate to ask."

"That's kind of you," Father said.

"You're quite welcome, sir. Leave your clothes here," Jensen said with a haughty proper tone, and with a wave of his hand, he pointed toward a narrow bench. His short black hair looked glossy and combed to perfection. He sported a thin moustache, also glossy, and curled the ends slightly upward. "I will see to it these are cleaned and pressed. When you have finished bathing, there are robes in the corner for you to wear."

"We've not yet checked in," I said. "Is there somewhere for me to pay for our stay."

Jensen turned on his heel and faced me, clasping his hands behind his back. He offered a reassuring smile. "You're a Hunter, are you not?"

I nodded with a confused frown.

"Ah, sir ... Forrest, is it?"

"Yes? How'd—"

His smile widened. "Your name isn't unknown in these parts. Our host has graciously extended his hospitality to you. We're to accommodate your every need. As his guests all is taken care of, and there is no charge to you and your party. Enjoy your hot bath in this fine mineral water that rises naturally from the hot springs below. Some insist it has healing properties. But if one is skeptical, perhaps it does not?"

Jensen left the room and closed the door behind him.

I cocked a brow and looked at Father. He grinned. "How did he know my name?"

"Jacques told you that Vampire Hunters have reputations that often precede them."

"True," I said, still frowning. "But, I've done nothing worthy of drawing attention to myself."

"I wouldn't worry too much over it," he replied. "Enjoy the notoriety. Everything's free."

"Nothing's free," I whispered. "There's always a price."

He chuckled. "Tonight it is, son. I don't know about you, but I want to wash all this sweat and grim off my body."

Father began undressing and looked at the large pool of water. He grinned and his brow rose. Eagerness brightened his eyes.

The water was white in color with thick steam rising off the surface. Although I had never seen anything like this in other cities, I felt like I had been here before. Most of the major cities we had traveled through had bathhouses, but never any that were filled with steaming white water. I supposed the minerals were the reason the water was white, but I found myself like Father and wanting to wash away days of sweat, grim, and in my case, dried blood from my cuts.

After I undressed and placed my filthy clothes on the bench, I slipped slowly into the hot water. I winced and gasped. At first it seemed too hot, almost like I was going to boil myself, but after I adjusted to the temperature, I leaned my back against the pool wall and closed my eyes.

The heat of the water soothed my aching muscles, bruises, and seeped into the healing cuts on my back. I took a deep breath and slowly exhaled. I felt so relaxed that it wouldn't have taken much to drift off to sleep.

Father sighed and splashed water as he sank. "They might have to pry me out of here, son. I've never felt this good since ... before my legs were severely broken. This hot water ... my legs aren't hurting at all."

Hidden by a curtain of steam, Thomas slipped into the pool at the other side.

"Have you been here before?" I asked the coachman.

"No, I haven't."

"What is this place?" Father asked.

"An inn," he replied. "That's what the sign said at the end of the lane. Based upon its structure, though, I think it must have been a castle prior."

Father glanced at me with a sly grin. "Probably quite expensive then? That is, of course, if we had to pay."

I shrugged. "Even if that wasn't the case, Father, we have more than enough to stay for a night."

"We might be here longer if the snow continues," Father replied.

"The sky was starting to clear before we came indoors," I said.

"That's good news," Thomas said. "Three days of traveling and we've not encountered another one of those demons. Has Penelope any theory for that?"

I shook my head. "No. She thinks she might have killed all that Albert had sent, or the river has been a deterrent. Who knows? Maybe his power doesn't extend this far."

"I keep looking when we're traveling. I'm too fearful to think there's no more."

"Don't let down your guard because we haven't."

"I don't plan to."

141

Father placed his face into the water and vigorously scrubbed it. Then he looked at me. "You think maybe the owner's generosity stems from him needing your services as a Hunter?"

I had not thought about that. "That might be possible."

"Seems a good barter, if that's the case," Father said.

Depends upon the vampire.

Father slumped deeper into the water until his head was fully submerged. He stayed under for nearly half a minute, and then he blew out long streams of bubbles before pushing himself above the water's surface again. Streams of water rolled down his face. He ran his hand through his beard, laughing, and then he wiped his eyes and stared at me. I had never seen him act so jovial before.

He pressed his back into the corner of the pool and rested each arm atop the bricked pool wall, lounging. "Forrest, you seem quite comfortable with the young lady. Penelope has taken a liking to you. Have you expressed your feelings for her?"

Even though my skin was already red from the heated water, I imagined that my cheeks had probably gotten redder. "We've talked. But most of our time we've kept ourselves more focused on keeping Thomas alive and killing ghouls and gargoyles, but those are things you're aware of."

"I'm not trying to embarrass you, son. Honest. I'm happy for you. I was simply trying to see if you've come to the place where it's not so difficult to tell her your feelings."

I nodded. "It's easier. A lot easier. I appreciate the advice you gave me, and for abruptly running off that morning and leaving us all alone when I was scared out of my mind."

He laughed. "It's like a bird teaching its young how to fly. It nudges the young one out of the nest. But they learn to fly on the way down, most of them."

"In my case, you kicked me off the side of a mountain with jagged rocks at the bottom."

"You're alive, aren't you? She's still traveling with us. If she didn't share your interests, you'd have parted ways well before now. She's never been uncomfortable around you."

"She's a little *too* close at times," I replied.

"And that bothers you?"

As much as I enjoyed traveling with Penelope beside me in the coach, I still struggled internally about things Father insisted I shouldn't. "I suppose not, but then ... as I told you before about my age—"

"Given what you are, son, and the knowledge you've attained, that isn't a relevant point for you," he said, pointing his finger at me. "And, not a matter that needs expressed right now."

He pointed toward where Thomas was hidden in the fog.

"The point is, son, the two of you are interested in one another. There's the courting process—"

I shook my head. "That's a bit premature."

"It needs considering."

"Maybe after all the dangers are past."

"Those never end for you, Forrest. You know that. Or her, either, considering the creatures she slays."

That was true.

"One step at a time," I said.

Father grinned. "You've never followed that route."

"What do you mean by that?"

"You never crawled as a child. You were walking quicker than others your age. And the next thing we all knew, you were grown."

I wondered what I had missed from bypassing my youth and immediately becoming a man at the age of eight. I had to admit I had to adapt rather quickly. In retrospect the hardest part was ignoring the childhood fears most children experienced. When you had to fight and slay vampires, you didn't have any choice except to quash those fears without allowing them time to fester and grow. In my situation the three major fears I contended with were: losing family members or friends to the undead, getting killed, or getting turned into a vampire. How did I deal with those? By slaying the vampires before they had a chance to act on any of those circumstances.

CHAPTER 22

$\mathcal{I}$ stayed in the hot water until the skin on my hands resembled a wrinkled plum. I'd have remained in the pool until deep in the night but I didn't know if Penelope and Madeline had returned to the room yet. I didn't want Penelope to feel uncomfortable. She had already expressed how Varak made her feel. I marveled that she, who killed demons, held an uneasiness toward the child like I did.

I grabbed one of the thick robes, put it on, and tied the belt around my waist. Already I missed the soothing warmth of the water. I could have stayed several more hours. At least the room was steamy and hot. Once I stepped back into the narrow hallway and headed to our room, I expected the temperature would decrease quite a bit. It wouldn't be as harrowingly cold as outside the castle for which I was thankful.

I returned to the room, opened the door, and entered at the same time Penelope came through the other bedroom door that led to the adjoining hall. Our eyes met and widen with shock. Neither of us had expected anyone else to be in the room, and she seemed as surprised as me that we were the only two here. Just us. Alone together. She was wearing a robe over a silken gown that flowed to her ankles. Even though we were fully covered, we both became uncomfortable and stared at the floor.

While gazing downward, I causally glanced up to watch her without raising my head. She was blushing, and she cupped her hands together and held them at her waist. She was overcome with shyness, as was I, but I noticed she was sneaking glances toward me, too. I had never felt so awkward. I was more at a loss for words than when Father had left us alone together at breakfast.

I finally braved looking up and opened my mouth to speak but Madeline came through the door and closed it behind her. She glanced toward Penelope.

"Where's Varak?" Madeline asked, nervously glancing around the room.

Penelope frowned. "I thought you had him?"

Madeline shook her head and placed a hand over her heart. "No. The maid said that she'd give him to you while I bathed."

"I've not seen him," she replied.

Madeline became frantic, covered her face with her hands, and turned toward the door. She gulped deep breaths and kept looking around the room as though she had no idea what she should do. This was the first time in weeks that she had not kept Varak within her sight. She held him most of the time except whenever we stayed in an inn, like now. When she could, she placed him on the floor and let him crawl. He was able to hold himself up when he found something sturdy to hang onto and had even taken several steps but wasn't able to walk on his own yet.

She paced side to side for a few moments before she finally decided to reach for the doorknob. The door opened and a maid stepped in with the infant. Madeline snatched the child from the woman's hands and hugged him close.

"He's a delightful little boy," the woman said with a smile. "We gave him a bath while you relaxed in yours. He's so adorable that I almost hate to hand him back. It's rare for us to see infants, so when we do, we want to hold onto them and pamper them."

Madeline scowled.

Varak held himself upright in Madeline's arms, staring around the room with his bright eyes. She carried him across the room to one of the cots but kept a wary stare toward the maid. Her attachment to Varak troubled me. Could we even get her to part with him once we reached the Archdiocese in Freiburg?

The child had already ensnared her to become his permanent care-taker. I wondered to what extent he controlled her or did he at all? Perhaps she had taken affection and sympathy toward him because he didn't have parents. He was an orphan. It wasn't impossible and seemed logical if I chose to ignore the possibility of the child already being able to tap into his charms.

Father and Thomas came into the room. The maid showed us where the cupboard was before giving the pot of stew several stirs with the large ladle.

"Should you need any assistance, ring that bell." She pointed to the brass table-bell on the reading table. "Have a good night."

Father combed his beard with his fingers. He looked around the room, studying the walls.

"Is something wrong?" I asked.

He made an odd face. "No. After getting cleaned up so well, I'd just like to trim this wild beard. I don't see any mirrors in here, either. You mind trimming it for me later?"

"Not at all," I replied. "You might want to eat first anyway."

"That only means you have to pick out bits of food, which is why it needs trimmed."

I shrugged. "It's only food."

Penelope had found the bowls and stood at the pot filling them. She was far different than the night we had first met. I had seen the rugged side of her that night, but almost ever since, she had presented herself with more elegancy than what my parents had taught me.

After we had eaten, Father set the map on the bed that detailed where the vampire resided in a small village in the Black Forest near Offenburg. Friedhof was the name of the village, according to the old man who had drawn it.

"Friedhof?" I said, glancing toward Thomas. Being inside the coach while he drove, we seldom were fortunate to see any of the road signs. "Are we anywhere near this place?"

Thomas paled and swallowed hard. He rubbed the side of his face. "We are *in* Friedhof."

Father frowned. "You're certain?"

The coachman nodded.

Father looked at me. "Do you think this inn is where the vampire resides?"

Everything about this room I recognized, even though I had never physically been here. I knew the details of this room, the bath pool, and some of the outside architecture looked familiar to me. From my dreams?

"He's here," I said in a near whisper. "I think he's the one who holds the deed and title to this castle."

Penelope sat on the edge of the bed and placed her hand on my arm.

"You're sure, son?"

I nodded.

"How do you know?" Thomas asked.

"I've dreamt vividly about this place several times since we left London."

"So the owner hasn't extended his open invitation to us to hire you?" Father asked.

I shook my head. "It doesn't seem so. Maybe he has invited me for a challenge?"

"What kind of challenge?" Penelope asked.

"To see which one of us survives our conflict."

CHAPTER 23

"How is there contention between the two of you when you've never met?" Penelope asked.

"Easy. He's a vampire, and I'm a Hunter."

"That automatically defines it?"

"Sums it up nicely in my book," I said.

"You've never pardoned a vampire?"

"Have you ever let a demon go free?"

Her eyes narrowed, and she quickly looked away.

"You have?" I asked.

"A few," she replied.

"Why?"

"It's difficult to explain."

"Try."

She huffed and her lips tightened. "I've allowed some to live in order to glean useful information."

"In what way?" Father asked.

I frowned. "How can you trust they'll even tell you the truth?"

Penelope sat on the edge of the bed and folded her hands on her lap. "I have the ability to enslave a demon under my control if I choose. Not a powerful demon, but an imp or some of the lessers. I link my mind to its, which is why I choose one with less strength. A mightier demon could reverse the link to enslave me or drive me to insanity or kill me."

"But how does that guarantee they tell the truth?" I asked.

"When I enslave them, they cannot lie or they burst into flames."

"What about those plague demons?" Thomas asked. "The ones trying to kill me. Can you enslave them?"

She shook her head and bit her lower lip. "Good Heavens, no. That'd be suicide. They'd infect me with the disease."

"Through your thoughts?" Father asked, perplexed. "How?"

She shrugged. "I don't know, but I've been warned never to do so through strong intuition, so I understand partly why Forrest reacts to some of his premonitions. But, Forrest, why do you consider all vampires to be evil and unworthy to be pardoned?"

"They have no soul. They're ruthless and feed upon other humans."

"You're blanketing all vampires to be exactly the same?"

"When it comes to how they stalk their prey and sire offspring, I see no difference in any of them. There's only one I've protected," I replied.

Her eyes flicked toward Varak and quickly back toward me.

I nodded. "And that's only because I swore to do so and you know the reason I cannot."

"Fair enough," she said.

"But the vampire in this village," I said. "There's no reason he should know me yet or that I'd even be headed—"

It dawned upon me.

"What is it, Forrest?" Father asked.

"Albert."

Father frowned. "You think he'd alert this vampire that you'd be passing this direction?"

"I can think of no other."

Penelope gave me a worried look.

"What's wrong, Penelope?" I asked.

"Then everything unfolds here tonight."

"What do you mean?" Thomas asked.

"The demons that had been sent after you have hidden, but I have a feeling they will emerge again soon to kill you."

A gentle rap came at the door. We all turned. Someone rapped again. "Yes?" I asked.

The door opened promptly.

Jensen, who had led us to the men's bathing pool, entered. In his arms was a neat stack of clothes. He acquiesced a slight nod and a friendly smile. In his elegant voice, he said, "I'm afraid your old coat is in tatters, Hunter, and all of your clothes were … shall we say, are not even useable as filthy rags. But your host has a gracious heart, offering new clothes his tailor fashioned well before your arrival."

"We can't accept these," I said. By accepting the apparel, in a sense he assured we were indebted to him. No words needed to enforce it. It was implied.

"He insists. In fact, he's offered his invitation for all of you to dine with him tonight at midnight."

"So late?" Father asked.

He laughed softly. "The night is just beginning for him."

"Who exactly is our host?" I asked.

"You don't know?" Jensen asked somewhat amused. "There is no mistake for your arrival here. He has been expecting you for quite some time, and this is the exact day he predicted you'd arrive."

"Who?"

"Count Lorcan," he replied. Jensen set the clothes on the cushioned bench. "Please be prompt arriving at the banquet hall. Not a second too late. Going through this door, you'll find the banquet hall straight down at the end of the corridor. Ladies, the wardrobe against the wall opens into a small changing room."

"How is it he knew of our arrival when we had never sought to come here until a few days ago?" I asked.

Jensen studied me with his brow raised for several moments before offering a polite smile. "My guess is you already know the answer to that question, dear Hunter, but if you haven't figure it out by the time you arrive at his table, certainly ask him. Lorcan is a man who greatly treasures the company of others and loves intriguing conversation. I'm certain the two of you will get along splendidly. He's talked for days about how he longs to meet you."

I could not ascertain whether that was intended as a threat or not. I had hoped Jensen would tell me how Lorcan knew such details as to validate my suspicions. I held no doubt that somehow Lorcan had reached through the netherworld of my dreams and tethered to my thoughts and plans. He could see me, but he had veiled himself where I could not visualize him. It proved he possessed a great deal of power and possibly more than any other vampire I'd faced prior. While these matters were imposing, my curiosity outweighed my fear.

Still smiling politely, Jensen walked to the door, grabbed the knob, and turned to face us before he closed it. "Remember, promptness, midnight."

I nodded.

Jensen closed the door.

Father's brow furrowed. "Son, I feel uneasy about this entire situation."

"As do I," Penelope said.

"There's not anything else we can do," I said.

"We could leave," Thomas suggested, glancing nervously to the door.

I shook my head. "How? We have no idea where those men took the horse. I assume it was the stables where they had gone, but we don't rightly know. And if we found the horse, we'd still need to find the wagon, hitch the horse to it … His guards or servants would apprehend us well before we could succeed in doing all of that."

Father sighed and wadded up the map. "You cannot exactly slay a vampire when he *knows* we've come to do so."

"Or since he's invited us to eat with him," Penelope said softly. "Not proper etiquette, now is it Forrest?"

I gave her a pretend stern glance, and she crinkled her nose, smiling. Even though we hadn't known one another long, I could tell when she was being playful. I chuckled.

Regardless of the dinner invitation, she didn't need to question my intent. She knew I'd not leave this former castle without attempting to stake Lorcan. I imagined he was thinking the same. I was quite certain he *knew*.

"Perhaps he wishes to eat *us* for dinner?" Thomas asked, and I knew his question was *not* in jest. I tried not to smile.

"But he's predicted your arrival for longer than we've known he existed," Father said. "You mentioned you've seen this place in your dreams? Have you ever seen him?"

"No. He's kept himself hidden from me. I sensed his power. He's strong. I sense him now. The most disturbing part of those dreams was the amount of bloodshed."

"You've witnessed him killing people in your dreams?" Penelope asked.

"No. I suppose what I'm trying to say is that I detected the volume of blood he's shed and drank from the numerous people he's killed during his lifetime as a vampire. My guess, it's in the hundreds."

Thomas looked uneasily. "Then we're nothing more than fodder."

"We have plenty of stakes," Father said. "We tuck them into our pockets, behind our belts—"

"Then he immediately views us as a threat," I said.

"And you don't him?"

I shrugged. "He is, but nothing in my dreams indicated he seeks to harm or kill me."

"Then *what*, son, would he want?"

I thought about his question for several moments. The answer came as if prompted to me, but not from a previous Hunter's wisdom. Lorcan whispered it to me.

"I think you were right earlier, Father. He wishes to hire me."

CHAPTER 24

"Hire you?" Father said with a most curious stare. "I've never known a vampire to hire a Hunter. The thought is preposterous."

"Even though you were the one who suggested it?" I asked with a wide grin.

He frowned and waved me off. "Just an old man foolishly thinking out loud, son. Wisdom comes with age, but so does senility. It was an absurd thought."

"Perhaps, but I don't think so," I replied. "The impression in my mind about tonight's invitation is the same gut feeling I've gotten in the past, and they've never been wrong before."

"So you're proposing that we go to his banquet room without *any* weapons at all? And what happens if we're not right about his invitation?"

"It's insane," Thomas said, shaking his head.

Penelope shook her head. "I think Forrest's right. Jensen insists that we're guests here. Lorcan's gifted us with new clothes, a lavish bath and room, and food. Why go through all that trouble only to kill and feast upon us?"

Thomas frowned at her. "Read Hansel and Gretel sometime. He's made us more presentable before he kills us. Could all this just be a part of his ritual?"

"Son, don't forget the most important issue of this argument. He's a vampire. It's too great a risk for us to enter his chambers or dining room without some sort of way to defend ourselves. Besides, I know you. You'd never allow yourself to be hired by a vampire."

I frowned and rubbed my bearded chin.

"Forrest?" Penelope said. "You wouldn't?"

"I'd like to hear his proposal," I replied. "He'd be hiring me to slay another vampire anyway."

"But what about what you said earlier?" she asked.

I placed my index finger to my lips and shook my head.

Her eyes and Father's widened, realizing the Count was possibly hearing everything we had said.

"When we reach the banquet hall," I said, "Remember *not* to gaze directly into his eyes or he can compel you."

They nodded. Thomas paled and visibly shook.

I slipped my hand around Penelope's. "You and Madeline need to change into the clothes Jensen brought."

Father walked to Madeline and took Varak from her. He smiled. "I can watch him while you dress."

She smiled with gratitude.

Penelope took the women's clothing and opened the wardrobe doors. The room on the other side was in complete darkness. She took a burning lamp off a table and walked through the hollow wardrobe. The lamp lit up the small room and she smiled at me before pulling the doors closed again.

I found my clothes easily since they were so much wider and larger than anyone else's. I hurried and slipped into them while the women were in the other room. Thomas did the same with his across the room near the hearth. Father sat on the edge of the bed with Varak on his knee. The child smiled and giggled and Father smiled in return. The largest part of my heart wanted Varak not to be what he was probably destined to become. I truly did.

While I buttoned my shirt, I wondered what Lorcan's motive was. I agreed with Penelope that Jensen kept insisting we were guests and according to him, Lorcan had been eagerly awaiting our arrival for some time. That was the same sensation I had felt in my dreams.

WE ARRIVED at the banquet hall a few minutes before midnight. In spite of the long room, the table was modest with ten finely carved high-back chairs positioned on each side. Count Lorcan's chair was at the far end and regal like a king's. The back and seat were thickly padded.

On the opposite stone wall were six large life-size paintings. Three were beautiful women dressed in ballroom dresses and wearing different gemstone necklaces, bracelets, and rings. The other three paintings were men dressed in elegant, if not regal, attire. They resembled one another enough for me to believe they must be siblings, perhaps Lorcan's own children?

Lorcan was already seated. He sat stiff and proper. His pale complexion glowed in contrast to his solid black long sleeved shirt. By the way the cloth shimmered beneath the candle chandelier, I assumed it was silk. He wore a ruby ring on his right hand and a sapphire ring on his left. He motioned to us and smiled. "Welcome guests! Please, come and be seated. And Forrest, please, sit here beside me. We've so much to discuss."

Thomas hurried to the farthest chair from Lorcan where place settings were. For some unexplained reason, he couldn't hide his nervousness in the presence of the vampire. I didn't quite understand his anxiety. Upon his first encounter with the plague demon, before Penelope had arrived and killed it, he had bravely accepted the potential fate of death from the plague demon calmer than whatever suspicions he believed he'd be dealt at the hands of Philip.

I sat to the left of Lorcan, Penelope sat beside me, and Father sat directly across from me. Madeline held Varak and sat beside Father.

An elegantly dressed manservant came to the table with a bottle of wine. Lorcan smiled at us while the man filled our glasses.

"This wine comes from my vineyards. I do hope you find the taste to your liking," he said. When all our glasses were filled, he lifted his glass to toast, and being polite, we did the same. "A toast! To possibilities."

I sipped the wine. It tasted sweet with the hint of a nutty flavor.

Lorcan set down his wine goblet and glanced at me. The skin on his face was tight, drawn in. For those who noticed this first, they'd be disturbed by his appearance, but I doubted anyone that made eye contact with him ever noticed his corpselike appearance. His striking blue eyes were piercing, almost icy white. A person's gaze was immediately drawn to them, which made them susceptible to his glamour. Fortunately, I didn't succumb to his charm.

He waved his hand toward the food on the table. "Please, help yourselves."

A roasted pheasant rested on a large plate with all types of side dishes and breads neatly placed around the bird. Everyone glanced nervously toward me for approval, or perhaps more their concern on whether eating the food was safe. Since I hadn't perceived any malice from Lorcan *yet*, I took one of the bird's legs and a piece of bread, placing them upon my plate.

After I took several bites, the others began putting food onto their plates.

Lorcan leaned toward me. "I trust that your journey through the Black Forest thus far has been a pleasant one?"

"Other than the heavy snow," I replied.

Lorcan laughed softly. "Ah, I'm afraid I have no control over that. How are you liking your stay at my castle?"

I offered a cordial smile, still concerned about being this close to a vampire and not having a weapon. "It's been nice so far."

"I sense your apprehension, Hunter. Relax. You wonder whether this hospitality is genuine or short-lived. I understand. But I assure you, this invitation comes with no strings attached."

Father frowned. "What exactly has no strings attached?"

Lorcan pursed his lips and forced a smile, glancing toward Father. He was annoyed by my father's interruption. "I have need of your *son's* services, which is a matter he and I need to discuss since *he* is the Hunter."

Normally, Father found offense in being considered less a vampire hunter than I, but he didn't seem to acknowledge the snide insult. "A vampire hiring a Hunter to kill another vampire?"

Lorcan's jaw tightened.

"Father, please."

Father shook his head and turned his attention to the food. "My apologies. And my compliments to your cook. Excellent food."

"Duly noted," Lorcan said. He turned toward me again.

"Is that what you're doing? Hiring me to kill another vampire?" I asked.

"It is an offer I'd like for you to consider. As I said, you may refuse to slay this vampire and be on your way in the morning without fear of *any* repercussions."

"Why have you chosen me? Certainly other Hunters have passed this way."

"Indeed they have, Forrest, but none have shown the integrity that you've displayed."

"And how did you learn of me?" I asked, tearing a piece of bread in half and dipping it into the wine sauce.

Lorcan smiled and folded his hands in a prayer-like manner. "We've visited, you and I, but on a different plane. I know you've sensed my presence."

I narrowed my eyes. "Yes, and *why* have you invaded my dreams? How have you done so?"

"I simply wished to learn more about you. Few Hunters have the ability to kill so many masters in such a short amount of time like you have. Of course, you should know that this would capture the attention of other vampires, especially that of other master vampires."

"Like yourself?"

He feigned a smile. "I'd be a fool if I didn't keep my best interests at heart, would I not? Learning of your success against three powerful masters stirred me with concern, as it has throughout the entire undead realm. You've caused a ripple-effect, which shall not go unnoticed, so I'd rather befriend you than find myself on the wrong side of your stake."

I suppressed my laughter. He'd always be an enemy to me regardless.

I refused to ever entertain the friendship of any vampire. I'd never allow myself to trust one. I had already seen the spite of masters and those had held no compassion toward others, and apparently not for their own kind if Lorcan was truly seeking to hire me to slay another vampire.

I chewed the bread, took a sip of the wine, and swallowed. "Tell me about this vampire you wish to have slain, and better yet, *why* do you seek his death? Can't you kill him?"

Lorcan eased to the side his chair, stuck his elbow on the armrest, and rested his chin atop his fist. "Diplomacy has its downsides amongst ruling vampires, Forrest. A master vampire who rips the head off a rival ruling vampire tends to lose favor with the great vampire council. In case you're unaware of the family that rules over the council, they are the upper echelon, those directly descended from Count Dracula himself."

"As I have understood," I replied, "Dracula's descendants have more to trouble themselves over than minor skirmishes like yours."

Lorcan's eyes narrowed. "And how would *you* know of such things?"

"Even vampires are known to namedrop when they're faced with death, thinking they'll strike fear into my heart and cause me to reconsider."

Lorcan leaned back in his seat and laughed. "So you don't negotiate?"

I stared into his eyes, unflinching. "With a vampire, never."

His laughter and smile ceased. He studied me for several moments. "I see. Does that limit you killing this other vampire for me then? As I said, you're free to decline my offer."

"You've yet given me a reason for why you view this master as a threat."

Lorcan smiled evenly. "He has plotted to kill my family members. More specifically, my children."

I nodded toward the six paintings on the wall. "I suppose these are they?"

Father turned and looked over his shoulder. His cheek was puffed with a hunk of bread. "Nice family."

Lorcan nodded. "Yes. My children."

"He has made attempts?"

"Yes."

"What are his reasons for doing so?"

"Territorial rights," Lorcan replied.

I frowned.

"By government treaties set by the Vlad's vampire council, the mountains of the Black Forest were deeded to me. Ambrose, the other master, does not like that I have six children and view them as a greater threat than myself."

"Why is that?" Father asked with a full mouth.

Lorcan's eyes narrowed, but he didn't bother looking in my father's direction. I simply shook my head at Father.

"Why does this Ambrose view them as a threat if the territory has already been deeded to you? And does that imply you rule over the human governments or are you the overseer?" I asked.

"I'm the overseer, but since I have six children, I can place them into prominent positions throughout the Black Forest," Lorcan replied. "Doing so prevents Ambrose from trying to infiltrate my lands with lesser vampires of his own."

"And where are your children now?"

Lorcan smiled. "They reside in this old castle with me. Until Ambrose has been … slain, I cannot establish their rightful places in the mountains. I had wanted them to dine with us tonight, but I thought that might be too *daunting* for all of you."

I gave a shrug and looked again at their pictures on the wall. Each woman was beautiful. Their eyes held intense confidence, and their smiles curled with tinges of mischief. The three men had stern gazes that could make a brave man cower. Their chiseled facial features displayed the coldness of their hearts. These men could be ruthless once they resided over an area of the Black Forest. They probably already were. Whoever the artist was, he or she had captured the essence of Lorcan's children.

"Where does Ambrose reside?" I asked.

"Schaffhausen, Switzerland."

"Is that his assigned territory?"

Lorcan nodded.

"And why is it not satisfactory to him?"

"It should be," he replied. "Splendid city. A fantastic place, but for whatever reason, he covets being farther north and wishes to settle within my forest."

"Have you not spoken with him? Offered a meeting to resolve the dispute?"

"We've exchanged letters, which is a *painfully* slow process, but we've never met in person."

"Then how do you know he wishes to have your children slain?"

"There have been attempts on each of them during this past year," Lorcan said softly. "Usually at banquets and balls with other esteemed rulers."

"How do you know it is Ambrose?"

Lorcan glanced toward Penelope and smiled. She looked away. "We captured each would-be slayer, compelled them, and they told us who had hired them."

"Other Hunters?"

Lorcan grinned and glanced toward my father. "No. He's not that resourceful. Common folks who *think* they are capable of killing vampires and nearly get themselves killed for attempting it." He glanced back to me. "I realize it is unorthodox for me to hire a Hunter to kill another vampire, but when it comes to protecting my children and preventing the wrath of the council from raining down upon me for taking the law into my own hands, I cannot find a greater ally than a Hunter."

Penelope slipped her hand under the table and squeezed my leg. I looked at her and she subtly shook her head.

"You have something you wish to contribute?" Lorcan asked her.

"I'm curious as to what your reward is?"

"Fair enough. One thousand gold marks."

Father's fork dropped from his hand and clattered against his plate. His eyes widened, and he coughed to prevent choking on whatever he had been trying to swallow. He pounded his chest with his fist a couple of times. His face reddened and tears moistened his eyes. He gave me a stern look that indicated that I should accept the offer.

"That's not enough?" Lorcan asked, giving Father an amused smile.

Father tried to clear his throat, but it was too scratchy for him to speak. He waved his hand, shook his head, and sipped the wine but still declined an answer.

Lorcan turned toward me. "Is that not a fair enough offer?"

I held no emotion on my face. I took a sip of wine and set down the goblet. "Might I inform you of my decision in the morning? Before we could even accept, we have to meet the archbishop in Freiburg."

He offered a courteous smile. "Of course. Again, there's no threat if you decide not to accept the offer. I will simply have to look for another Hunter."

"If you wish me to consider your offer, I have one stipulation."

Lorcan's brow rose. "And what is that, Hunter?"

"Stop your attempted intrusions into my mind while I sleep," I said evenly.

He held a smirk for several moments. "Attempted?"

"Any further attempts at all whether I'm awake or sleeping," I replied, "and I will not entertain your offer, and instead, regard you as a hostile enemy."

"You have my word," Lorcan said through gritted teeth.

I stood. "Thank you for extending your hospitality to us."

He rose as well. "Indeed, Hunter, this conversation has been quite ... informative."

CHAPTER 25

When we returned to our room and closed the door, Father shook his head in disbelief. He was panting from exhilaration, not exhaustion. "You need to *think* about this offer, Forrest?"

"Of course," I replied. "Why wouldn't I?"

"One *thousand* gold marks," he replied. "That's more than you and I could earn over the rest of our lifetimes."

"That's a huge exaggeration, Father. But we don't know that he's telling the truth," I whispered.

"Forrest's right," Penelope said. "We don't know."

I stood as close to them as possible. Speaking in whispers didn't guarantee the vampires couldn't hear us. Their magnified hearing was capable of eavesdropping for quite some distance. Besides that, most castles had hidden passageways, and as old as this one was, it was possible for someone to be listening on the other side of our walls where we couldn't see or detect them.

"We have another issue to consider," I whispered.

"What?" Father asked in a hushed tone.

"We're not dealing with just one vampire. There are seven. We are outnumbered. Even with our best weapons, should they turn on us, we're dead."

Father frowned. "You suspect he might do that? Don't you think his offer is legitimate?"

I shrugged. "He doesn't seem to be lying. I believe he genuinely wants Ambrose slain, but we cannot ignore the possibility of being attacked or killed by them."

"For the amount of money he's offering—"

"Look, Father, even *if* we are successful slaying Ambrose, who's to say Lorcan won't kill us when we return to collect his reward?"

Thomas sat on the edge of a cot and cleared his throat. His complexion was pasty pale. "Whatever you decide, Forrest, my journey ends when we reach Freiburg and you hand the child over to the Archdiocese, provided no additional plague demons arise and kill me."

I nodded. "I have no issue with that. Your obligation ends there."

"I'm sorry," he said softly.

"No need to be. We appreciate your services thus far."

"Albert never gave me any other choice."

I smiled. "Everyone has a choice. Action or inaction. You chose to act in order to survive, and we've chosen to protect you."

He offered a humble smile. "We've not reached Freiburg yet."

"Penelope and I will do all we can to ensure that we do."

She smiled at Thomas. "We will."

Frustrated, Father paced the floor. "Do you realize how much that money could help us? How long it would last?"

I'd never known my father to be greedy, but he wanted that money more than his next breath. We had always had a modest lifestyle. Things were lean at times, but no different than it had been for most other families in Romania. Poverty was rampant. People fought for survival, sometimes going a few days without eating a meal. One thousand gold marks was an extremely large amount of money for us. I understood that, but it put a strange glint in his eyes, worse than when he had fought his cravings against consuming strong drinks.

"The money issue is secondhand, Father. Everything else needs to be weighted."

"Son—"

"You and Jacques were the ones who hammered it into my head about *not* making hasty decisions, remember?"

He nodded.

"You were both right. If we go after Ambrose strictly because of greed, we're dead. A dead man cannot spend a thousand gold marks or even one. Money does a corpse no good at all," I said.

"Unless you're Lorcan," Penelope said with a wide grin.

"You know what my point is," I replied.

She nodded. "I know. Just trying to lessen the tension."

"Money should never be the main objective. Slaying the vampire and learning as much about him or her is what needs to be first on our minds. We need to calculate the risks and ensure we know where his lair is."

Father sat in a cushioned chair with a slight grin. "You're talking like you want to slay him?"

I sighed. "It's my obligation as a Hunter to rid the world of all vampires."

Penelope eased close and whispered, "Even Lorcan and his children?"

I nodded. "It's late. Everyone needs to get some sleep. I'll stand watch until morning."

"You need your sleep, too," she said.

"I'll sleep in the coach when we depart tomorrow morning. Someone needs to remain awake throughout the night."

I retrieved my Hunter box from near the door and set it on a reading table. I lay several sharp stakes beside the box for easy access. I placed several bottles of garlic juice on another table. I had two bottles of holy water left, which wasn't a lot when I faced the possibility of fighting seven vampires. Once we reached Freiburg, I needed to restock.

MORNING CAME without incident or confrontation. I never detected one sound in the outer hallways or behind any of our walls. While I had sat and waited, expecting the worst from Lorcan, my mind entertained the idea of what Penelope had suggested. Were all vampires pure evil? Was it unfair and unjust for me to place them all into the same category?

Hunters weren't given any guidelines. There wasn't a manual filled with commandments, at least none I had found. We had Hunter's instinct and intuition, but nowhere was it explicitly written that vampires were necessarily evil. Of course my first confrontation with Baron Randolph had left me with the impression that all vampires were self-serving, vain, and merciless. Then the next few reinforced those attributes. This prejudiced me to believe no vampire was capable of compassion or mercy.

Even one night's thoughts concerning the true nature of vampires didn't dissuade my self-proclaimed credo. They were vile creatures of darkness, soulless, and doomed for eternity. Perhaps they despised mortals because those of us who believed in an afterlife held to the hope they'd never have again. Who truly understood what fractured in their minds after they turned into vampires? The transformation affected their entire beings. Over time, most people's minds deteriorated some-what, and as I had noted with Philip, who was a Hunter and not a vampire, there was an actual threat to mankind whenever a mentally deranged person became a vampire. Although it was merely speculation on my part, I believed Philip had absorbed the mental inclinations of one of these lunatics. He no longer possessed rationality. But when it came to Varak, neither had I.

Penelope eased off her cot, slipped her robe on, and came to sit beside me. She smiled. Her curly hair was frizzed and looked like a damaged windblown daisy after an intense rain. She leaned her head against my shoulder. "You want to get some sleep? I can watch the door until we're ready to go."

"I'm fine. People have been moving outside in the hall. Servants, I suppose." I looked at the cuckoo clock. It was almost 5 a.m.

She stared up into my eyes in a way that made me feel funny inside. I stared at her lips, and she did mine. My stomach felt nervous. Without realizing I was moving, I leaned down to kiss her and Father abruptly wheezed and cleared his throat, startling she and I.

We pulled away from one another and turned to look at him. His eyes were still closed but he rolled over, facing our direction. He'd be awake within a few minutes. Once he tossed and turned, sleep lost its grip on him.

I released a long sigh. I glanced at her again, but the moment was lost.

Someone rapped at the door. Father sat up on the edge of the bed, as did Thomas and Madeline.

A few seconds later, the door opened. Jensen stepped into the room. His eyes regarded the stakes on the table. He suddenly looked concerned and partially confused. It showed a lack of gratitude toward Lorcan on our part.

His eyes shifted toward me. "I do hope you had a pleasant night's sleep. Count Lorcan has requested your presence for breakfast in the banquet hall. He has matters to discuss while the stable hands are getting your horse and coach ready for you to depart."

We nodded. After Jensen left, I packed my weapons into the box, and we hurriedly dressed. I don't believe anyone rushed because they wanted to eat. We were ready to leave the castle and travel to Freiburg.

"Have you made your decision?" Father asked.

"I have."

"And?"

"We will accept the offer."

Father's mouth dropped. His eyes grew fierce with excitement. He patted my shoulder with great enthusiasm.

"One thing, Father."

"What is it?" he asked.

"When we get to the banquet hall, let me do the talking. Lorcan was quite perturbed that you kept interrupting him earlier in the night."

Father grinned. "I'll be silent."

"And *try* not to divulge your zeal for the money, okay?"

He nodded, but I knew he'd never succeed. His eyes and smile were a direct reflection of how he felt inside. No matter how hard he tried, he'd never vanquish his lust for the reward.

CHAPTER 26

*L*orcan sat at the head of the table when we arrived. He didn't seem as jovial as he had been near midnight. I couldn't tell if he was angry or simply impatient at hearing my answer. Of course with sunrise approaching in a couple of hours, I imagined he was ready to retreat to the darkness of his casket or sepulcher. It stood to reason a vampire might get cranky like a mortal when he doesn't get rest.

After we took our seats, he rested his elbows upon the table and stared at me. "What have you decided?"

"We will slay Ambrose for you," I replied.

He grinned with satisfaction. "Splendid. How did you arrive at your decision, if I may ask?"

I crossed my arms and leaned back in my chair, attempting to look like I had spent a long time coming to my reasoning during the night. "I suppose if I had children and someone was trying to kill them, I'd find a way to eradicate such an enemy. And I wouldn't care whom I had to hire to carry it out. Although I've not met your children, I can tell they are of the utmost prominence based upon their portraits on the wall." Perhaps I had been too flattering, but I simply wanted to pack our belongings and travel on our way to Freiburg. Even though Lorcan had promised I could reject the offer without repercussions, I wanted to depart in the most amicable way possible.

"What is your business in Freiburg?" he asked. His eyes focused on Madeline and Varak. He suddenly seemed interested in them when earlier in the night he had not.

"Personal."

He frowned at me. "Ah, I see. No coaxing it out of you?"

"It is not of your concern."

Lorcan studied me for several moments in silence, trying to read me. He gave a disappointed smile. "You find it difficult to trust me?"

"Trust isn't something I readily offer anyone."

"You're wise, Hunter. Trust must be earned. A foolish man who trusts a stranger often suffers great loss and tragedy. That's why I have taken additional means in the hope I can prove my trustworthiness to you."

I frowned. "What do you mean?"

"Flora!" Lorcan shouted.

Our attention turned to the tall slender brunette standing at the side door beneath the paintings. Her long curly hair hung down around her shoulders. Flora wore an elegant royal blue gown like she had when the artist had painted her image onto the canvas. Her alabaster skin was flawless. With high cheekbones and a narrow-bridge nose, her face displayed aristocracy, more so than her father's did. My first impression was that she was haughty and regarded herself in a separate class altogether than any of us. Not that I could argue such a point because we were paupers in comparison.

A tall man stood limply at her side, standing *only* because she held him upright. In spite of her thin appearance, she was incredibly strong. The man must have been over twice her weight and stood about my height. She was holding him up by his shirt collar with one hand. Without much effort, she flung his body toward the table. He landed a few feet away, and the man didn't move. He wasn't breathing.

"Forrest?" Penelope whispered. "That's Philip, isn't it?"

I rose. Lorcan placed a fierce grip around my wrist, preventing me from leaving the table. If he chose, he could snap my arm with little effort. "Is he dead?"

Lorcan nodded. "Yes."

I pulled my arm, and he freed me of his hold.

"You killed him?"

He smiled. "You should be relieved."

"Why's that?" I asked.

"He came to the castle at 3 a.m. with the intent of finding and killing you. He arrived on horseback, covered with ice and snow. Determination was what had kept him going. A normal person would have died from the frigid cold. But not him. He was raving mad. What's odd, Forrest, is that he held no interest in slaying me or my children. He was, however, insistent on killing *you*." A strange amused smile curled on his lips. "What would possess a Hunter to kill another Hunter? I've never heard any reports of a Hunter turning against another within their league. Especially not with the passion he exhibited. He considered you his enemy. Why is that, Hunter?"

"He didn't tell you?" I asked.

Lorcan shook his head. "No. But it makes me wonder what trespasses you've committed against him?"

"None."

"And yet he's pursued you?"

I shrugged and tried to appear dumbstruck.

"Come now, Forrest. You're amongst friends. While none of us were able to compel him to get the answers we wanted, we know he has ruthlessly tracked you for quite some time. For what purpose?"

"We didn't see eye to eye."

"Apparently not," Lorcan said. "But there has to be more to this."

"Like what?" I asked.

"How'd he know you were in my castle of all places?"

"I don't know." And that was the truth. I didn't understand how he had escaped from the cemetery. Father had tied Philip better than I had the time before, and yet, he had somehow caught up to us. I didn't have any idea how he had done so, and certainly, I was dumbfounded at how he knew where we were lodging for the night. He had to have had help.

What worried me was who had helped him and guided him to us? Was it through another Hunter's intellect? Had we not stopped at this inn for the night, he would have found us on the road and confronted me probably for the last time.

Lorcan's eyes narrowed. "You really don't know, do you?"

I shook my head.

"Nonetheless, he was your mortal enemy, and we've ensured he won't ever make another attempt to kill you."

I walked around the table. Philip lay face down on the floor. I grabbed his shoulder and flipped him over. Rage had frozen in his facial expressions. He had not feared death or the vampires. He had probably tried to fight them off, but even he wasn't a match for Lorcan's children. His determination to defeat them was only so he could find where Varak was.

Two sets of bite marks were on his neck with two more sets near each wrist. If my guess was correct, Lorcan's children had drained him of his blood. They had feasted on a Hunter's blood, which boosted their strength far greater than normal. Now was not the time for me to make any accusations or even hope to combat any of his children. We were outnumbered, and with their increased strength, it would be like trying to fight a dozen or more vampires.

I checked Philip's mouth for blood but found none.

"And this is supposed to build my trust in you?" I asked.

"Shouldn't it? He was your enemy. We killed him. This is my way of showing loyalty to my oath. My gesture of good faith," Lorcan said with genuine pride in his voice.

I knelt in silence beside Philip's body. I grieved over his death, not for who he was as a person, but because another Hunter was dead. Because I had vowed to protect the hybrid infant, Philip was dead.

Lorcan turned in his seat, offering a reassuring smile. "Do you not realize that I sense your skepticism, and what Hunter wouldn't be skeptical making a pact with a vampire? It's not like you're dealing with the Devil."

I had my doubts about that.

Lorcan continued, "Just like another Hunter seeking to kill you, it's doubtful many vampires would dare consider the thought of a master vampire hiring a Hunter to kill another master. Perhaps this is why destiny crossed our paths. Hunters hate you and you have befriended the vampire who killed your enemy."

Anger stirred inside me. I wanted to blurt out how wrong he was and that he was forever my lifelong enemy. He certainly wasn't my friend. Killing the Hunter, which did prevent me from killing him or being killed, could be viewed more as a threat, his way of proving the strength of his family, which was daunting on a whole other level. Philip had far more experience slaying vampires than I did. I'm certain Lorcan was aware of that.

The more vampires I encountered, the better I had become at determining how old vampires were. The older the vampire, the greater his or her strength. I didn't know if vampires were able to determine the same thing about Hunters. I guessed it was possible, and if Lorcan could, he knew I was still a novice Hunter.

I kept an even expression on my face. The last thing I needed to show was my inner rage or the slightest hint of fear. I didn't have fear for myself, but for Penelope, my father, and the others. I feared what might happen to them if I didn't keep my temper in check. For the first time since I had expressed my feelings to Penelope, I recalled why I had predetermined the risks of falling in love. It wasn't my death that was the greatest loss. It was hers and the agony of living without her.

Father must have sensed the potential threat, too. He kept looking at Philip and then he glanced toward Flora who stood at the door. She held a defiant look when she gazed at me, almost like she wanted me to attack her father. I knew better. Lorcan had already shown me his strength when he had gripped my wrist. Without a weapon, I wasn't physically capable of fighting him or her. Flora could be at my throat before I saw her move, especially with her enhanced power.

I rose to my feet, standing beside Philip's corpse. "I appreciate you having an interest in my welfare." I expressed the words, but I was torn inside with gut-wrenching sickness. It troubled me that a Hunter was dead and in a way, I had offered thanks to the vampires who had killed him. It was difficult swallowing the vile taste of guilt.

Lorcan smiled. "It's not just your welfare, Hunter, but the rest of your party, too."

I frowned.

Lorcan stood. "Come. All of you. Let me show you."

He walked toward the door where his daughter stood. She slid her arm around the crook of his, and they led the way down the long dark corridor. The walls were made of massive stones. Every ten feet a lit iron sconce was fastened to the wall. This area was the older section of the castle and had not been renovated like our inn room and bathhouse had been.

The long hallway was cool with a dank smell. The path we walked seemed endless. I was reminded of the long outer wall when we had arrived. This arched tunnel must be inside that wall.

Lorcan glanced over his shoulder and smiled. "Not much farther."

Uneasiness settled over me. Father and Penelope both gave me nervous glances. Perhaps they felt the same as I did. Was he leading us into a trap?

Again we had left our weapons in the room, and I was already having second thoughts. I had never expected to see Philip dead at the hands—well the *fangs*, I suppose—of Lorcan's children. Even had I suspected they had killed another Hunter, I knew our weapons would not help us. Not at this particular moment anyway and not with their increased strength.

Philip might have been capable of defending himself against two of the siblings, but it was highly improbable that he had any knowledge of the total number of vampires in this castle. One master and six of his offspring. Of course, there could be even more than that, if each sibling had made sires, too. But depending upon how long the siblings had been vampires, their strength and prowess might equal that of a master. Philip never had a chance to survive against such odds. Even if I was fighting by his side, we'd have been easily defeated. The unity of these vampires was too powerful for a couple of Hunters. I wondered if Lorcan realized the dangers of assigning each of his children to a different section of his territory within the Black Forest. The farther away from one another they were, the weaker they became.

Lorcan and Flora turned to the right at the first hall that connected to the corridor we were walking along. This corridor was shorter and the iron bars on each side of the hall looked about as inviting as any prison cell might present itself to an unsuspecting victim.

But there weren't any prisoners here. Each barred room held a different torture device. If the rock walls could scream, I had a good idea of the terror they'd reveal. Spiked weapons, stretching racks, and metal enclosures that were placed over roaring fires to cook prisoners alive. Lorcan and his family were more demented than I had credited them. I suppose Philip had gotten off easier than previous prisoners.

We passed all of those rooms and entered the circular room at the end of the corridor. Inside this room a banister encircled a pit below. Flora placed her hands upon the smooth railing. Her father stood beside her.

"Look below."

Except for Madeline, the rest of us stepped to the side of the rail with extreme caution and gazed down. She remained outside the room, cradling Varak, gently rocking him. Down at the bottom of the pit were eight plague demons like the ones Penelope had killed. I frowned and caught Lorcan's intense stare.

He smiled. "Until your arrival, we've never encounter such demons within our halls. Like the Hunter, are these also your enemy, Forrest?"

I shook my head. "Not mine, but our coachman's."

"I see. And why is that?" he asked.

"You don't know?"

"I wouldn't be asking you if I did."

"You have no knowledge of Albert the Were-rat?" I asked warily.

He shook his head, slightly puzzled by the name. "No. What significance does this were-rat have with these demons?"

Until this moment, I truly had thought Lorcan had received word about me through Albert. While vampires could mask lies, I didn't perceive him as being dishonest. And the plague demons had seemed to have caught him off guard, too.

"Thomas?" I said.

Thomas nervously rubbed his moustache, swallowed hard, and held onto the banister to hold himself upright. "Albert sent these after me."

"Why?" Lorcan asked.

"As punishment for not repaying my debt to him."

"I see. So you have a death sentence hanging over you? Rather than face your rightful punishment, you've decided to flee?" Lorcan asked.

I shook my head. "No, the demons are more of a test, or in this case, a twisted game."

"Game?" Lorcan asked. "What sort of game?"

"If Thomas succeeds in getting us to Freiburg without getting killed by one of the plague demons, his debt is cleared."

Lorcan said, "I see. Interesting. Then if I were all of you, I'd gather your belongings and finish your journey to Freiburg. Your horse and coach should be ready and awaiting you at the entrance. These demons are trapped here and cannot escape to follow you."

Penelope looked at the demons in the pit with eagerness in her gaze. She wanted to kill them. I sensed her detestation toward them was the same as mine toward vampires. "Why are these demons confined to the pit?"

Flora said, "As a precaution for the castle's safety, there is a summoning circle on the pit floor that draws invading demons here."

"Who drew the circle?" Penelope asked.

"I did," Flora replied with a prideful smile.

Lorcan chuckled softly. "She has taken a keen interest in demons and other dark arts."

"You realize these demons carry the plague?"

Flora's smile didn't fade. "Indeed I do."

Penelope regarded Flora with a skeptical glare.

Flora pursed her lips. "It's not like I keep them as pets."

"Then why do you?"

"To study them and their behaviors."

"These have only one purpose, and that's to infect villages and cities with the Black Death."

Flora crinkled her nose. "They *are* the most *boring* of demons."

Penelope's brow rose. "Oh? What ones are interesting?"

"The incubus has been … shall I say, the most exciting," Flora replied with a sly grin before taking in a deep breath, closing her eyes, and shuddering.

Penelope turned toward me with a stunned expression. "Can we get out of here?"

Madeline gave me a worried look, too.

I glanced to the others. "Let's go."

They all turned to walk through the corridor filled with various torture chambers. Thomas hurried ahead of everyone, almost running. Apparently he didn't believe these demons were trapped and could escape. I held my own doubts about that as well.

Father limped beside Madeline and Penelope followed. I took a step toward the door, but Lorcan placed his hand firmly on my shoulder, turning me.

"Forrest?" Lorcan said. "One more thing?"

I faced him. "Yes?"

He handed me a leather pouch that was tied shut. "There are one hundred marks inside. An advance, if you will."

"We've not done anything yet," I replied. "I'd rather not take the money until after Ambrose has been slain."

"Forrest, Ambrose resides well on the other side of Freiburg. You'll have need of food and boarding expenses. Or are you considering forfeiting my offer altogether?"

"No, I accept. I never go back on my word."

Lorcan smiled, placed the pouch into the palm of my hand, and then gently folded my fingers over the pouch. "Good."

"And what do you wish for me to bring back as proof of his death?" I asked.

"Proof?"

I nodded.

"Ambrose wears an amber broach that encases a large stag beetle, and on his left hand is a ruby ring. Either of those or both should suffice," Lorcan said.

"Very well."

He smiled. "At least now you'll have less obstacles since the other

175

Hunter has suffered his demise. As for the demons, Flora will keep them bound in the pit."

"You didn't turn Philip, did you?"

Lorcan chuckled softly. "You've never seen my children eat. A Hunter's blood divided between six adult children? Not a drop was left. Besides, he was a raving lunatic. I certainly don't need someone else to keep on a leash."

Flora flicked her gaze toward me. Hunger shown in her eyes and my neck burned where she stared, longing to bite me. She seemed to have problems restraining her bloodlust. I wondered if she had recently become a vampire because she exhibited the signs of an untamed vampire, lacking control of her hunger. Regardless, she made me uncomfortable, but I tried not to show it. She licked her lips before smiling seductively, showing the slightest tips of her fangs. I'd have thought her much more attractive had she been human. Be that as it may, I couldn't wait to get outside the castle and travel farther away.

"How can you be certain this was all of the plague demons?" I asked.

Flora rested a hand on her hip and flipped her long curls to one side. "Whoever sent them, only sent eight."

"But Penelope has killed several of them."

"Yes. They dissolve into ash, but they can reappear elsewhere. But as long as they remain in physical form, they are confined inside the pit and cannot materialize elsewhere."

I hoped she was telling the truth and provided I didn't somehow offend her before our departure, maybe she'd ensure their confinement until we reached Freiburg. I couldn't know that she would, but I didn't dare ask, either. No sense intriguing her amusement since she seemed like one who enjoyed playing morbid games with mortals' lives. *Sort of like Albert ...*

"If I may ask," Lorcan said, "what is your state of affairs in Freiburg? Does it have to do with the child the maiden tends to?"

It was already partially a question he had asked before. I guessed he wanted to throw me off guard. I studied his eyes for several moments. I felt his power leap toward me, trying to penetrate my thoughts. I frowned and formed fists. "I *warned* you about trying to probe my thoughts."

Flora bore her fangs in an instant and hissed. Her eyes peered black and narrowed. She moved across the floor toward me.

"Daughter, no." Lorcan placed his hand between her and me. "My apologies, Forrest. Forgive me. Force of habit."

I relaxed my hands and nodded. Flora retracted her fangs, but she didn't look away from me. She attempted to look intimidating, but I ignored her. At this particular moment, I knew not to turn my back toward her.

"But it is the child. Why Freiburg? Why are you taking him there?"

"He's an orphan," I replied.

"There are orphanages and cathedrals all through the countries you've traveled, are there not? We have them here, even though we're a small village. And you're passing all of them in preference of Freiburg."

"I am. More than that, I cannot tell you."

"I find it strange that your journey has been plagued by such adversity," Lorcan said.

"And it hasn't ended yet," I replied.

"Flora and I shall escort you to your room. It has been a pleasure."

CHAPTER 27

*W*hen Thomas drove the coach through the castle gates, the snow was no longer falling. Winds during the night had blown a good portion of the snow off the road. The sun peeked at the top of the mountainside, presenting a pastel sky of reds, purples, and pinks. I was ecstatic that we were on our way.

Flora had made me uneasy. Vampires could compel most mortals, but a beautiful vampire held a stronger seduction, drawing unsuspecting victims to her by enticing their lusts first. Even at a young age, I realized people tended to judge others upon first glance, and often the plain common folk were quickly ignored while our interests were drawn to those with unnatural beauty and charisma. Sadly, some people sacrificed their dearest possessions in their pursuit of obtaining what they believed to be the perfect spouse; only to later find themselves wallowing in sorrow when they realized what was on the surface was far more beautiful than the monster contained within.

Flora was dangerous, and probably had been so before she had been turned, using her looks and charm to obtain the things she desired without question or argument. As a vampire she could influence others to do her bidding for hundreds of years, provided she wasn't slain well beforehand.

Father cleared his throat and adjusted himself in his seat. I tossed him the pouch of coins. He caught the pouch, frowned, and shook it in his hand. The sound of jostling coins brought a curious hopeful smile to his face. "What is this?"

"He gave us one hundred marks."

His mouth dropped in awe.

"You know what this means, don't you Father?"

"What?"

"Regardless of whether or not I've made the right decision in slaying Ambrose for Lorcan, there's no declining the offer now."

Penelope leaned her head against my shoulder. "His daughter seems more unpredictable than he is. I don't care if she did deny it, but she views demons as pets. She has a fetish for them. A vampire who holds affection for demons is quite unsettling. She has eight plague demons in her possession. Do you realize how great a threat that is to the population of neighboring towns and cities?"

"You think she'd use them to infect a city?" I asked.

"Don't you? Imagine how she could blackmail a king or queen into giving her whatever she wanted. If they denied her, she could use one demon to prove her point and keep the other seven in reserve."

I hadn't considered that. Manipulation was the agenda of most ruling vampires, and Flora definitely fit that mold. Mentally, she had a passion to watch others suffer. It wouldn't have surprised me to learn that the torture devices were toys she used on peasants whenever she became bored.

But Penelope was right. Flora could choose whatever city she desired and claim it for her own. She had been the only one of the six that we had met, and if she were the least dangerous of Lorcan's children, I couldn't imagine what Philip had faced when he had fought for his life. The others had conveniently excused themselves from our presence, which I considered more intimidating because it left us wondering about their true nature. All we really knew about them was what the paintings on the wall revealed.

Frowning, I said, "Once we reach Freiburg, won't these demons that

Albert sent after Thomas dissolve or return to wherever he had summoned them from?"

"We can hope but at this point, there's no way to know. If she's completely bound them to the circle in the pit, she now controls them."

Father shook his head. "What she could do with those demons is more frightening than the turmoil most vampires cause, if she chooses to use them to spread the plague."

"I agree. But we don't have time to concern ourselves over that just yet. We're a day and a half's journey from Freiburg. If what Lorcan says is true, then we don't have to worry ourselves with the plague demons. But that doesn't mean I don't have to worry about other Hunters trying to get Varak before we hand him over to the archbishop."

Madeline leveled a frightened stare at me while hugging the child tightly. The boy cooed and giggled, as innocently like any child his age would. How I wished I were able to see ahead in time to know what this child would become, so I could feel more at ease. My mind was torn between hope and sorrowful regret, as I longed to keep the world safer. But I knew I couldn't allow harm to come to Varak while he was in our possession. Once Varak was at the Archdiocese, I was released of my oath and hoped that in the future I didn't need to rectify the situation, but I knew in the back of my mind my worries would continue to linger.

With a broad smile, Father stacked the gold coins in his hand.

I rubbed my burning eyes and yawned. The coach rocked steadily, making it more difficult to stay awake. "I'm going to get some sleep since it will be several hours before we stop."

Father stared at the coins, not hearing a single word I had said. I shrugged and leaned against the wall. Penelope lay against me and placed her arm around my waist. The warmth the coach had absorbed from being stored inside Lorcan's stables was being drawn away by the winter's frosty grasp, in much the same way Death sucked the last fragments of life from a dying man or woman. I pulled a blanket over us to fight the chill that was building inside the coach, and I surrendered to sleep.

MY SLEEP HAD BEEN UNEVENTFUL. No dreams or nightmares came, and thankfully, no attempts from Lorcan to venture into my mind had occurred either. Perhaps he could keep his word, but only time would tell.

Nightfall had settled. I rubbed my eyes and shook my head. I was still groggy. Father held a small lantern and sat at the window. He pulled the curtain aside and looked outside.

"I've slept through the entire day?" I asked.

He nodded. "I'm surprised you never awakened yourself with all your raucous snoring. I'd have stuffed cotton in my ears if I'd had some."

"I was snoring?"

"Like a giant bear." Penelope playfully jabbed me with her elbow. "You kept me from sleeping."

Father smiled. "Her snoring wasn't as loud as yours, son, but she was trying hard to complete."

"What?" she asked. "I *don't* snore."

"Yes, young lady, you do," Father said.

I stared out the window. "Why are we still traveling?"

"My guess is that Thomas wants to get to Freiburg as quickly as possible. He's only stopped a few times to feed and water the horse."

"Even after the demons have been bound, he's reluctant to stay the night elsewhere?" I asked.

"Do you place full confidence in her claim that she will keep them bound?"

I sighed. "Not really, but he's going to freeze to death."

"Death comes to us all eventually, son. I'd rather freeze to death than die from the plague."

"Unfortunately, we don't always get to choose our time of death or how we die. I suppose it's best not to know, but some forewarning would be nice," I said.

He nodded. "And sometimes you survive against incredible odds. You live when you should have died."

I knew he was talking about his own near death experience.

"Get Thomas' attention," I said.

Father turned and hammered his fist against the top of the coach. Thomas shouted, "Whoa!"

A few seconds after the coach stopped, Thomas opened the door.

"Are we not stopping for the night?" I asked.

"We are approximately a half hour from reaching Freiburg," he replied.

"So soon?"

He smiled. "I have kept the horse at a faster gait. The road has been better than what it was during the previous few days. Less snow, so the extra speed shouldn't stress him. We're almost there."

A sense of relief passed through me. It was good this part of our journey was coming to an end. "Great news. Press on."

Thomas smiled and closed the door. A few seconds later, he shrieked. The volume of his terrified screams decreased as something dragged him into the forest.

Penelope grabbed her bow and flung open the door, but Thomas was nowhere in sight. I opened my Hunter box, searched through the contents, and stuffed various items into my coat pockets. With a stake in one hand and my loaded crossbow in the other, I squeezed through the door and stepped onto the icy road.

"Where is he?" I asked.

She shook her head and whispered, "I don't know."

"Demons?"

"I don't sense any."

The horse shuffled his feet back and forth, making nervous whinnies. His eyes were wide.

Penelope took her night spectacles and separated the lenses, handing me one of them.

Faint moonlight spilled overhead, cascading downward through the firs and leafless deciduous trees. Snarls came from the shadowed recesses within the trees. I stepped around Penelope to shield her while scanning the trees with the night goggle lens. Whatever had taken him had carried him behind the larger trees out of sight.

"Thomas!" I shouted, holding the stake tightly to my side.

"Is that *really* a good idea?" she asked.

"Be ready," I whispered.

"For what?" She took her half of the spectacles and used the long leather strap to tie and secure it against her right eye.

"A werewolf," I replied.

She pulled an arrow from her quiver and lined it up on her bow. "Will an arrow kill it?"

"No, but it causes a great deal of pain. Aim for a vulnerable spot."

"Like what exactly?"

"An eye or the throat."

"And that won't kill it?"

"No. It's difficult to kill a were creature."

Thomas wailed in agony. Claws slashed through him, making wet sloppy sounds. He was silent in an instant. He was dead.

Anger pulsed through me. For all Thomas had endured to reach Freiburg and to come this close, a werewolf killed him. Since Jacques was a werewolf, I tended to be more permissive and not view them as enemies. However, after meeting Ulrich I understood that not all werewolves were affable toward the human population or even to those they once considered to be a part of their pack.

"Thomas is dead," I whispered.

"That's what I feared." Her voice crackled.

"Whatever happens, do not get bitten or scratched," I said. "Or you'll become all hairy."

"Does that mean you'd like me less?"

"It would change things quite a bit for both of us."

Branches snapped on the other side of the coach. Thomas had been killed in the forest on this side of the road. "There's more than one."

"I heard the footsteps, too," she said. She turned and pressed her back against mine. "You watch that side and I'll watch this one."

The horse stamped its feet. I couldn't see where these creatures were or their advancement. Deep breaths came from the edge of the trees ahead of me, but this creature blended in with the darkness quite well.

I pressed the lens firmly against my eye and squinted to hold it like an ocular. I held the crossbow ahead of me, waiting for the slightest movement that helped pinpoint its location.

Father eased the coach door open. "Is everything okay out there?"

"Close the door," I whispered. "Thomas is dead."

He leaned forward and looked out. "Dead? How?"

"Werewolves," Penelope said softly.

Father eased the door closed.

"See anything?" I whispered.

She didn't reply. Her arm pressed against my back and the bowstring *twung*! A fierce growl softened to painful yelps, moaning and crying. "The eye *is* a soft spot."

The beast I faced growled and leapt from the shadows. It was massive and muscular, almost the size of a small bear. It charged, growling. I fired the crossbow, striking its upper thigh. It roared from the pain. The arrow slowed the creature's pace slightly, but it kept coming toward me, snarling and raising its sharp-clawed hands, ready to slice through me. Nothing heightened the anger of a werewolf like a painful injury.

I dropped the crossbow and pulled my revolver from my coat pocket, firing three rapid shots into its chest when only one was necessary. The werewolf dropped and spasmed on the road before stiffening in death.

I turned and nearly knocked Penelope down. I didn't realize how close she was standing to me. Her wide eyes stared at the one she had shot with her bow. I walked toward it. It was writhing on the road with an arrow protruding from its eye. It was so preoccupied trying to pry out the arrow that it never even noticed my approach. I aimed and fired one silver bullet into its forehead, ending its struggle permanently.

The smell of burnt gunpowder wafted on the air. The gunshots echoed deep into the forest, reverberating for miles.

"They're dead?" she asked.

"Yes. I used silver bullets. Automatically guarantees the death of werewolves." I listened for more movement along the forest floor but heard nothing. "Any other werewolves out here? I have more silver bullets if you'd like your fate to be like theirs. Show yourselves!"

Four sets of footsteps scrambled away from the road, all running in different directions. With their keen sense of smell and hearing, they had no doubt witnessed the death of these two on the road. Mostly likely one of the two I had killed was an alpha. Both could be alphas if one was male and the other female, but in this darkness, I wasn't about to check. Since one of them had killed Thomas, I really didn't care to know. Both deserved death and if any of the others returned, I'd shoot them without hesitation.

CHAPTER 28

I almost went into the forest to search for Thomas' body, but I couldn't bear to see his torn body. The ground was frozen cold, so we couldn't bury him. We certainly couldn't haul his eviscerated remains into the coach either. He had deserved a much better ending for his life. I had promised to protect him and had failed to keep him safe.

I grieved. Fighting burning tears of regret, I took a deep breath and opened the coach door.

"Is everything okay?" Father asked.

"Two of the werewolves are dead and the others have fled deeper into the forest. Do you know how to drive this coach, Father?"

He stared absently at me for several moments before giving a slight nod. "I can."

"We'll get you bundled to weather this cold. It's not too far until we reach the city," I said.

Penelope placed her hand on mine. "Ride up there with him, Forrest."

Father stepped out of the coach with the burning lantern in his hand. In the faint glow of the light, Father's nervousness was evident. He looked toward the trees at the edge of the dark road, possibly assuming he'd be the next to get attacked by one of the werewolves.

I offered my hand to Penelope to help her climb into the coach. After she seated herself, I secured the door.

Father glanced toward me. "You're sure Thomas is dead? Because if he isn't—"

"From the sounds of him being sliced open and his guts falling out? He's dead."

"Unless you've seen the body, son, you can't be absolutely certain."

I sighed. "Being as I don't know for certain where his body is, don't you think we'd put ourselves at greater risk by searching for him in the dark? I don't like the idea of leaving Penelope, Madeline, and the baby alone. The other werewolves fled, but it doesn't guarantee they won't return."

Howls echoed deeper in the forests. Seconds later, others answered. They were all around us on both sides of the road.

"You're right. As much as it pains me, it's best we travel on. Thomas was a good man."

"I agree. Here, let me help you up into the seat," I said.

Usually he adamantly insisted on doing any physical activity without assistance, but he offered no argument. I don't know if he realized he couldn't possibly balance and pull himself up the side of the coach or if he was more worried that the remaining werewolves were circling back.

Once he grabbed the rails, I boosted him to the top of the coach.

He glanced down. "You mind handing me the lantern?"

"We'll attract less attention without it," I replied.

Father grumbled obscenities under his breath. I draped a heavy rug over my shoulder, grabbed the rails, and climbed up the narrow steps.

"What are you doing?" he asked, scooting over on the bench.

"Keeping you company."

"Company? Out here?" His pretend protest wasn't too convincing.

I took the thick rug and covered his legs with it. "It was Penelope's suggestion."

I caught his wide grin in the dim moonlight. "You'd best not ruin what you have with her, son. You won't find another as grand."

"And what do I have?" I asked with a grin. "You just like her because she insists that you're taken care of."

Father laughed, released the wheel brake, and tapped the reins on the horse's back. "What's wrong with that?"

The horse trudged forward and gradually increased its pace. The cold night air stung my face. I was glad my full beard covered my chin and cheeks to lessen the cold. I marveled at how Thomas had withstood the brutal cold. He had been extremely thin but never complained. Surprisingly, he'd never suffered any frostbite either.

I glanced toward the trees where I estimated he had died, but I was unable to see his remains even from the high seat. I couldn't believe less than ten minutes earlier he had been breathing, alive, and so quickly, gone. Life was fragile.

Father offered me a shrewd stare and shook his gloved finger. "Don't tell me you don't realize what you have with Penelope, son. She feels for you the same as you do her. Neither of you can hide it. There was a reason for the two of you to meet, and it wasn't those plague demons, either. Have you told her that you love her?"

"You said that it was evident."

"Have you told her?"

"No, well, yes, a little, but not at great length. But from how you describe us, if it's evident to you, she already knows."

"That's not the same thing. A woman needs to hear it, son. Hell, we all need to hear it." His voice cracked. He wiped away a tear. "Cause there comes a time when the woman you love might no longer be with you. No other pain in this world hurts as badly as that. Trust me. I know."

I placed my arm across my father's back and hugged him close. In comparison to my size, he was small, but whenever painful memories of Momma tugged his heartstrings, he seemed so much smaller. "I know, Father."

He sobbed and patted my hand. "So you need to tell her."

"I will."

The horse picked up its pace. The moonlight spilled through the trees, forming odd shadows as the coach rolled down the road. Patches of ice shimmered. Riding atop the coach offered an incredible sense of freedom. The breezing wind exhilarated me in spite of its biting cold. I watched the shadows, half expecting the werewolf pack to regroup and attack, but they never did. If anything, they had probably returned to the road to claim their dead.

Father sat in silence for several miles. His thoughts were on Momma. He remained torn inside over her loss. Those scars had never healed, and I never expected them to during his living years. It was times like this when I truly hoped a Heaven existed. A place where people crossed a threshold after they died to be reunited with their deceased loved ones. That was the hope the common folks clung to and what the cathedral priests insisted to be true, provided you followed their strict doctrines. Indeed, the thoughts of such a place offered peace and reassurance, which was something every person needed. True love never died, even after someone had. Love and memories lived on.

"I'm sorry, son," Father said.

"For what?"

The hurt in his voice prevented him from saying more.

"Father, I love you, and I hurt inside because of your pain. I cannot imagine how much you ache inside."

"You don't miss her?" he asked. "Doesn't your heart break because you cannot tell her you love her, too?"

"Of course I miss her. I wish I could tell her every day, but the love you shared with Momma was different than a son's love for his mother. That's part of why I'm reluctant telling Penelope my feelings and letting her know that I love her. I see how this still haunts and affects you, and I —I don't think I'm strong enough to sustain that kind of loss and pain."

Father turned in the coach seat and faced me. "Do you know what would have hurt me more? If I had never told her how I felt, we'd never have fallen in love, and instead of this loss, I'd be living with the regret of what I would have otherwise missed in life. It's okay to hurt inside. It's okay to grieve, but it's not okay to cower and never take that chance to find true love. Remember that."

He slapped my leg hard and looked toward the road again.

I thought about Penelope and how close we had come together within such a short amount of time. We were good friends and strange as it seemed, we didn't need to fully express our feelings in words. We had melded that understanding in our minds and our emotions, but Father was right. I needed to express to her more than I had over breakfast that morning. We never knew how short our lives would be. Thomas was a prime example of unexpected death. It could have been any one of us though, and we still had a few more hours of traveling before we reached Freiburg.

We rode without speaking for a long while. The tree lines on both sides of the road grew thinner. I suspected we were getting closer to the outskirts of Freiburg. I felt the sudden relief lessen the tension in my shoulders.

The coach axles creaked and scraped as the wheels passed over holes and loose stones. Father stiffened in the seat and pulled back on the reins. The horse planted its feet, but due to the road's descent and the icy patches, it skidded, trying to stop. The poor horse slid for several yards as the weight of the wagon pressed against it. Father pulled the wagon brake.

I glanced toward him. "What is it?"

"Don't you see them?" He pointed.

From the edges of the road, four people dressed in hooded robes stepped directly across our path. They each held lanterns that glowed to life.

"I see them," I replied, placing my hand on my revolver and stood. "State your purpose. I have a revolver."

The second one from my right stepped forward, lowered his hood, and lifted an empty hand. "Sir, may I approach? We offer no harm to any man. But what I must ask is vitally urgent."

"Yes, come ahead," I replied.

As he came closer, the moonlight and the light from his lantern reflected off the large silver cross hanging on his necklace. Not a werewolf. That was always good to know upfront. In his other hand he rubbed rosary beads. His nimble steps and his facial expression revealed he was more nervous than I was.

He stopped less than five yards from the horse. From the distance it was difficult to determine his age. His head was bald. "Is your destination to visit the archbishop at the Archdiocese?"

"It is," I replied. "Who asks?"

"Father Lucas. Would you be Forrest?"

My eyes narrowed. I pulled the gun from my coat pocket.

"Son!" Father scolded in a harsh whisper. "He's a priest for God's sake."

"So he says," I whispered. I kept my eyes on the man. We had had enough unpleasant surprises on our journey. "How do you know my name?"

"The archbishop has sent us to intercept you."

"Intercept us? Why? Is he prohibiting our visit?"

Lucas graciously smiled and shook his head. "No, it's nothing like that. He's offering your group refuge, but getting there requires a slight alternate route."

"Why?"

"Because there are people who wish to kill you before you get to the Archdiocese."

"What people?"

The priest stepped closer, rubbing the beads harder. "They call themselves Hunters. They have every entrance into the cathedral guarded. The archbishop has sent us to offer you safe passage as he is concerned about possible bloodshed."

"As am I," I replied.

The priest offered a slight smile and nodded. "But first, he has asked me to seek the reason for your arrival. To see if our accompanying you is acceptable in the eyes of our Lord."

I frowned, not exactly sure how to take that statement. How would asking our purpose now make any difference to their God? What prompted the archbishop to send these priests then, if not for some type of conviction to aid us? Questions for another time. "We have an orphaned child, and we were asked to deliver him to the archbishop in Freiburg."

"Why there particularly?"

"Father, I wish I knew. It was a request and I swore I'd honor it. With my life if necessary."

"A noble gesture. I'm certain the archbishop will be pleased to hear, but we must hurry."

"If all the entrances are being guarded, how did the four of you even get past them?"

The priest smiled. "We have our ways, Forrest."

"Did you receive word about our arrival before these Hunters came?"

He shook his head.

"But they told you my name?"

"Yes. And they asked of the child, but never disclosed why they wanted him. The archbishop does not want any blood spilled on our sanctuary grounds. Such contradicts the sole reason for the cathedral's existence."

Father cleared his throat. "So, can you guarantee our safety?"

Lucas walked toward the coach. "With the guidance and strength of our Lord, we will do all we can. If you permit us, we will drive the carriage into the city and keep you hidden inside the coach."

"Won't people find it odd for priests to be driving the coach?" I asked.

"Not at all. The men are looking for you. Not us."

"The Hunters will be suspicious seeing this coach under the control of priests."

Lucas smiled. "They will never see us."

"Come on, son," Father said. "Let's climb down."

Father checked the brake and tied the lead lines around the brake handle. He turned and lowered one foot onto the first step. I took his hand and helped keep him steady as he slowly made his way down to the bottom. By the time I reached the road, the other three priests had gathered beside the horse.

I didn't sense any threat from them. Nothing at all indicated they had come to cause us problems or further delay, but I was uncomfortable being near them. Perhaps it could have been their association to the cathedral I was most wary of, simply because I didn't understand the reasons behind their undying loyalty to a religion that clashed violently against other religions around the world, trying to quash and obliterate them. While they openly told their parishioners to love one another, the direct leadership practiced something entirely different by killing all who opposed them, sometimes entire villages and civilizations. I had witnessed it in Bucharest and had never forgotten it.

I stubbornly refused to cast aside the folk traditions my mother had taught me in favor of the cathedrals, especially since their goal was to annihilate all of the other world beliefs. It seemed ungodly to me.

Two of the priests climbed to the box seat and sat. The other two awkwardly positioned themselves atop the baggage compartment at the rear of the coach and held to metal handles while Father and I climbed back inside the coach.

I didn't have any idea how they planned to sneak us past the Hunters, but for the moment, I was thankful to be back inside, out of the cold.

CHAPTER 29

*P*enelope looked concern when Father and I climbed back into the coach and sat down. When the horse began pulling us, she peered out the window. "Why are we moving?"

I explained the situation.

"Hunters are waiting at the cathedral?" she asked.

I nodded.

She placed her hand into mine. "How did they know we were coming? Albert?"

While I believed Albert had sent Philip after me, and nothing had swayed my thoughts about that, I didn't think Albert had informed the Hunters waiting in Freiburg. But since Varak was a hybrid child, still innocent, an uninformed Hunter would never perceive this child any differently than a normal child. If I didn't know the boy's heritage, I'd never suspect the child to be half vampire. Everything about him on the surface demonstrated a typical infant incapable of any wrongdoing. So I really had no idea why these Hunters knew, except being told through Hunter's intellect, which to my understanding should not occur.

"I'm not sure," I replied.

"But you're still delivering Varak to the archbishop?"

"Yes. Afterwards, I have no further obligations."

Penelope leaned her head against my shoulder. Since I had slept through the entire day, I wasn't tired. I peered out the window. We were outside the forest now. The faint moonlight was enough to reveal the city buildings.

The driver slowed the horse several blocks into the city, turned onto a narrow side street, and stopped the coach in the darkness. The coach jostled as the priests climbed down.

The door opened. "Come. Everyone out."

"Where are we going?" I asked.

"We cannot risk driving the coach any closer to the cathedral," he replied. "We take the underground tunnels while the city sleeps."

Madeline hugged Varak. "Will it be safe?"

"It's the route we took to not be seen," the priest replied. "Please, hurry."

I grabbed my Hunter box while Penelope collected her bow and quiver. Father got out and helped Madeline climb down with Varak. The baby cried. She rocked him and gently shushed in his ear.

The cold night air and the eerie silence of the dark streets seemed almost worse than when we had stopped on the forest road. In some ways, I expected it to be more harrowing since these Hunters were all that stood between the Archdiocese and us.

"How many Hunters are here?" I asked the priest closest to me.

"At least a dozen," he replied.

"It is *exactly* a dozen," Father Lucas said. "Aren't you a Hunter, too?"

"I am."

He sighed. "It must be a heavy burden you bear."

"What's that?" I asked.

"To be hunted by your own." He walked to me, took something from his pocket, and then rubbed an oily substance on my forehead. He spoke a blessing in Latin, which basically asked God's blessings upon my soul. "The longer we linger above ground, the more danger you're in. Come. With a dozen men, they have enough to patrol the area, looking for you."

He turned and walked away.

A dozen Hunters in one place? Such was unheard of. Dominus had spoken about Hunters fighting in pairs, and he was the only Hunter I had ever fought side by side with. But a dozen? To kill me and this child? At this point, I didn't expect any negotiations. They'd kill me on sight. Nothing deterred their obsession and since I hadn't given the child to Philip, I was marked for death, too, because sending a dozen Hunters against one was overkill.

I was confused. They knew our destination, my name. How? Dominus might know, but he wasn't here to ask. Again, I missed receiving Jacques' advice. Something seemed amiss, and as usual, when I needed Hunter's insight the most, the spirits remained silent.

Bells gonged across the city, signifying the time. An hour before midnight. Perhaps it wasn't as bad as being midnight, but each heavy gong echoed an eerie tone, shattering the stillness of the night.

I stopped at the side of a building and reached into my pocket.

"What are you doing?" Penelope asked.

"Loading my gun and the crossbow."

"You plan to fight them?"

"To keep you, Father, and the others safe, I'll do whatever's necessary. I'll even die if I must to protect you."

Penelope placed her hand against my stomach. "You're not fighting them alone, Forrest."

She leaned up and kissed me. With my huge hands fumbling with the bullets in the dark, I didn't respond readily, so she turned to follow the swaying lanterns the priests carried.

Once the gun was loaded, I hurried to catch up to her. There were so many things I longed to tell her, but this wasn't the proper time or place. I wished I could stop everything else around us to talk heart to heart with her without outside interruptions.

A lot of changes were about to take place that I had never expected, and even if I possessed the foresight, I doubted the outcomes would have been any different.

CHAPTER 30

The underground tunnels were better maintained than the ones we had seen in London. Flickering torches inserted into iron sconces dimly lit the arched corridors. The torches were few and scattered, offering enough light to see the paths to each side of the water trenches. The dark shadowed recesses remained ample places for attackers to hide.

Iron lattices closed off some of the smaller side tunnels but didn't seem to be locked. Water gently flowed along the stone channels; the sound was deceptively reminiscent of a slow moving stream meandering through a mossy forest. Within the darkness it was easy to imagine being in such a place, but my attention focused more on potential enemies emerging with the intent of killing us.

The priests walked four abreast in a determined march. They moved fast enough that Father had a difficult time keeping up with them. Had they not carried oil lanterns, Father and Madeline would have probably lost sight of them. Penelope and I were able to use her night spectacles, which helped, but with only one lens each, it also limited us.

Madeline cradled Varak as she walked. He seemed to be asleep. Father fought to stay beside her while they walked.

Penelope and I stayed behind everyone else, constantly looking over our shoulders or toward the upcoming side tunnels. If any Hunters were down here, we wanted to see them before they attacked.

Since I didn't have any knowledge of the city layout, I didn't know how far from the Archdiocese we were. These tunnels intersected and probably covered several miles. Without guidance it wasn't difficult to get lost. I imagined a person could walk in circles for days and die of starvation before finding a way out.

Water splashed about twenty yards ahead of us. The four priests stopped and pressed themselves shoulder to shoulder, forming a tight human wall.

I moved closer to them. "What was that?"

"An intruder," Lucas said.

"A Hunter?"

"Possibly," he replied. "We're less than two blocks from the cathedral."

A large shadowed outline of a man moved past the lit sconce toward us and stopped.

"If it is one of them," I said, "make certain you get the child to the archbishop."

He nodded.

I jumped and stepped across the trench. Penelope followed without hesitation. The man remained near the light. I had the feeling that he stood in the path where we needed to go, and he didn't have any intention of moving. There wasn't anything we could do to avoid a confrontation with him.

He stepped away from the light and toward me. "Hunter, give us the child. Whatever you had hoped to accomplish has failed. Your hope and your life ends here."

I held my crossbow in my left hand aimed toward the rock floor. I raised my revolver and aimed for his chest. He was a massive man but a shot through the heart killed almost anything except the undead. He reared back his head and roared with laughter. I've never understood why someone would laugh when a loaded gun was pointed directly at him. Myself, I'd be looking for the quickest way to avoid getting shot. As large as he was, he wasn't swift enough to avoid the bullet's path or escape its speed, but he didn't seem to care. He kept laughing.

My finger tightened on the trigger, but the Hunter didn't make any effort to move. Before I squeezed the trigger, I was struck from my blindside, heaved into the air, and slammed to the ground on the other side of the trench. My crossbow dropped from my hand the moment I was hit. Upon landing, my gun jarred loose and slid across the floor until it hit the wall.

"Forrest!" Penelope shouted.

"Son!"

Something heavy landed atop me, pinning me down. I struggled to pull free, but my arms were wrapped tightly. I gnashed my teeth and growled, flexing my muscles, fighting to break free of his strong grip. I rolled to one side, pulling my assailant up slightly, and then I slung myself the opposite directions. His hold loosened enough that I was able to pull my right arm back and then I came around, clutching his throat. It was then I realized my attacker had been a second Hunter. Where he had come from, I didn't know because I had not seen anyone standing at the wall.

Tightening my grip around his neck, I slammed him against the wall a few feet from one of the torches. Both of his hands wrapped around my wrist as he fought to break my hold. I punched his gut several times with my left fist. He groaned and jerked with each blow. His throat muscles tightened and from the strange rasping sounds coming from his open mouth, his breathing was being cut off.

"Forrest, look out!" Father said.

I turned to the side, narrowly escaping the knife's blade. The knife thrown by the other Hunter struck the one I was choking in the chest, causing him to immediately release my wrist. His eyes widened as he realized what had happened. He slumped against the wall with his head bobbing slightly side to side. Instinctively, his hands made a feeble attempt to grip the hilt of the knife, but his zeal to fight was gone. His hands dropped to his sides. I watched the last moments of his life fade from his drooping eyes before I finally allowed his heavy body to collapse on the ground, which shoved the blade deeper into his chest.

Before the other Hunter attacked or threw another knife, I scooped my revolver off the ground. I turned toward him and fired. The bullet lodged into his shoulder. He growled in pain and rushed toward me. An arrow caught him in the throat. He staggered forward, gasping and wrapping his hand around the arrow shaft, but he kept coming. Anger and determination set in his crazed eyes.

I rushed toward him and struck his jaw with a harsh right. He fell backwards. In spite of the arrow, he tried to catch himself before he hit the ground but failed. He landed on his back, and I planted my knee on his chest.

He snapped the arrow shaft flush at this throat. Blood spurted from the hole. He gasped. His eyes grew fierce. His voice deepened. "You won't succeed. You cannot get past all of us."

"He's a child," I whispered near his ear.

"We know. That's why you must hand him over." He lifted his head off the floor, grabbed the arrow tip protruding out the back of his neck, and yanked it out before lowering his head. Blood spilled into a pool beneath him. Deep laughter rumbled in his throat, eventually going silent.

I rose to my feet and glanced toward the priests. They had surrounded Madeline and Varak and stood with their backs toward her. They appeared ready to fight to protect her, even though they had no visible weapons.

Father stepped beside me. He looked down and shook his head in regret. "Two dead Hunters."

Nausea welled inside of me. Although I hadn't killed either one of them, I couldn't shake the guilt pressing down on me.

Penelope frowned at the dead Hunter with disgust. "Had to break my arrow, didn't you?"

I sighed. These Hunters wouldn't have come to Freiburg if I hadn't brought Varak. I walked over to pick up my crossbow, which by some miracle had not fired when I dropped it.

"Are you okay?" Penelope asked.

"No. Hunters are dying because of me."

"Only because they are unwilling to look at your viewpoint," she replied.

I shrugged. "That doesn't matter. Vampire Hunters are not plentiful."

"And yet a dozen have shown here to oppose you?" she asked.

I glanced at Father. "Have you ever heard of anything like this? A dozen Hunters seeking to execute another Hunter?"

"No, son. Never. Nor have I seen more than a pair working together at a time, and that was to slay vampires, not one another."

I felt tears burning in my eyes. My shoulders drooped. A dozen Hunters had been summoned to kill me. And three dead were because of me. I had never imagined I'd be on the wrong side of the Chosen. I hadn't been a Hunter for more than a year. The burden of what was occurring was too much to withstand.

I was ready to surrender myself to the remaining Hunters and allow them to decide my fate before any more of them were killed. If protecting and keeping Varak alive was worthy of death, my life needed to end now. Perhaps I had carried this mission too far. I had tarnished my calling and was no longer worthy of being one of the Chosen.

"Forrest?" Penelope said softly. She knelt beside the Hunter she had shot with an arrow.

I looked at her. Surprise widened her eyes. "What is it?"

She took a deep breath and licked her lips. "These men ... they're not Hunters."

I frowned and came closer. "What do you mean?"

Father stepped nearer, too.

"See this mark?" She turned the man's hand palm up. On his wrist a dark symbol was inked into his skin. It resembled an eye, but not a human one. Something darker and evil.

"What is that?" I asked.

"A demon mark. The Mark of Krowl. Check the other man."

I hurried and turned his right hand up. The same mark was on this man's wrist, too.

I whispered, "If they're not Hunters, why do they want Varak?"

"I don't believe these men have any intention to kill him."

"They want him because of *what* he is?"

She nodded. "They are the cult worshippers of the demon Krowl. At the very least, they've taken his mark in return for gain, depending upon their level of loyalty."

"Loyalty?"

"Yes. They offer animal sacrifices to appease Krowl. The greater length they go to praise him, the larger their reward. These men are on the highest tier."

"Why?"

"They've been sent after Varak, knowing they must be willing to sacrifice their lives to get him. They cannot retreat. Krowl has probably blessed them and extracted all fear from their minds. They have no fear of dying. In their minds, death holds a great reward if they die while killing you."

"So there's nothing I can say to convince them to abandon their pursuit?"

She shook their head. "No. But if they get the child … they will use his power to destroy everything the Papacy views as holy."

"The Papacy? Why?"

"Because Jesuits discovered their cult years ago and tried to convert them. When they refused to worship in the manner the Jesuits insisted, the priests slaughtered nearly all of the Krowl worshippers as worthless infidels. A few dozen escaped."

"How do you know about this?" Father asked.

"As a Demon-hunter, I seek out all the information I can find about the demons. I have ancient tomes stored and hidden at my homestead. Books my father purchased around the world while he was slaying vampires. He brought them to me as gifts. I've studied them thoroughly. My father warned me about this group and told me the story. The reason they know we're here and what Varak is, is because their minds have become attuned to Krowl's."

I frowned. "By attuned, do you mean that he speaks directly to them?"

"Yes, and *through* them. He controls their minds and greatly influences their actions."

"Then Krowl knows these two men were killed?"

"I'm afraid so."

Lucas and the other priests came to us. "We can't stay in these tunnels any longer. We don't mind escorting you to the Archdiocese, but we aren't willing to sacrifice our lives by simply standing in one spot."

"I agree," I said.

"Too many passages converge into this one. If those two have already found you, the others will come soon," he said. "We must go."

He turned and walked away. The priests walked ahead with Madeline close behind. Father lingered behind with us as we walked. I didn't believe we'd reach the cathedral without encountering more cultists. The two had been difficult to take down, but if Krowl had actually seen his servants die, he'd sent more than two the next time. A lot more than two.

CHAPTER 31

"Why are Krowl's zealots posing as Hunters?" I asked.

"We might not ever know the true reason, but I think it is to confuse you," she said.

"Confuse me?"

"You mentioned it before. A true Hunter wouldn't set out to kill another Hunter. For a dozen Hunters to come after you, threatening to kill you, that's more than enough to shake anyone's resolve. Hasn't that made you question whether you're doing the right thing by delivering Varak to the Archdiocese?"

I nodded.

It was exactly how I felt. I had come to the point of laying down my life for my disobedience in bringing Varak to Freiburg. Other than Albert's prediction of what the child would become, I had never been warned about sparing the hybrid. It had been sternly implied by Albert and myself. Even now, I hadn't received any direct insight to inform me of exactly what should be done. I only knew what I believed to be the right solution.

Ahead of us the tunnel brightened. I smelled burnt sulfur. A thin layer of smoke hung overhead. Fire flickered along the passageway floor. In between the building smoke and the rising flames, the large shadows of six zealots standing side by side loomed. All were dressed like Hunters and every one of them was an imposter.

Father Lucas and the other priests stopped walking. They shielded Madeline and Varak behind themselves. Each priest took his silver cross in hand and held them up where these Krowl followers could see them, which gave me an idea.

One of the shadowed men said, "Give us the child."

I threw a globe-shaped bottle of holy water as hard as I could, striking the man's forehead. The glass shattered, splashing the water on his face and neck. Some of the holy water struck a man to each side of him. The man's limp body dropped.

I didn't expect the holy water to have the same effect on these men as it would vampires, but it did something I had hoped might occur. The other two men dropped to their knees, clutching their heads in their hands, screaming at the top of their lungs.

"What did you do?" Penelope asked.

"You said that Krowl was linked to their minds?"

She nodded.

"I figured since priests used holy water when they excised demons, the water should work on these cultists as well." I pulled my silver cross from my pocket.

"But they're not possessed by evil spirits, Forrest," she said. "He's only linking himself to their minds. It's not the same thing."

"Then how do you explain that?" I pointed to the three men on their knees in anguish.

"I—I don't know."

I shrugged. "I don't either. Maybe the holy water blocks his link?"

Lucas glanced toward us with a confused stare.

"Do you know a rite of exorcism?" Penelope asked him.

He nodded. "Of course we do. Why?"

"Forrest splashed them with holy water to sever the demon's control over them. Maybe if you excise it will finish breaking Krowl's bond with them."

Lucas turned toward the anguished men and chanted in Latin. The other three priests joined in. As their voices rose in unison, the cultists fell facedown on the floor in agony, squeezing the sides of their heads. They weren't about to recover enough to attack us anytime soon.

I took my last bottle of holy water from my pocket and flung it toward the other three men who had stepped away from their ailing companions. The bottle struck the man's cheek. The impact knocked him unconscious. He dropped to the floor, but the bottle didn't break. The two men beside him leaned down and shook him, trying to awaken him. Getting no response, they turned toward us.

Penelope fired an arrow into the closest man's chest. He gasped and spiraled around, but he didn't fall. His thick overcoat might have prevented the arrow from going deep enough to be fatal. By my estimate, she had missed his heart but had probably punctured his lung. Without my noticing she pulled another arrow and fired again. This arrow caught his shoulder. He clumsily spun and fell backwards into the burning debris on the floor. He wailed, tried to push himself out of the fire, but instead, he fell deeper into the flames.

The three cultists that the priests were chanting a rite over lay still. I didn't know if they were dead or not, but at least for now, we didn't need to worry about fighting them.

That left only one more who was uninjured in the tunnel we needed to be concerned about. With my silver cross dagger, I rushed toward the cultist and yelled at Lucas, "Take Madeline and the baby into the Archdiocese!"

The Krowl worshipper snarled at me. He widened his stance, expecting me to plow into him, but instead, I reached down for the unbroken vial of holy water. I uncorked it and flung most of the contents into his face. As he dropped to his knees, I pressed the silver cross to his forehead. Even though I didn't know a whole lot about combating demons, I had the impression they fled from whatever people believed to be holy.

When the cross touched his flesh, he struggled momentarily. He clutched my wrist with both hands, but his fingers trembled too badly for him to maintain a strong enough grip. Before he collapsed into unconsciousness, a deep voice bellowed through the man's mouth in a language I didn't recognize.

Penelope stood beside me. "We need to catch up to them."

I glanced around. "Where's Father?"

"He went with Madeline."

"Did you hear that strange voice?"

"Yes."

"Any idea what he said?"

"Since it was Krowl, I imagine it wasn't good," she replied. "Probably a curse."

We ran along the narrow path near the right-hand wall to avoid the smoldering debris. The fire had died down, but the smoke became a lot thicker. My eyes and throat burned. Tears blurred my vision, further obstructing my view through the smoky haze. Once we made our way outside the smoke-filled section of the tunnel, the priests' lanterns became visible. They were making their way up a spiral set of stairs.

I wiped the tears from my eyes and slowed my pace, carefully searching through the shadows and behind us, wondering if more cultists might make a last effort to stop us, but none did.

We hurried up the stairs and stepped out inside the front entrance of the cathedral. Father stood next to Madeline and Varak. We stopped beside them near a large bowl of water. Burning candles flickered everywhere, on the walls, the tables, and railings, lighting the entire sanctuary. The vaulted ceilings seemed to rise forever without end, as the glow of the candles didn't carry that far.

The four priests were talking to a man wearing an elegant red robe in the wide center aisle. I assumed this to be the archbishop. The priests appeared to show humbleness as they stood before him. They spoke in hushed tones, occasionally glancing in our direction. After several minutes, the archbishop motioned us toward him.

He was tall, thin, and slightly stooped. His short gray hair was almost hidden beneath the tall mitre hat he wore. The smoothness of his face indicated he was probably in his early forties. His kind smile and peaceful gaze dispensed comfort, almost making you forget your deepest fears and worries. I had met few men with such charismatic appeal.

"According to Father Lucas," the archbishop said, "you have incapacitated eight of the twelve cultists who have attempted to imprison us because of your intended arrival. You're safe in our sanctuary. They cannot pass through these doors."

"But they can," Penelope said.

The man shook his head and offered a kind smile. "Child, you mustn't worry. They cannot. They arrived in a group of twelve. A cult's strength is strongest when they gather all thirteen of their highest council. They only brought twelve."

She shook her head. "No. There *are* thirteen. Krowl is the thirteenth. He came with them. He was linked inside each of them."

The archbishop narrowed his eyes for a moment, thinking, and then he returned to his peaceful, reassuring smile. "This is a holy sanctuary, blessed by God and our priests. The doors have been locked and secured. Even if the demon broke through the doors, he cannot cross the threshold into our cathedral."

"Krowl can," she said.

The archbishop's smile partially faded. He didn't like his authority challenged. His voice became angry. "The demon you speak of cannot defile our holy sanctuary. I believe I know more about demons than you."

A brief flash of anger stirred in her eyes. She took a quick deep breath, somehow calming herself. "I'm a Demon-hunter. I've killed various types of demons. The majority of them cannot enter into your sanctuary, but Krowl is different. He can, and if you don't help me, he's going to burst through that door and kill all of us."

"*How* is he any different than other demons? How can he defile our cathedral and not be instantly destroyed by the holiness of our Lord?"

"Because of the Papacy," she replied.

"What?" the archbishop frowned. "How dare you speak such blasphemy."

Father Lucas stepped up and took her by the arm forcefully. "It's time that you should leave."

Penelope yanked free of his hold. "No. I've not finished explaining. Krowl is a demon dedicated to destroying everything you hold holy. He has no fear of what you've blessed because of the Jesuit priests who slaughtered his worshippers."

"Those cultists were infidels, unbelievers, and worthy of the fate they received," the archbishop replied.

She shook her head. "To call such judgment puts you into God's place, but you're *not* God. You're a man."

The four priests gasped in horror. They looked around in fear as if the earth would shake and lightning hurled from the ceilings.

Anger tightened her brow. "Krowl knows this. He sees this. His vile hatred and lust for revenge is far greater than your petty faith. He will take great pleasure in torturing you until you are dead. And unless I get your cooperation, he's coming to kill all of us, but especially *you*."

Father Lucas frowned at her. "We took care of eight of the cultists in the passageway. That should have made him weaker."

She smiled and shook her head. "No, it has made him stronger."

"How?"

"Krowl had possessed the twelve men, so his power and strength were spread out amongst them. Each time his power was cast out of one, the others increased in power. After driving Krowl out of the other eight, instead of us weakening him, we have allowed him to grow stronger inside the other four. He's outside the door. I sense him and his anger is growing, but if you'll help me, I can draw him out and kill him."

Lucas flicked his gaze to the archbishop. The pale archbishop wiped perspiration from his brow and nodded.

"What do you need?" Lucas asked.

"Blessed salt. At least a pound of it," she replied.

Lucas motioned to one of the other priests. He hurried down a side aisle and through another door.

Penelope lowered her quiver to the floor and untied a side pouch I'd never noticed. She removed her silver dagger with odd symbols etched into its blade and handle. "Everyone clear the center aisle. This is where I plan to capture him."

The archbishop gave her a skeptical gaze. "Capture him? Exactly what do you mean?"

She didn't reply with word or gesture. Instead, she busied herself with various tools inside the pouch.

"Wait," I whispered to her.

"What, Forrest?" She beamed with her cute smile. "I don't have much time."

"You're not planning to use the symbol the healer gave you, are you?"

"I'm left with little choice."

"It might not work or it might cause something more catastrophic."

She shook her head. "No. I studied the one Flora had trapped those plague demons with. I believe the same circle will work. Trust me?"

With my life, apparently. I looked at the archbishop. "Just do what she says."

He held a strange side-glance toward me. His face flushed red, from anger I guessed. It was easy to see he didn't like someone else telling him what to do. At this point, I really didn't care. I wanted this demon destroyed before he had a chance to take Varak and commit horrible atrocities against mankind. Penelope was the best hope we had to destroy Krowl, provided she had been given the correct symbol to use.

CHAPTER 32

 e cleared the center aisle and positioned ourselves along the outer edge of the cathedral pews. I took a few minutes to admire the vaulted ceilings, the towering pillars, and the stained glass windows. The artwork was breathtaking. I'd been in a few cathedrals, but of all the ones I had ever entered, this was the most picturesque one. Great detail had been painstakingly patterned into every facet with untiring dedication.

The priest returned with a large bag of salt and handed it to Penelope. She untied the drawstring and carefully formed a large circle on the floor. The layer of salt was at least an inch thick and three inches wide. Once she finished the circle, she began making smaller symbols inside the circle. She paused after she completed each one, closed her eyes, and chanted before starting the next one.

No one spoke while she worked. I was too intrigued, wondering what each symbol meant. Her delicate artwork was quite exquisite and an amazing talent I wasn't aware that she possessed. After she finished, she walked to the altar, took three lit candles, and positioned them equal distance from one another around the outside of the circle. She studied her layout for several moments. She walked to the edge of the circle and seemed careful not to allow the toes of her shoes to touch the salt. She outstretched her left hand over the salt symbols and pricked her finger with the dagger until several drops of blood dropped, combining with the salt.

The four priests and the archbishop looked appalled. They frowned with curiosity, whispering amongst themselves.

Penelope positioned herself between the salt circle and the altar. "Everyone be prepared. He's coming."

The front entrance doors rattled, shook. The intensity increased, shaking with violent urgency. The priests looked at one another in terror as the doors splintered inward and showered into millions of tiny wood fragments. The last four cultists stood side by side at the threshold. These men appeared much larger than all the others. Pure evil hardened their faces. Their attention was on Penelope, but none of them moved.

"See?" the archbishop said. His voice was haughty. His smile was more prideful than a humble man's should be. He stood, holding his elegant staff in hand. "They cannot come inside."

Penelope ignored him.

No sooner had he spoken the words than did these four men rush through the door. The archbishop released a high-pitched scream. His staff clattered on the floor.

The four men ran down the center aisle straight for Penelope. All four spoke in unison with loud bellowing voices that weren't theirs and echoed off the walls and the vaulted ceiling. It was Krowl speaking through all of them. "Today your blood spills as a sacrifice to me unless you kneel and offer me your homage."

Two of the priests fainted between the pews. The other two paled and held their crosses out before them. The archbishop was stunned. He lowered himself into the pew. His lips trembled. When he glanced toward me, I shook my head with disappointment. I wondered why Albert wanted the child to be brought to this particular cathedral. This man was a coward and apparently lacked real faith in his god.

"Neither are happening, Krowl," Penelope said sternly.

The four men stood near the circle but dared not attempt to cross it.

She raised her hands and spoke phrases in Latin. The hundreds of burning candles in the sanctuary were snuffed in an instant. We stood in complete darkness. A deep guttural growl bellowed near where Penelope stood in the aisle. Bluish-white flickering sparks permeated off a giant demon's horn-covered back. Full of muscle and thickly scaled skin, Krowl towered ten feet in height. His hideous face had sharp tusks that hung from his odd shaped mouth. Drool dripped from his mouth. He was the most hideous creature I had ever seen.

Penelope stood less than a foot away from him, unafraid. To me, it seemed he could have struck her with the palm of his hand and probably killed her instantly, but he didn't budge. He was trapped inside the salt symbol she had drawn, frozen.

She lifted the dagger high in her right hand. "To the abyss!"

"Fool!" Krowl shouted, writhing in pain as flames licked up from the floor and blazed around his legs. "Banishing me to the abyss has sealed your fate for far worse curses in your life. You shall know undying misery. You foolish, foolish girl!"

The flames rose and engulfed him. He released a high-pitched howl, bursting several of the stain-glassed windows. In an instant, he vanished.

The two conscious Priests rushed with their lanterns toward the center aisle. The four men lay dead on the floor. Apparently when he was pulled from their minds, they were unable to withstand it.

Penelope lay on the floor. I hurried and knelt beside her. She was panting. Her eyes were closed. Sweat covered her face. What she had done seemed to have drained her strength. She was exhausted. I sat beside her, and she curled herself against me, resting her head against my chest.

"I told you it would work," she said with a wide grin.

"That you did."

The two priests began lighting candles.

Father came to us. "Are you okay?"

She gave a slight nod.

After a few minutes, the archbishop found the courage to stand and left the bench where he had sat terrified while she banished the demon.

"What is this magic you have cast within our sanctuary?" he demanded.

"What?" I asked, glaring at him.

"No magic," she said weakly.

"The symbol," he replied. "Your blood offering upon it. These are things witches perform, not saints. Not Christians."

Penelope took a deep breath, frowned. She attempted to push herself up but still didn't have adequate strength. "I am not a witch. I'm a Demon-hunter."

The archbishop glanced around the sanctuary. "Where are the others of your coven?"

"Coven?" she said. "I have no coven."

"You must. Where are the other twelve? Otherwise, you'd not possess such power."

"You said that about Krowl's circle, too," she said softly. "Thirteen for power? Is that what you consider a coven to be?"

"Yes. It's what the Papacy has known for centuries. Twelve is the absolute," he replied. "Thirteen is—"

"Is it now?" Penelope replied, finding enough strength to sit on her knees. Fury creased her brow. "Then what you claim as reasons for your faith is nothing more than covens, too."

"How dare you make such claims. You blasphemer."

"It's in your scriptures," she replied. "Twelve tribes of Israel plus one God equals thirteen. Jesus and twelve disciples equals thirteen. Is that not the same mathematics you're using?"

The archbishop paled. His posture stiffened and his jaw tightened. Perhaps he had never looked at those groups in the same light as she described. He didn't offer a rebuttal.

"You seem resentful that I was the one who banished him and not you," she said. "But it's not a competition. I don't cast evil spirits out. I kill or banish demons. When they are banished they are trapped inside a fiery pocket in the center of the earth where they cannot escape. What you and your fellow priests do by excising the evil spirits you *incorrectly call demons* doesn't kill them, it sends them out to find a new host to possess. You don't eliminate the problem. Instead you allow the demon to torment another poor soul."

"I watched you add your blood to whatever you had drawn on the floor. How is that not magic? Dark sorcery?" he asked with a less accusatory tone. "And do you not use a spell of some sort?"

"No different than any prayer you offer for blessings, healing, or a divine touch."

"Are you comparing yourself with me?" he asked in a condescending manner.

"Not at all," she replied.

Father looked at me. "Are you certain we should leave Varak with this man? A man who has no appreciation for what Penelope has done to save not only our lives, but *his*? She risked her life to confront Krowl and banish him, and rather than acknowledging her success, he's retorted with accusations and condemnation. I've never seen such an ungrateful sack of bones in my entire life, and one who considers himself *holy* at that. He's a disgrace for what the Archdiocese deserves to have as an Archbishop, and I perceive *nothing* holy about him."

Those words cut deep. The archbishop looked genuinely disconcerted and hurt. His sad eyes regarded each of us, one by one. "My apologies. You're right. I've placed my authority equal to God and unfairly judged your actions."

"True," I replied. "You did. And even worse is your cowardice after the demon appeared. Surely one who believes in the power of his God would not have trembled in the presence of something that should be considered weaker. Yet, you did, and two of your priests fainted. I view you as someone far less worthy of the position granted to you by the ones who placed you in this cathedral."

I stood and helped Penelope to her feet. Even after she stood, she clung tightly to my hand. Her legs were still weak and without holding onto me, she'd have collapsed. I helped her to the closest pew where she quickly sat down.

"I oversee a lot of issues as the archbishop, within the church and with city officials, but understand that it's not every day a priest or bishop expects to encounter a fiendish demon from the pits of Hell.

Even those of us who excise demons must have a pure heart by offering penance and confessing our sins before our Lord. Without doing so, we are not worthy challengers to even rebuke the weakest demon. If we're not spotless and without blemish, an unleashed demon can rip us to shreds or worse, it can possess us."

I frowned. "Are you saying that you weren't afraid of Krowl?"

"No. I was terrified."

"Because you lack faith?"

"No. As I said, I had not offered penance or confessed my sins for the day."

"And what sins would a man of your status be subjected to?" I asked.

"Every man is assaulted by various lusts and stray thoughts, even I. Entertaining such thoughts for a long amount of time is considered sin in itself. Gaining excess money, power, or even misleading others are dangerous temptations, especially when the one who benefits from these actions are intentionally committing them. Some would also say even if they aren't intentional, they are sin just the same."

"And such are what held you back this evening?" I asked.

He shook his head. "No. I'm simply expressing there's a wild array of enticements. Minds wander. Had I known I was about to face a demon face-to-face, I could have been prepared. But, since Krowl emerged through his believers, my mind was racing to determine if I could face him."

I didn't believe him. What I had seen was genuine fear, and that wasn't something so easily dismissed. But he was in a high position within the Catholic Church and was trying to find a redeemable way to make his actions seem less cowardice. Reacting in fear like he had wasn't easily counterfeited. It was real. Since I was tired and didn't wish to be in Freiburg any longer than necessary, I decided not to press the issue further. He held no authority over me, so his spinelessness wasn't necessarily my concern.

The archbishop offered a friendly smile. "I realize I've made a horrible first impression, and for that, I simply ask your forgiveness. I'm sincerely sorry for my behavior." The archbishop tucked his chin to his chest and closed his eyes.

I glanced toward Father and then to Penelope. Both shrugged. I believed they were as exhausted and ready to leave as I was.

"Accepted," I replied.

The archbishop opened his eyes. Both Father and Penelope nodded toward him. "You truly are gracious. You've traveled a long distance to bring me this child. The only forewarning of your arrival was Krowl's cultists who had come to take him by force. The child must be of some importance for a demon to bring twelve men to try to kill you. Do you mind explaining exactly why the demon wanted him and why this particular place was chosen?"

Sadly, the archbishop could never know the truth about the child. The consequences were too severe. I shook my head. "Penelope should have asked while she held him captive in the circle and before she banished him forever."

He frowned. "You don't know?"

"I'm afraid that knowledge went into the abyss with the demon."

"Then what is your purpose for bringing him to this Archdiocese?"

"He's an orphan," I replied.

"Yes, Father Lucas informed me. But our curiosity begs one question, 'Why this cathedral?'"

"It was a request, and nothing more can I provide. What matters is that we've fulfilled our part by getting him here safely," I replied.

"And why should I accept this child? Do you realize the cost of rearing a child and having someone nurture and oversee the child's welfare?"

"Varak has a caretaker. Madeline is more than happy to tend to his needs."

Madeline walked over to us, rocking the boy in her arms. Varak slept in absolute peace with a little smile curled on his lips.

The archbishop stared down at the child and then to her. "Is this true? You'll care for the child if we provide a place for him?"

She smiled eagerly, in spite of the tears moistening her eyes. "Of course. I cannot picture my life without him."

A tender smile came to his face. He could tell the love she held for the child, as could we, but in ways, I wondered if her love wasn't actually an *obsession*.

A short time later, Father Lucas showed us to the rooms where we could stay the night. I had insisted we get rooms in town, but the priests assured us that all the inns had closed for the night. I was content knowing we had succeeded in getting the hybrid child to Freiburg, and more elated to learn that I hadn't been the direct target of other Hunters. However, my sleep wasn't any more peaceful.

CHAPTER 33

The following morning the priests were gracious enough to fill my empty vials with holy water. They had witnessed how effective a weapon it was against the cultists, but after I explained how it aided me against vampires, they were happy to bless as much water as I needed.

We left the Archdiocese and walked to the nearest lodge where we could buy a hearty breakfast. We discussed our plans to reach Schaffhausen to slay Ambrose. A train could get us to the city within a few hours. Father expressed selling the horse and coach so we weren't constantly reminded of Thomas. In a way, I agreed, but I didn't want to dismiss Thomas' contribution for how close he had gotten us to Freiburg. It was a shame he had died like he had, but dying from the plague would have been far worse.

With Madeline remaining at the Archdiocese, we were down to three, which was more manageable and reduced our costs greatly.

As we rose to leave, Penelope noticed a newspaper on the table next to ours. The two sailors who had been eating at the table had gone and left the paper behind. Strangely the newspaper was from America and the date more recent than I might have expected, being as no one could have traveled to Schaffhausen from the west coast of America in so little time.

Penelope read the headlines about a great fire in Seattle, Washington in the United States. She scanned through the various photographs in the newspaper. Her eyes widened.

"What is it?" I asked.

She pointed at the photo. "Look."

I frowned, looking closer, nodding. "The city was engulfed in flames. What else am I missing?"

"The demon. Don't you see him? In the midst of the flames."

I shook my head. "No."

She gasped.

"What's wrong?"

Penelope looked at me with fear in her eyes. She pointed to different places in the photograph. "There are dozens of them, Forrest. The fire that burned Seattle occurred because a portal to Hell had been opened."

"What?" I asked, slightly grinning.

"You don't believe me?" She looked hurt. "Do you think I'd jest about that?"

"I don't see any demons in the photographs," I replied. "Honest."

She bit her lower lip and closed her eyes. When she opened them, she studied the pictures again, shaking her head. "Maybe you can't see them because you aren't a Demon-hunter?"

I shrugged. "I suppose that could be why. But I really don't see them. I see fire, smoke, and steam from the water hitting the flames. Nothing else. Sorry. But did you notice the date of the paper?"

She glanced at it. "So? You think this is a hoax?"

"It might be. I cannot see how a traveler from America could arrive here in such a short amount of time. That would be beyond record time for the world's fastest ship. It cannot be done."

"Perhaps it's a sign by a higher force, giving me the information so I can act quickly."

"Or it's a trap."

"A trap? How and by whom?" she asked.

"Penelope, you just banished a powerful demon who placed a curse upon you before it was silenced from our world."

"And you think this newspaper would be the curse? The story is very troubling."

I shrugged. "I don't know much about curses and how they work."

She stared at the paper for several minutes, flipping from page to page, and then she neatly folded it where the front story was the only article visible. "Forrest, I don't think it's a curse. I believe there's a reason I've been given the information, even though, like you said, it doesn't seem possible to get this newspaper so quickly except my help is required."

"In what way, Penelope?" I asked, taking her hand into mine.

"To seal it? I'm not sure, but I have to travel to Seattle to be certain."

"Why?"

"If the portal has been opened and hasn't been closed, the world edges toward total destruction. Come with me?"

Father frowned at her. "We have plans to take the train to Schaffhausen. Can't this wait until after—"

She shook her head. "No. Don't you understand how dangerous such a portal is?"

"I imagine it presents an enormous danger." I rubbed my thumb against the back of her hand. "Penelope, as much as I want to help, I'm not a Demon-hunter. Father isn't either. We'd be useless in such a battle."

She placed her hands over her eyes and shook her head. After a few seconds, she pulled back her hair and paced the floor. "It's my duty to go, Forrest."

"It's suicide if you go alone," I said. "Please stay with us? After we slay Ambrose, we'll all travel to Seattle. We'll have more than enough money to board a fast ship."

Penelope looked at me. She was torn inside. Her eyes reflected her inner turmoil. "I want to, Forrest. I think I'm falling in ... No, I *am* in love with you. I've never felt this way before."

Father's face reddened. He gave me a hopeful smile and walked out the door, giving us added privacy.

"Penelope, I've never felt this strongly about anyone else, either," I replied. "I know I love you, too. Father and I have vowed to slay Ambrose. We could use your help. Had Lorcan not already given us a deposit, we'd leave with you now. Accompany us, and once we've slain him, we will sail with you to Seattle."

I pulled her close and embraced her. She buried her face against the center of my chest. Hot tears soaked into my undershirt.

"We cannot wait that long," she said. "As it is, even if I leave on a ship tomorrow, it will be months before I reach Seattle. By then, I might be too late."

I hugged her tighter and whispered into her ear. "Then don't go. Won't Demon-hunters nearer to Seattle be alerted and travel there to eradicate these demons?"

Penelope pulled back and looked up into my eyes. "It's possible, but again, the dangers of an open portal to Hell are catastrophic."

"If you're the only one who arrives in Seattle, the portal will have been opened for at least three months before you can get a chance to close it."

"It's better than no one sealing it at all."

"Do you even know how to seal a portal?" I asked.

She looked away.

"You don't, do you?"

Her eyes flicked to mine. "I'll find a way."

"Won't demons guard and protect the portal, so more of their kind can pass through?"

Her tiny shoulders shrugged. "I don't know, Forrest. I've never dealt with a situation like this before."

"All the more reason why you don't need to go alone."

She sighed. "I don't see any alternative. I must obey my instinct and my calling."

I recognized the determination in her eyes. I couldn't talk her out of going or delaying her departure. I forced a smile and embraced her tightly. With her in my arms, I ached terribly inside. Tears etched down my cheeks. I shook, and her arms tightened around my waist. She sobbed, too.

I paid for our breakfast, and we met Father outside. He stood in a corner of the building smoking his pipe outside of the brisk wind. When his gaze met mine, his eyes saddened. I suppose he read the pain in my eyes.

"What's your decision?" he asked her.

Penelope bit her lower lip and looked away.

"Father, do you mind letting us have some time to ourselves?"

He puffed his pipe, offered a forced smile, and nodded. "I will go get the horse and coach and see if I can get a decent offer at one of the stables. Where shall we meet later?"

I pulled my watch from my pocket and checked the time. "Here, for lunch?"

He nodded. The sadness in his eyes didn't lessen, but he didn't try to persuade Penelope with arguments. I imagine he expected I already had. He turned and walked down the street.

She and I took a short walk, found a bench, and in spite of the cold winter wind, we sat huddled together. Few words were exchanged between us. We held one another close, and after neither of us could shed any more tears, I stared into her beautiful eyes for the longest time. I couldn't shake the hurt inside. I had told her how much I loved her and how I needed her to be a part of my life. Nothing persuaded her to stay, even though she said that she felt the same. I felt like there was more I needed to tell her, but I had said everything I could think of. I suppose there aren't any proper sequences of words that can explain the cries of a tattered heart as it struggles to piece itself whole once more.

She placed her hand to my cheek and smiled. I swallowed hard, trying to make the painful lump in my throat disappear. I leaned closer to her, and we shared our first real kiss. Her warm lips were soft and salty from her tears. A flood of emotions poured through me as her lips pressed against mine and she wrapped her arms around my neck. If I could have picked a moment to last forever, this would have been it.

I wrapped my arms around her waist and never wanted to let her go. I loved everything about her and feared releasing her. But it was getting close to noon. The sun slipped behind thick dismal clouds. "Are you certain you cannot wait until after Father and I kill the vampire?"

She placed both hands on my cheeks. Fresh tears dampened her eyes. "I want to, truly I do, but what if you learned about a city being overrun by vampires. Would you stay with me or go fulfill the duty you've been chosen to do?"

I closed my eyes, unable to answer.

"See?" she said. "You'd do what you needed to do and what you believed was required of you."

I nodded. I tried to sound bold, but the tears and pain fractured my voice. "Penelope, we've not known one another long, but I've never wanted to part ways since we've met. I certainly didn't expect one of us to leave this soon."

She leaned her head against my chest and sighed. She didn't say anything more. I stood and hefted her in my arms, carrying her back to the lodge. Father stood in the corner out of the wind, cleaning out his pipe. He had my Hunter box and her quiver. How he managed to bring all of our belongings by himself was beyond me.

Penelope stepped inside the lodge to get our table while I helped Father gather our things.

"I sold the horse and coach. Not for what they were worth, but we're pressed for time—"

"That's good, Father. Something's better than nothing."

Father asked a lot of questions, but I hurt too much inside to offer any answers. He nodded and offered a sympathetic smile. "When you need to talk, son, I'll be here to listen. Heartaches are hell."

I felt lost and numb inside. My stomach ached worse than any other time I could remember. I wanted to hold her so badly and never let her go, but I knew I couldn't. It wouldn't be right. She'd resent me if I kept her from going.

I had even considered getting rooms for the night and hoped by morning, a new premonition might occur to convince her to stay. But I feared if we stayed together another night, we'd give into our intimacy for one another to consume our sorrow. I wasn't anywhere near ready in my mind to leap that chasm, especially since we were parting ways, and perhaps she wasn't either, even though we both seemed to be dying on the inside.

CHAPTER 34

$\mathcal{W}$ hile we sat at the table for lunch, I had no appetite at all. I was experiencing the worst stomach and chest pains imaginable, so I pushed my plate aside. Whenever I glanced toward her, tears burned my eyes. Tears leaked down her cheeks. I tried to speak, but no words came. Even Father didn't attempt to start conversation. He face was flushed. He wasn't able to look at either of us.

After the quietest lunch ever, Father and I walked her to the river's dock where she purchased a ticket. Father stood beside me on the dock. Penelope took my hands and stared into my eyes. Sadness and regret filled her eyes.

"Are you certain you cannot delay your departure until after we slay Ambrose?" I asked.

She shook her head. "I wish I could."

I considered abandoning the pursuit of Ambrose until later, but I had already taken Lorcan's deposit. I'm certain the vampire would consider that theft, if he learned we had left for North America.

"I want you to have these," she said, untying the goggles from around her neck. "I know how much you like them."

I shook my head. "Penelope ... I can't take these. You need them when you're fighting."

She placed them into my hands and closed my fingers over them. "I can get another pair. Besides, I want you to have something to remember me until I return."

"Do you really think I could ever forget you, Penelope? I never shall. You possess my heart, and still I ask that you wait until we can accompany you."

She rose on tiptoe and kissed my lips softly. I leaned down and we kissed more passionately. When she pulled back, she said, "This isn't goodbye, Forrest. It's just that I need obey what I know in my heart I must do. Like you did when you brought Varak to the Archdiocese in spite of all the obstacles. Our paths will cross again."

Penelope hurried toward the plank. I noticed Father wiping away tears as she boarded the ship. I ached inside even though I could still see her, but seeing her walking away, getting farther from my touch, I thought my heart would cease beating or explode from the intensifying ache. Inside, I wanted to run after her. I should have gone with her to help her like she had helped us.

She had promised once she had gone and sealed the portal in Seattle that she would board the next ship and sail to meet me in Bucharest. I feared it would never happen. I didn't believe I'd ever see her again. My doubts reinforced my former oath to walk this world alone and not to give my heart to another.

Penelope had helped us get Varak to Freiburg and safely inside the Archdiocese where the archbishop and nuns could protect him. We had protected the child against great odds and from the attack of a dozen demon cultists, which had forced Penelope to kill a powerful demon that had marked her with a curse. But I had never fathomed she'd leave my side to become vulnerable to something she considered an actual threat. I had thought we'd fight the battles together.

We were both similar in our projected dark destinies. Before it was revealed that the cultists weren't actual Hunters who had been sent to kill me because I had committed a major transgression against the Chosen, I had accepted that my punishment was being issued. I was to compensate for what could be no less than direct disobedience against those who had called me into their Order as a Vampire Hunter. The dangers of allowing a half-blood vampire human was too great a risk and worthy of my death. Because of that, I feared tremendous loss in my life, overshadowing doom, and heartache unlike what I was experiencing right now. Deep inside, I truly didn't believe I'd escape unscathed for protecting Varak. Bad events were coming. I sensed it. And Penelope could become my first painful loss.

A day away from her would be painful, but the voyage along various rivers and across the seas was months in one direction. I didn't have any way to reach her or to know the outcome when she eventually faced the demons. All I could do was wonder what had occurred until ... *if* ... we ever met again. Could she get the portal sealed before a horde of demons killed her? Evil spirits had never possessed her, but from what I understood, these demons must be stronger than any she had faced before if they torn open a portal from Hell.

Father and I stood, waving. Penelope waved back. After a half hour of watching the ship sail down the river, Father wiped tears from his eyes. "I'm sorry, son. There was nothing to convince her to stay?"

"No, Father. She holds to her obligations as stubbornly as I do. I suppose we were right for one another." My voice broke, and I wiped tears from my eyes.

Father sniffed and rubbed his nose with the back of his hand. "There are no words at a time like this. I'm sorry."

I shrugged and stared at the spectacles she had given me.

"Come on," he said. "Let me buy you a drink. It won't erase your pain, but it might numb it a bit."

I clasped my father's shoulder. "No, Father. That's okay. I need to experience this pain and hope it eases over time. Numbing it only prolongs it."

He smiled. His bloodshot eyes remained wet from his crying. "Son, you are indeed a man."

CHAPTER 35

*T*here are many levels of pain. Some are physical injuries that heal slowly over time. Those brutal inflictions to the heart and mind and soul seldom heal enough to completely vanish. They might fade, but often memories jar and bump the bruise again, causing the tenderness to swell. An anguish soul never heals. One just has to deal with it the best way possible.

The first two days aboard the train were steady but slow. I believed we could have ridden on horseback to our destination faster than the steam engine train traveled, but not during the harsh winter weather.

Father and I sat across from one another. He read a couple of books he had purchased before our departure in Freiburg and seldom spoke while I stared out the window thinking about Penelope. I was thankful for the quiet and enjoyed the scenery outside the window.

I reserved crying until after he had fallen asleep. Tears seemed the greatest comfort, and I wondered about Penelope and how she was faring. I felt absurd, wondering if she had already forgotten me. Her absence hurt so much.

I stared at my Hunter box between my feet and thought back to the night when the vampire had attacked Father, and I had learned my fate. While I had faulted my father for several months for not having told me sooner, I understood why he had not and his purpose for not doing so. I was his son, his only child. All he wanted was to protect me from the grief and agony that came from being a Vampire Hunter. His delay had not been strictly from selfishness or jealousy, as I had believed. It was parental love in its purest form.

The train pulled into the Schaffhausen station a few hours before sunset. As we stepped off the train, Father said, "Did you enjoy the ride?"

"It was pleasant enough," I said, tightening my coat collar and straightening my hat to brace myself from the harsh cold wind.

He tapped tobacco into his pipe and smiled. "I tried not to disturb you since you have so much on your mind."

"I appreciate that, Father."

Father lighted his pipe and puffed small streams of smoke. "Shall we find an inn first?"

I nodded. "That would be good. We get settled first, find somewhere to dine, and then follow that map to where Ambrose's lair is. Provided Lorcan has been honest with us."

"You're skeptical about everything, son."

"It pays to be if you wish to live a long life. Besides, he's a vampire, and I will never trust one of them."

"When do you wish to attempt to slay him?" Father asked.

"If his lair is where the map indicates, we do it while it's still daylight. I'd rather stake him while he's resting in his coffin. Quicker, quieter, and easier."

Father grinned.

"What?"

"You only want to get this done faster so you can take a ship to catch up with Penelope."

I shrugged. "I do, but we still have to collect the bounty from Lorcan before I can consider sailing to Seattle. We cannot afford to leave any loose ends. Besides, such a trip will be costly since we have no idea how long we'll need to reside in America. We'll need the rest of the money."

"That's true."

By the time we found an inn and put our belongings inside, the sun was an hour from setting. We happened upon a man who had a horse harnessed to a small wagon. He was young, probably still in his late teens, and lanky. He offered us a ride near our destination for a small fee. I gladly accepted because with Father's stiff legs, it'd take us three times longer on foot.

After a half hour, the driver turned toward us. "From where have you two traveled?"

"London," I replied.

"You've journeyed far," he replied.

"We have."

He frowned. "What's your interest in this old mountain trail? Most folks in the city won't come anywhere near the trail. They believe the surrounding woods are haunted. A lot of tourists have come to this trail but most have never returned."

"Really?" Father asked.

"Yes. Near the top, I am told, is a cave that overlooks the Rhine River. But with all the stories, I'd never attempt walking along the trail. I certainly would never *enter* the cave."

He stopped the wagon near an old cemetery. Most of the carved grave markers were crude crosses. "This is as far as I will take you. My old horse, if he gets spooked, I'd never catch him. I could, however, wait for your return down the mountain, if you'd like. Money upfront, of course, being as so few ever return."

I smiled and shook my head. "No, thanks. We might be here for a while."

His eyes widened. "Overnight?"

I shrugged. "Depends upon the circumstances."

The young man shook his head. "No amount of money could tempt me to stay out here in the dark."

"Then you had best hurry," Father said.

The driver laughed nervously. He tapped the reins several times and made the horse turn around. "When you return to the city, if you need my services again, you can find me at the same place."

I waved. "Thanks. Be safe."

"Worry more for yourselves!" He snapped a whip over the horse's head, making the horse move even faster.

Father glanced toward the narrow road that wound along the river's edge and then abruptly cut upward through tall leafless trees. The steep incline looked to be more than Father could handle. He gave me a nervous glance.

"I can go inspect it, Father, if you'd like?"

He sternly shook his head, which I expected. "I'll be fine. Ever since that hot bath at Lorcan's castle, my legs haven't hurt as badly."

"Is that so?"

He nodded.

"Let's see if we can reach the area where the road levels off. That might be where the cave is." I placed my crossbow into a holster on the back of my coat, picked up my Hunter box, and walked ahead of him.

After fifteen minutes of brisk walking, sweat rolled off me in spite of the cold. Somehow, Father had managed to keep up with me. He panted and puffed, wiping profuse sweat from his face with his hand-kerchief.

"Are you okay?" I asked.

He leaned forward, placing his hands on his knees, and took several deep gulps of air. "Never better."

I grinned and released a deep laugh.

Father frowned and pointed a shaking finger. "Since my legs were crushed, I should add."

"Okay," I said.

"I did keep up with you, and considering everything else, that's pretty good for your old man."

"You did great. At least going down will be easier," I replied.

Father glanced at the steep descending path and wiped his brow again, shaking his head. He mumbled curses under his breath.

At the sharp curve of the road was a clear view of the Rhine River. Roaring water echoed where the falls cascaded. Clouds of water spray hung in the air, and even though the winter air was frosty, I almost wanted to swim after the exhausting climb we had endured.

The road split to the left and the right at the top of the hill. The tall leafless trees forked their way into the darkening sky. At the end of the left path was a dark oval cut into the side of the rocks. If the map was true, this was Ambrose's lair.

I thought it odd that Ambrose would choose a cave for a lair when Lorcan had an entire castle. Of course, from what the young driver had told us, people believed the area to be haunted, which allowed more privacy, but still ... a cave?

I sat on a large boulder and patted the area beside me. "Let's rest for a few minutes. That climb took a lot out of me."

"Me, too."

Wiping sweat from my brow, I said, "The morning would be better for us to slay him, Father."

He panted and shrugged. "But we're here now. Why ride out tonight if you wanted to wait until morning."

I chuckled. "For one, I didn't really believe a cave existed up here. And if we didn't find one, we could easily camp the night and catch a ride back to town in the morning."

"So what now? Inspect the cave or camp out?"

I stared at the cave entrance for several moments. It seemed quiet. Even though it was dark enough outdoors, most vampires didn't tend to rise until closer to midnight. I suppose there was no hard tenet for that, but it would be best to know the size of the cave ahead of time and since it was still early, I doubted we'd encounter vampires near the opening.

"I want to look inside the cave."

"Now?" Father's brow rose and his eyes widened.

I nodded.

Father took his handkerchief and wiped sweat from his face. The fear in his eyes was evident even in the darkness. His breathing changed, too. He was nervous.

I opened my box, took out my revolver, and checked the chamber. Loaded. I slid it into my coat pocket. I grabbed two weighted stakes.

"Here," Father said, placing the sack of gold marks into the box. "I don't want to lose them if we're forced to run."

I nodded.

"That's a *lot* of holy water," Father said, still wiping sweat from his brow.

"Let's hope we don't need to use it all tonight." I slid several bottles into my pocket.

He glanced nervously toward the cave opening. "You think we will?"

"I really don't believe we're going to encounter any vampires this early in the night, but we need to prepare ourselves, just in case." I handed him two vials of holy water. Dusk was settling over us. "Let's go."

CHAPTER 36

$\mathcal{I}$ adjusted the straps on the spectacles Penelope had given me, so they'd fit my large head properly. Instantly, everything around me appeared to be surrounded by light. Right inside the ominous cave I found an oil lantern left by the last victim that had dared to enter. The skeletal remains of his hand and arm were still attached to the lantern.

I shook the lantern and the finger bones dropped to the dusty cave floor. I wanted to inspect the cave while we were here. There was enough oil in the lantern to burn at least a half hour, which I hoped was more than adequate time to slay Ambrose and leave when we returned in the morning light.

Father struck a match against the cave wall and lit the wick. I let him hold the lantern, and I adjusted the Penelope's night goggles to fit my head and put them on. With the goggles I had no need of the lantern, but Father did.

Strange scraping sounds fluttered and whooshed outside the cave. We peered out to see large winged creatures circling the trees. They looked like giant bats. Some of them flitted toward the bare tree branches, attached their clawed feet around the limbs, and hung upside down.

"In God's name," Father whispered.

"I don't think they're associated with God," I replied.

Father gave me an angered side-glance. "Nor do I. We need to hurry back down the path, son."

"No. Let's hurry and inspect this part of the cave. We might be fortunate enough to find Ambrose's coffin, so I can stake him before he has awakened."

"Okay. But even if we kill Ambrose, how do you propose we get past those demon beasts?" he asked.

"A problem we deal with afterwards."

The cave began as a narrow tunnel and widened into a large room. I noticed several sepulchers carved from stone. Two of them were already open.

I scanned the room holding a stake in hand, trying to find where the awakened vampires were. Three sepulchers away stood one of them. She was a beautiful voluptuous woman with her dark hair curled into a bunt. Her piercing dark eyes were alluring and her smile captivated me. It was like she could reach inside my soul and remove all my pain. She whispered coaxing words with her smooth sultry voice kissing at the edge of my ears. The lure of her beauty spellbound me. I didn't see the vampire. I saw a beautiful woman.

Slowly, I lowered the stake in my hand. I felt at peace.

She licked her lips and glided toward me, stopping inches from me. I couldn't take my eyes off her beauty.

"I could never abandon you," she whispered. "Not like Penelope did."

The mention of Penelope's name shook me, breaking me from her charm. It was then I noticed my father's stern whispers. "Forrest! Forrest! Snap out of it! She's trying to compel you."

I blinked, suddenly seeing a hideously wrinkled woman instead of the mirage she had presented. The vampire continued smiling as if I were still under her lure. She eased closer and I brought up the stake and plunged it through her heart. Her eyes widened. She shrieked a second before collapsing to dust.

Never had a vampire glamoured me. She could have easily killed me. All I could guess was that she was much older than any vampire I had encountered prior. The fact she held me within inches of biting my throat frightened me.

"Forrest!" Father shouted.

I turned to see a male vampire rushing at him. Father held a stake, but he was too hesitant. I flung a bottle of holy water. It missed the vampire but it shattered on the rock ceiling. The holy water splashed onto its face. It hissed, gnashing its fangs, and immediately turned its attention toward me.

As it rushed toward me, I reached over my shoulder and took my crossbow. Before the vampire was halfway across the room, I fired. The enchanted arrow struck through the vampire's heart. I retrieved the arrow and reloaded the crossbow. I loved those enchanted arrow stakes and wished I had cut dozens of them when I had been in London.

Father hurried to where I stood. The scraping wings of the massive bat creatures outside the cave were getting louder. It sounded like hundreds of them had gathered in the trees. Retreating was probably as dangerous as sliding the lids off the sepulchers and staking the vampires.

I gripped the corner of another sepulcher lid and pried it slowly to the side. Inside lay another beautiful female. Her eyes were closed. Her hands were crossed over her stomach. She didn't move or breathe. In essence, she appeared to be a corpse. Dead. But after the other two, I knew she was an undead. A vampire.

I positioned the stake over her heart and drove it hard and fast through her chest. Her eyes widened and she flashed fangs before turning to ash.

"Fools!"

I turned toward the narrow passage way that lead farther into the cave. The silver-haired vampire loomed large and angered. He wore an amber broach with a stage beetle enclosed inside like Lorcan had described. It was Ambrose.

"Who has sent you, Hunter?" he demanded. "Lorcan?"

I turned and faced him. "Yes. He hired me to slay you."

Ambrose frowned. "I don't know which comes as a greater surprise: A Hunter who has allowed himself to be hired by a vampire, or a master vampire too afraid to slay an opposing master, so he hires someone else to do it."

"Lorcan did indicate that he hoped to bewilder you in such a way," I replied.

"I do hope he paid you handsomely," Ambrose said in a cold even tone. "No amount of gold is worth your death though, is it? But having you as one of my children, Hunter, I must commend Lorcan for gifting me a prize far greater than whatever gold coins he has offered you."

"Son," Father said softly. "I—I don't think we're getting out of this alive. Just know, I love you. I've always been proud of you. You're the best son I could have ever hoped for."

Ambrose laughed. "How touching. Your father fears death, but you Hunter, you do not?"

I pulled Father behind me and turned my head slightly. "Run for the door."

"With those creatures outside?"

"The lesser of two evils," Ambrose said. "Either way, you have no hope."

"Go, Father," I whispered. "Know I love you, too."

"Children, rise!" Ambrose shouted. "We have intruders! Kill them!"

The lids of the sepulchers burst into the air all around the room. Father turned and ran for the cave entrance. I pulled my revolver and shot three vampires in the head. Although silver bullets won't kill vampires, they inflict a great deal of pain. These three dropped to the dusty floor, writhing in pain. I fired three more shots, aiming toward any vampire running toward Father.

I was struck in the back hard, plowed to the ground by a vampire, but I rolled to the side swiftly. The vampire lost its grip. I yanked a stake from behind my belt and drove it through the beast's heart. It crumbled.

Father was almost to the door, still holding the lantern. A vampire grabbed him from behind and twisted his arm in an unnatural way. Bones snapped.

Father screamed.

I shoved myself to my feet and ran toward him. Tears burned in my eyes. I plunged a stake through another vampire that was approaching my father. I missed the heart, but caused enough pain to stop its pursuit.

Three more vampires rushed to cut me off, preventing me from reaching Father. Pain creased on his face as vampires clawed through his clothing. Rage burned inside of me, but I couldn't push through the vampires holding me back.

I clutched one vampire by the throat, lifted his light body into the air, and staked him. I reached for the next and did the same. Glancing around the room, dozens of vampires had entered the room. There must have been over a hundred of them inside this cave. The odds were too great, even if Penelope had come to aid us. I reached into my coat pocket and tossed four enchanted arrows into the air.

The arrows were swift to take down the four closest vampires. Once the vampires dropped as ash, the arrows quickly zipped through the air in search of four more. I holstered my crossbow and made it to my father. He lay on the dusty floor. Blood spilled out from several nasty wounds. He didn't see me. He was in shock. His eyes were distant. With the blood pouring from him, I didn't see any way he was going to survive, but I wasn't about to leave him behind. I heaved him up off the floor and placed him over my shoulder. I grabbed my Hunter box and ran for the entrance.

I glanced back before leaving the cave. Most of the vampires had retreated through the passageway where Ambrose had emerged. The four enchanted arrows whooshed through the air, killing any vampire within their vicinity. The good thing was that none of the vampires were pursuing. They had seen how effective the arrows were. Ambrose had apparently decided to hide as well.

The giant winged bat creatures were hanging all through the tree branches. Several dozen of them were in the high branches right outside the cave. I lay Father onto the large boulder where we had sat earlier.

"Hold on, Father. Please, don't die." Tears trickled down my cheeks. "I can't lose you, too."

But he wasn't moving. His eyes peered at me, frozen in death. I placed my ear to his nose. No breath.

My heart hammered in my chest. I took in huge gulps of air. With the help of the goggles, I quickly inspected his throat. No vampire had bitten him. I don't think any had intended to.

I placed my ear to his chest, hoping for the slightest heartbeat. Nothing. I bunched up his blood soaked shirt inside my fists, sobbing.

I rose with rage inside me. I grabbed my box and started back for the cave entrance when something huge slapped my chest, lifting me off the ground. I landed on my back, all the air escaping my lungs. A loud roar bellowed. I grabbed my box, preparing to get to my father, so I could carry his body down the narrow path, but was yanked off the ground by one of the winged creatures.

Its huge talons pressed into my shoulders. It lifted upwards, narrowly missing the treetops, which probably would have shredded through me. The creature soared past the tree line and over the river. I lowered the box between my thighs and squeezed together to prevent it from falling. I slid my dagger from its sheath and stabbed at the thing's leg.

It shrieked and lowered its head toward me, trying to bite me. I plunged the dagger through the softness of its neck and cut sharply to the left. It plummeted downward. Its wings drooped over my head. Taking its claw-like appendages at the tips of its wings, I spread my arms out, trying to catch the air, hoping to glide away from the water, but it was useless.

The creature and I plummeted, striking the icy cold water. Darkness engulfed me.

CHAPTER 37

$\mathcal{I}$ drifted halfway between consciousness and what I considered touching Death's door. My body ached, especially along my ribs and the back of my head. I couldn't feel anything below my waist. Try as I might, I couldn't even wiggle a toe.

"He's coming around, Ian. I told you he wouldn't die easily. He's a big strong man, full of muscle."

"Brother, he is busted up pretty badly. He has severe bruising all down his spine. Doubtful he can ever walk again. And as bad as he is, he probably won't last a week."

"Ah, but you're wrong. I know it." He cackled with bizarre laughter. "Look. Look. Here. Look here."

"What is it, Gunner?" Ian asked with a tone of disgust.

"These marks. They be made by a bear!"

I attempted to open my eyes but only got that in-between blurred phase like looking through the murky water of a stream. These two men … I could barely see the outlines of their faces. I must have hit my head harder than the pain registered. These two men were hideously disfigured, mainly their teeth. Their teeth were long and twisted, yellowed. Surely I was still trapped inside a nightmare, and if I were, I didn't see any way of climbing out.

"A bear? We have very few bears near us," Ian said firmly. "The waterfall is too harsh."

Gunner laughed in what sounded like chattering. "That's what's so unique. You know—you know what it means?"

"What? You bumbling fool?"

"He's … he's going to become one of them."

"One of who?"

"Like us. He's going to change."

"The scars are most likely from something else, like a jagged tree branch where the river current dragged him over the falls."

"No, it's a bear," Gunner said undeterred.

Ian sighed. He leaned closer to my chest where Gunner had pointed and started sniffing what I assumed must be claw marks because I wasn't capable of rising up and looking. His clammy hands touched my chest muscles. I tensed. He sniffed.

"You're right, Gunner. A bear."

Gunner giggled and clapped his hands. "He's going to change then."

"We can't be certain, but we can be hopeful. If he does, at least his body should heal of these injuries."

"And if he don't?"

"He'll probably die."

Gunner made a sad groan. "Mustn't give up hope. Say, where'd you put that box we found?"

"Near the door," Ian replied.

Gunner rushed away. A few moments later he dragged the box across the floor. "Hefty damn thing to tote. Wonder what be inside?"

"Might as well look."

The latches unsnapped and the hinges creaked. "My, my, Ian."

"What is it?"

"Ah, he be a Vampire Hunter!" His voice rose to a near squeal. He came to my side and placed his cold hands on my shoulder and looked down at my face. Still a blurred image. "Keep fighting to live, mate."

My lips moved, but only slight scratchy sounds came out.

"All his vials are intact," Gunner said. "Nothing wet inside. Ooh, look."

"What?" Ian said.

"He has a sack of coins."

"So?"

"No reason. Just ... he must kill a lot of vampires to get money like this. I've always wanted to hunt vampires."

"Look at him, Gunner! Look at the shape he's in. Is this how you'd like to end up?"

Gunner huffed. "Well, no. Not particularly, no."

"Vampire hunting isn't a profession you pick. It picks you."

Gunner came back to my side and patted my shoulder.

"Rest easy, friend," Gunner said. "It's two weeks until the next full moon. We'll keep you safe while you recover. Took a nasty fall off the cliffside, you did. That rocky waterfall didn't do ya any favors, either. But when the full moon rises, new blessings befall ya, they will."

I moaned and tried to raise my head. Couldn't.

"Let him be, Gunner. Let him rest. Pawing at him won't help the situation none."

"But ... a Were-bear. Doesn't that excite you?"

"Not particularly, no."

"Why not?"

"Because he could *eat* us."

"Always thinking the downside, aren't you? Never look at the good."

Ian growled. "What's good about it? Poor chap nearly falls to his death, you jump into the frigid water and pull him out, but the only real mercy might have been if you'd have left 'em to die."

"Ian? Surely, you don't mean that?"

"Gunner, what if he wasn't scratched by a shifter bear? Hmm? He's never going to go anywhere. For him to survive, requires our waiting on him hand and foot, day after day, and if that happens—"

"I'll tend to him. *Me*."

"Every detail?" Ian asked.

"Every one."

"Then for your sake and his, I pray the bear was a shifter. It's all the hope you both have."

Gunner clapped his hands softly. "He'll turn, Ian. He'll turn. You'll see. The great Vampire Hunter will transform into a bear."

"Come on, Gunner. Let him be. We need to catch fish for the day and find some dry firewood. Since the cave gets cold at night, we need to make it warmer for him. He's injured so he'll need food. Soup. Fish soup. Find some healing roots if you can."

"On it, brother!" Gunner hurried away.

Had I heard him correctly? I had been attacked by a bear-shifter? I never encountered a bear … Wait. Something huge had struck me not too far outside the cave. That much I did remember, but I never saw what it had been.

I wanted to snap fully awake to get a grip on reality, to discover the truth. I healed quickly or at least I always had in the past. But I'd never lost the feeling in my legs before. That concerned me.

After I no longer heard the brothers talking, I tried to rise up again, but to no avail. I sobbed. Tears crested in my eyes and spilled down my cheeks. I couldn't stop their flow. Everything I held dear in my life was gone. First Momma, now Father, and Penelope … she was sailing across the world to face a possible horde of demons alone. I feared I'd never see her again.

I lay here, helpless and unable to move. I couldn't even talk. Had those who had chosen me to be a Hunter turned their backs on me? Was I cursed because I had kept Varak alive? Every step of our journey from London to Freiburg had been filled with misfortune, and as I had feared, a heavy price would be demanded for keeping the hybrid child alive. I couldn't image a heftier cost because my life was all I had left. Death would have been a blessing instead of suffering this anguish inside.

Lorcan had betrayed us. He was the reason Father was dead. The whole slay-his-enemy had been a scheme geared—I reasoned—to kill me because I was a Hunter. Perhaps Flora wasn't the only one who enjoyed torture games. I had been used as a gift offering to Ambrose from Lorcan. I doubted it was for peace, but Lorcan wanted to keep his children safe. For a vampire, there was no greater energy surge than for one to drink a Hunter's blood. But Ambrose had mentioned that he planned to turn me. Either way, had Ambrose succeeded, Lorcan had never intended for me to stake Ambrose. He knew the odds were too high for me and my father to be victorious. It was a suicide mission on our part.

Albert had offered to turn me into a were-rat on several occasions, insisting that I'd gain incredible strength and foresight by doing so. I had denied his offer each time. Now that I understood a bear were-creature might have attacked me, I hoped it was true. If there was one thing an angry bear possessed, it was rage. After all the sorrowful ordeals I had survived, my rage was building and longed to be released. Combining my rage with the rage of a massive bear, it would be far more magnified than I could ever hope to contain.

The events since we had left London flashed through my mind. My hot tears ceased, and for years to come, I didn't expect to experience the comfort of tears to soothe any of my inner emotional pains or loss. Coldness had suddenly frozen my tear well and slowly gripped my heart.

Yes, I hoped what Ian had predicted about the claw marks coming from a shifter was true. And if it were, I was about to evolve into something ruthless and unforgiving. I was going after Lorcan, his children, Ambrose and even Albert. There would be nothing to stop me. Each would suffer my rage. I'd pursue them to the ends of the earth if necessary, but I would find and slay each one.

My first transformation was two weeks away, if a bear shifter had actually infected me, and for some unexplained reason, I believed this to be true. Two weeks was a long time to fume over the atrocities others had committed against me and my family. When my rage eventually released, it would explode like a volcano. Ultimate destruction followed. A lot of undead and paranormal creatures were going to die at my hands. I'd never stop until I found each one of them and held them accountable for their transgressions.

I had nothing else of value in this life except my soul. With the raging anger festering inside, I even dared Death to attempt his claim before I had satisfied my vengeance. For a while, his role would become my occupation. I'd bury those he had failed to remove from the earth and turn them to ash.

In the territories where the undead reigned, they'd fear my coming. Some vampires might stake themselves rather than face my wrath. As Jacques had mentioned almost a year earlier, my reputation eventually preceded me. While that might ultimately prove to be true, I hoped it occurred after my rage began to settle. The last thing I wanted was for Ambrose, Lorcan, or Albert to know I was coming for them. If Death could creep into homes unseen and unheard in the dead of night, perhaps I could do the same. The undead were about to witness their greatest unexpected nightmare. Me. But unlike Death, I'd show my enemies no mercy. They had taken from me, and now they'd know the ultimate price they'd pay.

THE END

AFTERWORD

[Author's Note: The hardest part in writing this book was the death of Forrest's father after the two of them had finally gotten closer. However, in *Succubus: Shadows of the Beast*, where Forrest first appears (almost 120 years later), this is how he mentioned his father's passing. I knew John's fate when I started this book and dreaded when the scene took place. I shed tears, but Forrest's losses are what changes him and hardens his view against the undead even more. Due to all his losses, he undergoes a transformation that coincides with his character, not just physically, but mentally and spiritually as well. Internal hardships and struggles are what change all of us. Life isn't necessarily fair, or how we often wish it were. But whenever we come to a crossroads, we have a choice to make: Which path should I take? In this book, Forrest encountered a lot of crossroads. His decisions for each are what he must reflect for the rest of his life. While he cannot change them, he will learn from them.

Forthcoming:
Forrest Wollinsky Vampire Hunter [Blood Pact] Book 4

ABOUT THE AUTHOR

Leonard D. Hilley II grew up a quiet, shy kid with an inquisitive mind. Learning to read at an early age, he fell in love with books. He read every book he could get his hands on and stacks of dark comics about ghosts, monsters, and creepy things that stalk the night.

Like a lot of boys, he caught beetles, wooly bears, butterflies, and had an ant farm. When he was ten, his interests in science increased even more after seeing a professor's insect collection. Soon he set out on his quest to build his own collection. He also learned to rear butterflies and moths to obtain perfect specimens. He learned botany, gardening, and set his goal to become an entomologist.

At eleven, he watched the original Star Wars on the big screen. His imagination soared. Soon after, he discovered Roger Zelazny's Chronicles of Amber. Six months later, he had written the first draft of a novel. A novel he later discarded, but the characters stuck with him. Years later, these characters came to life in Shawndirea, which Hilley intended to be a novella for Devils Den. The characters, however, refused to be ignored and took the opportunity to unveil Aetheaon in their first epic fantasy. Lady Squire: Dawn's Ascension was quick to follow.

Shawndirea was Hilley's farewell to butterfly collecting, and those who have read the novel understand why. He has taken Ray Bradbury's advice to heart: "Follow the characters." He does. He follows, listens, and take notes—often never knowing where they're going to take him, but he's never been disappointed in the results.

Hilley earned a B.S. in Biology and an MFA in Creative Writing to combine his love of science and writing.

Sci-fi Titles: Predators of Darkness: Aftermath, Beyond the Darkness, The Game of Pawns, Death's Valley, The Deimos Virus.

Epic Fantasy: Shawndirea (Aetheaon Chronicles: Book One), Lady Squire (Aetheaon Chronicles: Book Two), Frosthammer (Aetheaon Chronicles: Book Three), Shadowfae (Aetheaon Chronicles: Book Four), and Devils Den.

UF/PR: Succubus: Shadows of the Beast (Nocturnal Trinity Series: Book One), Raven (Nocturnal Trinity Series: Book Two), A Touch of the Familiar (Nocturnal Trinity Series: Book Three)

YA UF/Paranormal: Forrest Wollinsky Vampire Hunter; Forrest Wollinsky: Blood Mists of London; Forrest Wollinsky: Predestined Crossroads.

9 781950 485093